Shattered Pieces

South Hillsbend Series
TK Sunderland

Stone Ledge Publishing, LLC

Cover Design by Melissa Doughty - Mel D. Designs melissadoughty.com

1st edition 2026

Shattered Pieces
ISBN Paperback: 978-1-971115-00-9
ISBN E-book: 978-1-971115-01-6

To my children, who frequently had to share me with the residents of South Hillsbend. My thanks go out to my "little" sister and NWG who read this book and pushed me to publish. And to my mother, who helped me in the beginning by answering my random medical questions, wondering why I was asking such things. Cancer took you before you could see why.

Note to the Reader

Please be aware that this story includes flashbacks depicting past domestic violence and emotional abuse. Please prioritize your mental well-being while reading.

For a specific list of pages to skip, please visit my website: tksunderland.com/content-care

If you or someone you know is experiencing domestic violence, help is available. In the US, you can call the National Domestic Violence Hotline at 800-799-SAFE (7233).

PROLOGUE

Three a.m.

THE OPPRESSIVE SILENCE WOKE her. She lay unmoving, wishing this time the quiet wouldn't be there, praying that if she opened her eyes, things would be different. Sluggishly, she reached her hand across the bed and found it empty. The cold of the space next to her seeped into her body.

Her heart refused to accept this new reality, that her world had been so utterly destroyed. She kept her eyes closed, feeling the room around her. There was no sound, no life. It was empty. She was alone.

Her eyes opened to the near-complete darkness of her room. She forced herself to pull back the covers from her body and get up to look. As she swung her legs over the side of the mattress, her tangled hair wrapped around her shoulder and down her back. She hadn't brushed it in days. The nightshirt hung limp from her thinning body. It was the only clothing she had worn this week. There was no reason to change. No one was here to care.

Slowly, she placed her feet on the floor and stood. Dizziness overtook her, but she fought to stay standing. Her body cried out from the lack of care and nutrition. Her muscles tight, she waited for her vision to clear. With each step, her legs and bare feet felt like lead as they dragged across the wood floor of her bedroom, pulling her toward the reality she now faced.

She didn't hear the expected sound of calm, steady water in the shower. The bathroom door stood open, the room was dark, and the scent of him was missing from the air. Stepping into the doorway triggered the small motion-activated night light, creating a faint illumination over his brush and shaving items. Her fingers traced over his bar of soap in its dish on the counter. The ache in her chest grew, step by tedious step, out to the hallway.

Darkness enveloped her as she stepped out into the living room, where they would curl up together every evening to watch the news and talk about their days. A chill wrapped around her as she looked to the empty table in the dining room, where they ate together, planning out their week ahead. The kitchen was dark, with no pans banging on the stove grates and no plates clattering onto the granite counter as quietly as possible to not wake her. No smells of breakfast and coffee awaited her when it was her time to get up and ready for work.

Step by agonizing step, she opened the door and looked out into the garage. His car was still there, waiting for its owner. Waiting to witness him holding her hand on the way to even the most mundane errands. He wasn't here, though. He was never going to be in this house again. She would never hear his voice again, nor would she ever feel his touch. Someone had taken that from her.

Her legs no longer held her as she crumpled to the floor in agonizing tears. Pain ripped through her chest, and the sobs took her breath away. They took him from her. It wasn't fair that he was gone and she was still here. She had tried. She had wanted to save him, but they took him from her. She curled into a ball on the floor, not wanting to move, wishing he were there to lift her to her feet, hold her, and whisper to her that everything was fine, this was just a nightmare.

When her tears ran out, she rose to her hands and knees, slowly crawling back to her room. She didn't want to go on anymore. She didn't want to be in this world alone. There was only one person she could count on to help before it got out of control again. Lying on the frigid wood floor, her hand shaking, she reached for the phone on the nightstand. She pulled up her contacts and pressed the top person.

A sleepy male voice answered, "Baby-girl," on the third ring.

"Charlie, please, I..." The sobs overtook her.

"Where are you?"

"It doesn't matter."

A deep sigh. "Yes, it does. Where are you?"

She tried to pull in a deep breath. "On the floor in my room."

The sound of sheets moving on the other end of the line made her imagine him sitting up in his bed, so far away. "We're going to do this together, okay? I need you to sit up."

She concentrated, placed one palm on the floor, and pushed herself to her knees. Her muscles protested every movement. "I'm up."

"Good job. Now, I need you to crawl into bed."

Even though he couldn't see it, she shook her head. "It's so cold."

"I know, but you also know you need to rest, and your bed is the best place to do that."

She slowly slid her body into her bed, then pulled the blankets over herself. The bed was frozen and empty. "Charlie, he's not here. I don't want to be alone."

"I'm not going to hang up. Go back to sleep. I'll be here with you."

"I love you, Charlie."

"I love you too. Let's get some sleep."

She turned over with the phone in her hand. The sounds of Charlie shuffling in his bed came across from the other end of the line. He was her light in this abysmal darkness. The one person she could always rely on. His breathing slowed to a more relaxed pace, and the sound of it lulled her back to sleep.

ONE

THE MID-MORNING SUN SHONE across the windows, and the breeze brought a sharp crispness to the air. Unlocking the front door of his restaurant, Blackwood Grill, Tai Jackson let himself inside. The staff would be coming in soon, but this was his moment of peace before the flurry of activity began. He walked the length of the bar, his eyes scanning the neatly ordered stock on the back shelves. Passing through the doorway into the silent kitchen, he made a beeline for his office. The paperwork wouldn't handle itself.

The light came on as he flicked the switch, then he turned to close the door before making his way back to his desk. As his computer started, he opened the blinds on the row of windows across the room. The view was limited to just the back parking lot and alley, with no glimpse of the distant mountains. Still, he liked knowing what the weather was doing while he worked at his desk.

A pile of color-coded files, the tasks he needed to complete, sat on his desk. He'd laid everything out last night to make things easier today. Long after he settled in to start payroll, a chime sounded to his right, and the security monitors lit up. The staff was beginning to arrive. Tai quickly silenced the alerts. Otherwise, they'd chime incessantly with every person entering and moving through the space.

As he worked, Tai could hear the muffled voices of the kitchen staff preparing their stations for the day ahead. Customers would arrive within the hour, so everyone had to be ready. Tai worked through each task he set out for himself, and as he closed and put away the last folder, he blew out a calming breath. He despised this part of his job. The fact that his employees depended on him was the only thing keeping him from setting fire to it all.

Standing, Tai shut off his computer, made sure his shirt was tucked and straight, then went to the office door for the part he enjoyed the most. Being out with his staff and customers, moving with the crowd's flow, never failed to bring him energy each day.

Tai opened his office door and stepped into the kitchen, where he heard Benji and the staff already starting lunch. Plates clanked, knives chopped, and voices called out orders. The aroma of the wood-fired grill reached Tai first, the delicious scent of meat sizzling in the flames. The sharp tang of onions followed, then the warmth of baking bread and burger buns. This, he thought, was the real start of the day.

Operating the grill was Benji, a man with mostly white hair streaked with brown, smile lines at the corners of his mouth, and a jolly laugh that made his round belly bounce. "Hey, Tai!"

"Hey, Benji, is it busy for lunch today?"

Benji shrugged. "Pretty normal so far. I'm good."

Through the pass-through window, he could see that the visible dining areas were already full of happily chatting customers.

Tai gave a quick nod to his kitchen manager. "Good to hear. Let's keep things moving smoothly."

Tai moved to the right and through the doorway behind the bar. Immediately, the hum of customers conversing at the tables replaced the loud kitchen noises.

From his left, a happy male voice shouted, "Heya, Sugar Daddy!"

Tai stopped, placed his hands on his hips, and turned to the man moving drinks efficiently across the bar. "Charlie, we have talked about this. I'm your boss, not your sugar daddy. Please stop calling me that."

From the opposite end of the bar, Vanessa piped up, "Charlie, one of these days, he's gonna pummel you." The tiny blond ball of pure energy zipped to the kitchen window to grab plates, then dashed off again.

Charlie flashed his biggest grin and puppy eyes at Tai. "Naaaaah. He likes me way too much." All Tai could do was roll his eyes, which was the exact reaction Charlie was looking for.

Charlie was the best bartender Tai ever had. He could manage multiple customers without breaking a sweat. Tai watched now as Charlie leaned over the bar, his hazel eyes sparkling, and a bright smile on his face, to talk to a couple, causing them both to laugh. Tai's lips lifted into a wry smile. Charlie was the reason why half of the regulars kept coming back and why Tai let him get away with so much.

Tai walked the bar's length, greeting customers he recognized before moving to the dining room. Out here, in the midst of his customers, he felt alive. He moved from group to group, the hum of happy conversation fueling him. For ten years, seeing people enjoy the fruits of his hard work gave him an immense sense of pride.

At each table, he stopped to introduce himself and ensure all was well. With the tourist season wrapping up and traffic starting to drop off, locals occupied most of the seating. They loved to bring Tai into their conversations, chatting about the local gossip he tried to avoid. It took him some time, but he eventually assisted Vanessa and her team in clearing tables, allowing them to focus on service.

He saw Vanessa zip behind him with a tray of meals. "Thanks, Tai! It's been pretty busy today."

"That's what I like to hear. Are you good?"

"Yep, it's starting to wind down now, as usual, so I'll be able to catch my breath in a bit."

With Tai and his staff constantly moving, the lunch crowd slowly dwindled to a couple of occupied spots and a lone patron at the bar. Vanessa, her team, and Tai cleaned the empty areas, wiped them down, and gave the dishes to Benji's staff to wash. They had to reset every space and prepare for the next round.

The calm over the place was a time to catch their breath before the dinner rush started. It never got old for him. Years of working for others in the business and learning everything from the ground up gave him an immense appreciation for his staff.

As usual, Charlie leaned over the bar, chatting up his customer. The man finished, paid his tab, stood, and headed for the door. Tai waved farewell to him, then returned to placing fresh silverware at each table. When he looked up, his gaze fell on the sidewalk outside.

Through the many windows, Tai watched a woman walk unhurriedly along the sidewalk. She emerged from the back lot, moved along the side of the building, and then turned to cross the front of his restaurant. His movements stilled as she approached. She hesitated, timidly pulled the door open, and stepped inside. He'd never seen this woman before. He would have remembered. Her unusually tall, slim build was unforgettable. Her jeans traced the line of her incredibly long legs, and a dark maroon sweater accentuated the deeper tones of her skin.

She removed her sunglasses to reveal dark eyes. As she turned to look around the space with palpable uncertainty, her long, silky, brown hair cascaded down her back, gently curling at the ends just below her waist. Her hands were now tightly clasped in front, so tight that Tai could see the knuckles were white.

Tai froze, utterly unaware of the world around him. The chatter of his staff dimmed to a mere hum. He stood there until his brain sputtered back to life. *Welcome her!* But before he could move, a loud shout erupted from the bar area. The woman turned toward the noise, her guard dropping. Her hands fell open, a brilliant light replaced the uncertainty in her dark eyes, and her lips parted in a smile so warm it seemed to chase the chill from the air. The transformation left Tai breathless.

Out of the corner of his eye, Tai saw a tall blur of Charlie dash from behind the bar, arms wide open, straight to the woman. "Baby-girl!" Charlie enveloped her in a full bear hug. As she wrapped her arms around his neck, he spun her around and planted a kiss on her lips.

Tai felt Vanessa step beside him, whispering, "Um, I thought Charlie was gay..."

Tai stood there, mouth agape, watching the woman's body relax against Charlie's. He could only manage, "You and me both."

It took almost everything Laci Capwell had to drive alone across a good portion of the country, but she made it. Now, instead of being at home, surrounded by memories, she was here in the mountain valley town of South Hillsbend with Charlie. She desperately needed her best friend's help. With the help of her adult children, Charlie had whittled away at her refusals and finally convinced her to stay with him.

His joy, as he sprinted toward her, yelling the funny nickname he'd created in high school, made her heart burst with love.

He'll know what to do. He can help me fix this. He has to.

The strength of his hug created a welcome shield around her. No one could touch her as long as Charlie was at her side. She didn't want him to let go.

He finally put her down, releasing her from the kiss. Cupping Laci's face, Charlie looked her straight in the eye and dropped his voice to a whisper meant only for her. "You and I are going to get through this. We're together again."

She touched her forehead to his, offering a timid smile. "Yes, Charlie, we're going to do this. But was the kiss necessary?"

The mischievous twinkle in his eye and bright smile spoke volumes. It lightened her heart, knowing he could finally be his playful self here in his new home, no longer locked away as he had been growing up.

He wrapped her in another bear hug, and she clung to him, absorbing the love he offered. Laci felt a tiny piece of her armor fall away, knowing she could depend on him to share some of the burden. When he stepped back, his gaze swept over her with concern. She shot him a glare, a silent, sharp warning. He understood and said nothing, but the concern in his eyes lingered. He would ask her later.

While Laci focused on Charlie, she more felt than heard a deep baritone voice rumble from over his shoulder, "Charlie, this is a new level of greeting customers. It might work for some, but most won't appreciate it."

Instinctively, her body stiffened. The voice had shattered the safe bubble Charlie had wrapped her in, starkly reminding Laci they were not alone.

Charlie chuckled, turning, but keeping Laci tight against his side. "Well, you won't let me greet you this way, so I have to direct it somewhere!"

Laci turned toward the voice. A man stepped forward from the back left corner of the space, head hanging, laughing. His smile revealed a constant amusement between him and Charlie. Despite their easy camaraderie, Laci's guard immediately snapped back into place. The long drive had left her on edge, and every stranger was a potential threat she had to evaluate. Her mind worked overtime, actively instructing her. *Smile, steady breaths, just look normal.* Without constant focus, the looming threat of panic would shatter her calm.

When Laci initially stepped inside, she'd spotted the giant standing in the back even before he approached. She was considerably tall at six feet, and Charlie was an inch taller, but this man towered over them both.

Laci quickly assessed him, her mind racing to determine a possible threat level. His broad chest filled the simple black cotton dress shirt, and rolled sleeves revealed muscular arms with rich, golden-brown skin. Though he was clearly a man who worked out regularly, he wasn't aggressively muscled. On his wrist, a simple black wristwatch. Everything about him suggested a professional, comfortable appearance, not a desire to show off. Nothing about him screamed threat to her.

Deep brown eyes watched her, not with a controlling gaze, but with kindness and interest. Laci's brain shorted out a little. Making eye contact was rare for her lately, and this felt overwhelming. Her eyes found a spot under his chin to focus on, a trick to appear as if she were looking at him.

"Laci," Charlie said, his voice warm, "this is my boss and the owner, Tai. Tai, this is my best friend, Laci."

Tai reached out. Laci had to consciously order her arm to move, to shake his hand. The warmth wrapped around her cold hand, and somehow it traveled up her arm. She immediately retreated. The effort of commanding her body to perform even the most basic movements was a frustrating, meticulous process, but it was how she'd survived these past few months. Each step, each word, was a conscious act of will.

Stepping back, it seemed to Laci that Tai knew his size was intimidating. Attempting a calm smile while her heart slammed in her chest, Laci regulated her voice. "It's nice to meet you. Charlie has told me only good things about you and working here." *Good, that sounded like something a perfectly average person would say.*

When he smiled at her compliment, the crinkling lines around his eyes revealed he often smiled like this. "Well, that's wonderful to hear," Tai said. "He's one of my three top employees."

A woman from the background spoke up. "Ha!" Her amused voice rang out across the space. "You only have three full-time employees!" She approached the group, extending a hand to Laci. "Hi, I'm Vanessa. I manage the front. Forgive us, but we rarely hear about Charlie's friends, which makes this a bit of a shock."

Compared to the two men, this younger woman, five and a half feet tall, thin, with spikey platinum blond hair, stood out like a woodland elf or pixie among trees. The only thing keeping her from fitting a child's fairy tale image was the colorful sleeves of tattoos along both her arms, peeking from beneath her black tee. Yet, something about her connected with Laci.

An older man with a cheerful, round face poked out from a window behind the bar. "Agreed. This is quite a shock!" He waved. "Hi, I'm Benji!"

Laci offered a light wave. "I guess I've now met the staff."

Tai smiled. "Yes, you have indeed. And some have customers to attend to." Vanessa saluted Tai and quickly skittered off.

Charlie turned to Laci. "Want something to eat? My treat. Then you can settle into the house."

"Sure, but not your treat. I'll pay." She refused to be entirely dependent on him.

"How about if there's no bill to pay?" Tai spoke up, stepping closer. "Consider it a welcome to our town. Any friend of Charlie's is a friend of ours. Pick whatever you like, on the house."

Laci turned in Charlie's arm to face Tai, her breath catching a bit, the size of the man still overwhelming. "Wow, um, thank you."

Charlie guided her from the center walkway, lined with short, red-brick planters, to the right side of the room, toward the bar, and pulled out a chair. Handing her a menu, Charlie leaned in, whispering quite loudly, "I can't recommend anything..." He sent a sly peek toward Tai, who was now frowning, "because it's seriously all delicious. Benji is an amazing cook." A deep chuckle from behind Laci reverberated through the room.

As she chatted with Charlie, Laci admired the restaurant's deep wood tones, black leather, intimate lighting, and exposed red brick walls, which rose high to the industrial black ceiling. The cozy atmosphere wrapped her in a small cocoon, even though she sat in this vast space. Charlie moved behind the bar, washing glasses and restocking shelves. Vanessa paused occasionally to join their conversation. Laci also noticed Tai kept his distance, though he glanced over several times.

While Laci dined, customers slowly filled the surrounding tables. Realizing the dinner hour was about to start, her nerves amped up again. Doing her best to keep her voice calm despite her hands shaking, Laci quietly grabbed Charlie's attention and murmured, "Why don't you give me a house key? I'll get out of your hair. You have customers to attend, and I need to unpack my car."

Sensing her unease with the crowd, Charlie looked up and over her shoulder. "Can I have thirty minutes to get her settled?"

Laci turned, a scream catching in her throat. Tai stood directly behind her. So close. How had he moved so silently? Her heart hammered in her chest, startled by his sudden nearness.

Tai seemed to ignore her jump. "Sure," he said. "Take your time." He moved behind the bar. "I'll cover."

Untying the apron around his waist, Charlie walked around the bar. He held out an arm. Laci got up to walk with him.

Her ramped-up nerves made her speak too quickly, words tumbling out of control. "Thank you, Tai, for the meal," she said. "I appreciate it. It was delicious."

He grinned warmly at her. "You're very welcome," Tai said. "And I hope to see you here again soon."

Laci offered a faint, quick smile back at him, then turned to walk with Charlie out the door.

TWO

SHARP PRICKLING SENSATIONS LIKE ants ran up and down Laci's skin. The hum of the dining customers transformed into a wave of noise, throwing her vision off kilter. Her heart fluttered in her chest, and she focused on regulating her breathing with slow, deliberate inhales and exhales. With every step, her eyes were fixed on the door, her hands grasped together to fight the urge to pull at her hair. Pushing outside, the cooler air washed away the prickling on her skin and gave her a sense of release as her heart finally stopped its frantic flutter.

"Come on, I've got you," Charlie whispered to her.

While walking around the front of the building, Laci did her best to take full, deep breaths, the mountain air carrying a hint of pine. The wall of windows encompassed the entire exterior of the restaurant, making her fully visible to everyone inside. She pushed her shoulders back and tried to keep her head held up, facing forward. The afternoon sun was fading, and the town's atmosphere grew dim. She did not want to be out here in the dark. *Bad things happen in the dark.*

Every face they passed seemed to stare directly at Laci, their eyes dissecting her, seeing the frantic fear inside. The parking lot gave her a glimmer of hope. *Car. I need to get to my car.* Once inside, she finally took a deep, cleansing breath. Laci sat for a moment, opening and closing her hands, feeling the cold leather against her back. Her heart slowed to its normal, steady pace. The rising tears neared the surface, but she tamped them down again. Charlie said nothing as he sat in the passenger seat, knowing she needed a minute.

Once she was relaxed enough, she started the engine and pulled out toward the main road. Though she could have parked at his house and walked to the restaurant, like Charlie, she needed the comfort of her vehicle nearby. It was her mobile safe zone for this first visit.

Following his directions, Laci pulled into a lovely neighborhood lined with trees, their branches bare in the fall season. It was her first time seeing the house in person since Charlie had moved here four years ago, and she couldn't help but feel proud of her friend and how far he had come.

"That's the house!" He pointed, and she pulled up to a modern two-story bungalow home with gray siding and white trim. The house was clearly Charlie's pride. The lawn was sharply edged, the flowerbeds clean, and every exterior light shone bright and clear. Parking her car in the short driveway, she appreciated the lit sconces on either side of the garage door. Small lights lined the walkway to the front entry, which sat back from the garage. Charlie led her to the navy blue front door and opened it for her.

He led her into a cozy foyer, the space flanked by stairs rising to the second floor and a smaller room. Inside the front door, a small side table served as a catch-all for change and keys. Silver-framed photos of the two of them decorated the surface, spanning years of their friendship. She smiled as she looked over the pictures, particularly the ones her mom had taken of them in fourth grade. Laci had the same photos displayed in her house.

"The kids in those photos had no idea how sharply life could turn, huh?" Charlie asked.

Glancing up at him, Laci gave him a sad half-smile. "No, they didn't. Those two were more interested in playing in the yard together and watching Saturday morning cartoons."

Looking around, the house felt almost like home because Charlie had used the same deep earth tones as she had in her own home.

"This is my gaming room," he said, pointing to the front room to her right. He led her down a hall that ran between the room and the stairs. The hall opened into a great room where the dining area sat to her right, the kitchen was tucked into the corner to her left, and the living room spanned the back. "And this is the main living area. This is your home now, so you use whatever you want."

With very little sunlight left, the urgency to be safely locked inside the house pulled at her. "I need to unpack my car."

"Sure, let's go through here." Charlie opened a door in the back wall of the kitchen and hit the opener on the wall next to the door.

After she pulled her car in, he closed the door behind her. Not wanting him to see everything she brought, she had him take one of her larger suitcases while she carried another. Then, they walked upstairs.

"This is my room." He pointed to the left to a room spanning the space above the garage, decorated in shades of purple. "I have my own bathroom, so you can use this one."

He pointed to the one at the end of the hall. "Then you have two rooms you can choose from."

Choosing the bedroom in the back right corner, she and Charlie dropped her bags beside the bed.

"I have to get back to work," Charlie said, pulling her into a hug. "I'll lock the front door when I leave. I won't be home until around one, so don't wait up for me." He released her and patted her shoulder. "I'm so glad you're here with me."

"Me too," she said, stepping back. "Now go. I'll be fine."

As Charlie walked downstairs, the click of the front door locking echoed through the quiet house, a sound of finality and safety. After a few more trips to the car, she finally got everything upstairs and into her room.

Sleep was winning the battle in Laci's body. After nineteen hours of being up and moving, with most of that time spent driving, she was exhausted. Laci quickly changed into her T-shirt and boxers, then climbed into what had to be the most comfortable bed she'd ever slept in. The fluffy mattress seemed to swallow her up, and Charlie had provided her with a weighted blanket. She smiled to herself, thinking that if Charlie ever wanted to get rid of her, she was taking the bed with her.

⚶

"Charlie, how come you never told us about Laci? How long have you two been friends?" Vanessa asked, wiping down the tables, but her eyes were fixed on him. Tai paused his work, not surprised in the least that V was the one to ask. He'd been wondering the same thing. He watched Charlie for a response.

"We met in third grade and have been inseparable ever since," Charlie replied, washing glasses behind the bar. He glanced at Vanessa. "I moved here to get away from a lot of crap back home. Laci was the one thing that kept me going. I guess she's the one part of my old life I've wanted to hold close and not share."

"Ok, so what changed?" Vanessa continued to poke.

Tai caught the barely noticeable flicker of pain on Charlie's face before Charlie covered it up and shrugged. "You know how it is. Life changes, and she could finally come to visit me. I usually visit her, but this time she's staying with me for a while. Don't worry. You'll see her again, I'm sure."

"Well, she seems sweet," Vanessa said. "Does she like movies or playing board games? I wouldn't mind if she joined our group."

Tai recalled how Vanessa had chatted with Laci while she ate, and Charlie tended to customers. Tai had stayed back a bit because he had the distinct feeling Laci wasn't as comfortable with him as she was chatting with another woman.

"Thanks, V, she does, and I'll ask her. But it will probably be mainly her and me for a while. We have a lot to catch up on, and I want to show her around the area a bit so she knows where to go while I'm working in case she gets tired of staying home and reading all the time." He glanced up at her and smiled.

"Oh, I completely get that. Laci needs to know how to navigate unless you're planning to lock her in the house forever! How long will she be staying?"

Charlie shrugged. "At this point, there is no end date set. She's staying as long as she wants."

Vanessa grinned. "Aw, well then, she needs other people besides you to hang with!"

"No doubt, but let's get her settled first and let me have my bestie time with her."

Charlie took the pile of dirty towels from the bar area to the kitchen bin. When he stepped out again, Benji was with him, and Vanessa waited by the door. Tai waved goodnight to the three and locked the door behind them.

So, Laci would be here for a while. Tai couldn't shake the image of her smiling at Charlie. The warmth in that one smile had done something to him. It was like some switch had been flipped deep inside him. He went through the motions of closing up, his mind still on her. He shut down his computer, laid out everything for the next day, and grabbed his keys from his desk. As he moved through the quiet building, checking every space, he heard only the echo of his shoes on the flooring. At the bar, he keyed in the code to arm the security system, then walked to the front, locking the door before heading to his car.

At just after one in the morning, he was the only one in the lot. The lampposts cast a bright glow, and he could see his breath in the cold night air.

Images of Laci rolled through his mind as he drove home. From a distance, he'd memorized the soft smiles to Charlie, how her hands made sweeping gestures through the air as she talked, and the few times she glanced back at him, he felt the weight of her gaze. Her hair shifted like waves of silk with every turn of her head, and the sight sent a jolt through him, a desire to run his fingers through the soft strands made his pulse quicken. He'd never reacted so strongly to any woman who walked into his business.

Tai was no idiot. He always followed one simple rule. Never sleep with a woman who came into his restaurant or lived nearby. It was crucial to keep his business and his employees' livelihoods safe from an encounter that could go sideways. When he traveled, he might find a temporary partner, but never near home. So why did this one woman cause him to fixate, to want to throw caution to the wind? *What is it about her?*

The risk was even higher because she was Charlie's best friend. Tai respected Charlie. The last thing he wanted was to cause issues with his bartender. The way Charlie held onto her suggested their connection was clearly tighter than that of typical friends.

Tai had watched her unease grow as the restaurant filled for dinner. As patrons began filling tables, he caught her rapid glances. Her shoulders stiffened when Dale, a local contractor who stopped in for a beer every Tuesday, sat down two chairs away. The guy was harmless. Tai had known him for years, but Laci shifted on her chair, inching away as if he were a threat. It confused the hell out of him.

When she said goodbye, her words came out in a rush, her eyes flashing between his chest and the door as if expecting an attack. He watched her pass by the windows on her way to the parking lot, clasping her hands, her head swiveling from side to side, her focus intense on the path ahead. With every person they passed, she seemed to tighten up even more.

What could have possibly caused that fear? He wanted to know everything about what made this beautiful woman so frightened in a sleepy mountain town where virtually nothing ever happened.

Pulling into his garage, Tai shut the car off and entered his house. He stripped out of his clothes as he crossed the floor and climbed the stairs, tossing them into the hamper in his room. His mind was still turning as he stepped into the shower, washing away the day's activities. Her deep, dark eyes and smiling face flashed in his mind again, and he felt a sharp need to see her smile directed at him.

Laci was a complication. A beautiful, tempting complication. Tai was a man who got what he wanted when he focused on it, but that wouldn't work here. He couldn't overwhelm a woman who looked at him with fear and navigated her world so timidly. He'd have to rein in his typical pursuit, regulate his approach. The next time he saw her, he would use all his control to keep himself in check. He needed more information, so he'd rely on what bits Charlie dished out. It would have to be enough.

THREE

LACI WOKE BUT DIDN'T move. She lay still, listening. The comforting splash of the shower was missing. In its place, the silence was a heavy blanket, thick and smothering. A cold, tight knot of panic twisted in her stomach. Where was he? Was he running late?

Finally, forcing her eyes open, she took in the dim space around her. A faint light hinted at unfamiliar shapes. She could make out a tall oak dresser in the corner and a chair with a blanket draped over the back near the foot of the bed, but these were not her things. This wasn't her room. The pale light, she realized, seeped in from a hallway she didn't know. Her breath hitched. *Where am I?*

Laci sat up. A dark figure hovered at the top of the stairs, silhouetted against the hall light. She froze, her heart pounding in her ears. "It's me. I just got home from work," the male voice called out to her.

For a moment, her mind couldn't comprehend the words. Her body coiled, ready to fight, until she recognized Charlie. The endless ribbon of highway, the blur of passing trees, the neon glow of a late-night diner, all the images of her drive to Charlie's house filtered in. She wasn't at home, alone. She wasn't alone anymore, but Charlie wasn't the man she wanted. The man she wanted was gone forever. Tears started, sobs wracking her body, and she buried her face in her hands. When Charlie sat, the side of the bed sank, and he pulled her into his arms.

Charlie reached up, his thumbs wiping away her tears. His voice was a soft rumble against her ear. "I know you miss him…"

She continued to sob into his chest, the damp cotton of his shirt soaking up her tears. He kissed her forehead and ran his fingers through her hair, the strands tangling slightly before smoothing out. The warm, earthy scent of him mixed with the smell of the wood-fired grills soothed her. Exhaustion finally overtook Laci, a heavy weight pulling her down, and she fell asleep against his chest, the tears still on her cheeks.

This time, sunshine woke her. It seeped in around the blinds, casting golden rays across the floor. Laci was belly-down, stretched as much as possible across half of the bed.

The bed rocked when a large body landed on the other half. Just like the old days, Charlie had undoubtedly taken a running leap to launch himself onto her bed, the way he always woke her when they lived together. It pulled her back to simpler, happier times.

Rolling over onto her back and stretching her arms over her head, Laci turned her head toward Charlie, and he gave her a huge smile. "Morning!"

Tilting her head up, Laci looked into his eyes. "Am I eighteen again? That would be great. There are so many things I could change."

He chuckled in response. "No, as much as I enjoyed those years with you in our apartment, we're not eighteen again. But I can keep this back-to-the-past theme going and make you my special pancakes for breakfast. How does that sound?"

Her stomach growled. "I guess that's a yes, please. But what time did you get in? Is it too early for you to get up? I can wait if you need more sleep."

She then realized she had no idea what time it was. Charlie raised his arm to look at his watch. "No, it's eight. I'm good. I got enough sleep. Tai got us out a little early so I could get home to you."

Laci grinned up at him. "You two work well together." She poked him in the shoulder. "Tai seems to dish out just as much as he gets from you."

"Yeah, we do. One time, I came in to find all the bottles at the bar with their labels facing backward. I knew they were all facing forward when I closed the night before. As I was turning them around, I saw him laughing in the kitchen."

Charlie looked down at her and gave a warm smile. "He's a good man, and since I'm sure you'll be hanging with me at the restaurant, I'm letting you know you can trust him, okay?"

She cringed a little. "I guess I didn't stop my body from locking up well enough."

One of his eyebrows rose sharply. "I can understand why you're on high alert. While you're here, I'll tell you who you can and can't trust. Tai is a good one through and through."

His smile grew. "You might even have some things to discuss, given your business background. Tai built his from the ground up. He takes care of his staff like family."

Laci took a breath. She knew she had overreacted yesterday, but couldn't help the involuntary response. "I got the feeling he was a good guy. But I don't trust my gut feelings about people right now. You know I trust you, and yes, I'll try to trust Tai too, since you said so."

"Thank you. Now, how about those pancakes?"

"Oh, hell yeah!"

They both dressed and made their way downstairs. As Laci set the table, Charlie put on a show for her, flipping pancakes high into the air, catching them with a sizzle in the pan. The smell of batter and butter filled the kitchen. She'd missed his infectious energy. On one flip, before the golden-brown disc could land, Laci shot her hand out, plucking the fluffy pancake from the air. She took a huge bite, grinning around her mouthful.

The breakfast was quick and full of laughter, a welcome change from the quiet meals she was used to. After they finished, Charlie gave her a tour of the house. When they got to the basement, Laci couldn't believe her eyes. "Wow, Charlie, you have a complete gym setup down here!"

Charlie beamed. "Yep! I was thrilled to move in here and purchase everything I needed. I can't be looking flabby if I'm going to find myself a hot man!"

Laci giggled and rolled her eyes. "Yeah, yeah."

Later, Charlie dressed and headed to work. Laci, still trying to rest from her travels the day before, stayed at the house. This place was a comfortable refuge for her now.

Curled up on the couch, she turned on the TV to an old movie. If this had been a typical day a year ago, she would have been sitting in her office, probably in a meeting with the global finance managers who reported to her. A stark contrast to weeks ago, when she forced herself to put on a brave face and look like she was enjoying a movie with her kids after they had moved back home. But the emptiness had consumed her from within. So much so that her children enlisted Charlie's help to get Laci away from the memories, give her a fresh place to start over.

On Saturday, Charlie wanted to familiarize Laci with the town so she would know where things were. They were quickly ready to head out into the crisp morning. Neighbors filled the air with the whine of leaf blowers, and a few conversations were heard off in the distance. The sounds were familiar, echoes of her neighborhood back home, and yet, here they seemed much more intimate.

On her first day, she hadn't realized the town center's layout had led her to take a much longer, roundabout route to get from one point to another. Walking was much faster, as they only had to stroll to the end of the street and through a path directly at the end of the cul-de-sac, which put them straight out into town.

"The town was built for walkers, not drivers," Charlie explained as they strolled. "Residential streets connect only via walkways, not roads, to encourage pedestrian traffic. The hotels and motels are on the edge of town to reduce cars. Tai lives way out, more up in the hills, so he has to drive in. Vanessa, Benji, and I all walk to work. Because we all live within walking distance, we often have movie and game nights at Benji's. Vanessa's boyfriend is a good guy, and Benji's wife is amazing too. Vanessa is already begging me to ask you to join our get-togethers."

"I enjoyed chatting with her and Benji, but I'm not sure about doing a big social event."

"No worries. I was able to convince her that you and I need our time together first. There's no pressure for you to jump right into it."

Charlie had witnessed the collapse of her mental health over the past months. The way he deflected Vanessa's invitation took the pressure off of Laci. She was fortunate to have him with her as her shield and protector. Back in their early days, Laci was the one protecting Charlie from the kids who picked on him. Now, the roles had reversed, and here he was, protecting her.

She knew she was a shell of her former self. If this had been a trip before her collapse, she would be walking around town, talking to people, taking every opportunity to get to know locals. But now, her trust in the human race had been obliterated. Happiness ripped from her hands. The only people she could trust now were Charlie and her kids. It felt like the early days again, when it was just the four of them against the world.

Being around people put an extreme strain on her energy. All her life, she'd sensed the emotions people tried to hide. Looking into their eyes, she could see their souls, their life experiences. Now, she could barely look anyone in the eye, terrified they would see the broken person inside. Only Charlie and her kids remained. Here, everywhere she looked, faces were blank, a blur, a giant mass instead of the unique individuals she used to see. A profound emptiness swelled in her chest, a constant reminder of what she had lost. Every time Laci's breathing picked up, Charlie would instinctively rub her back or pat her arm to calm her.

As they walked, Laci spotted a little store off to the right, with photographs on display. The magnificent images in the window stopped her in her tracks. Charlie pointed out that a few of the photos were from places in town. Then, a petite woman stepped out of the door and smiled at them. She had gray hair pulled back in a bun and wore a handmade white sweater with flowers along the bottom and a long, floral-embellished skirt.

"Enjoying the photos?"

"Yes," Laci replied, "these are impressive."

"Why, thank you. I took them all along my travels."

In the top right corner was one that captured Laci's attention. Animals or people were the subject of most of the pictures, but this one was a glorious sunset view from a high point across a small town. The image captured the last of the sun's rays, giving the sky above the town an ethereal glow. The woman grinned. "That one is from a lookout place on a hiking trail that winds up the hill over there. It's about a quarter-mile up and looks over the town here. Beautiful to go there in the fall and see all the colors of the trees."

Laci got an idea. "You sell photography equipment here?"

The woman gave her a big grin. "Yes, I do."

Charlie's face lit up, knowing exactly why she asked.

She turned to the woman. "Please, can we come in?"

The woman swept her arm back toward the door. "Come right in."

They stepped into the small shop, its walls adorned with photographs, lighting equipment, and camera lenses. The woman moved behind the main counter and toward the back of the store, where the most expensive pieces, including the cameras, were housed.

"My name is Carla, by the way."

As Laci approached the counter, she leaned into Charlie, and he wrapped his arm around her for support. "I'm Laci, and this is my friend Charlie."

"Oh yes, Charlie, I know you from the Blackwood Grill down the way. You always have a smile on your face when you're serving your customers."

Charlie beamed at Carla. "Yes, ma'am, I love my job. It allows me to talk a lot, which is my main hobby!"

Carla chuckled. Then she turned her attention back to Laci and asked, "So, Miss Laci, what can I do for you today?"

They spent another thirty minutes with Carla, reviewing the cameras, accessories, and everything she had available. Laci purchased a very nice package, and Carla even gave her tips on locations near the town where she could take beautiful photos to practice.

They stepped out of Carla's shop and back onto the main street. Laci leaned heavily into Charlie. Even an interaction with a kind stranger had been exhausting. To distract her, Charlie continued showing Laci around. There were small shops specializing in hobbies and cafés offering light dining. He explained that during the warmer months, the cafes and restaurants in town would set up carts providing small snacks and quick bites. It was convenient for tourists and employees working in the office spaces above the stores. Given she'd arrived toward the end of fall and nearly winter, it would be a while before she could experience this.

Each time they took a turn, at each store they visited, Charlie would ensure Laci was oriented back to the walkway leading to his street. No matter where she turned within the town, she knew how to get back home. As their walk went on, mapping things out in her head helped. She appreciated the town's simplicity. The pedestrian-friendly layout meant she no longer needed her car. Walking everywhere was a new experience, which calmed her nerves. The absence of traffic was a quiet relief, and for the first time in months, she looked forward to the small, solitary victory of running an errand on her own.

FOUR

LACI WALKED WITH CHARLIE to Blackwood. She planned to grab a quick bite, maybe fidget with her new camera, and then head home.

As they stepped through the door, Vanessa whizzed past with a tray of plates. "Heya, Charlie, hi, Laci!"

"Hi, Vanessa!" they replied in unison.

Laci glanced toward the bar, wondering if Charlie's absence was causing problems. Tai was serving customers, and he looked up, offering her a quick smile and a nod. She returned it hesitantly. *Charlie said you could trust him.* She wanted to trust him. But her instincts still screamed she couldn't afford to.

Charlie led her to the small booth in the corner by the window, which had a clear view of the bar. She took the seat with her back to the brick wall, a familiar, automatic precaution that kept the entire space in her view. Laci planned to eat quickly and get home before it got too busy.

Charlie hopped over to the bar and returned with a drink. "I have to get to work. Poor Tai has a lot to do in his office, so I need to help him out. Vanessa will be happy to get you anything you want, okay?"

"Thank you, Charlie."

With a squeeze to her shoulder, he turned toward the bar. As Charlie walked off, she heard him call out, "Tai, I know you missed me, my big hunk-a…"

"Get your butt to work, Charlie!"

"Yes, sir!" Charlie gave an overly dramatic salute.

Tai looked at Charlie with a big grin and a shake of his head. The two really did have fun with each other, just as Charlie had said. Laci felt some of the tension drain from her body. When Tai turned and gave her a warm grin and a wink, she did her best to return it.

A short time later, Vanessa stopped and sat opposite her at her table. "Laci! Sorry, I didn't get to you sooner. What would you like me to get you?"

"I'm good, I promise," Laci said with a wink, before giving her order. Vanessa scribbled it down and zipped away toward the kitchen.

After a quick scan of the space, Laci noticed it wasn't quite busy yet, with only three other tables occupied. She relaxed a bit and pulled out her new camera. This version was much more high-tech than the ones she used in college, but the familiar click when she twisted the lens into place comforted her.

Before she realized it, Vanessa was at her table again with her meal and another drink refill. "Do you mind if I sit with you for a minute or two? My customers are good for now."

Laci waved to the other seat. "By all means, rest your feet a moment."

Vanessa once again sat across from Laci, surveying the new camera equipment she had out. "Purchase a new toy?"

"Yeah, I saw this photography shop while Charlie showed me around town. I figured I could pick up an old hobby again and learn the town a bit more by exploring photo-taking locations."

Vanessa's smile grew. "That sounds like an amazing idea. As winter approaches, the park will look majestic, covered in snow first thing in the morning. It's so quiet, and the sunrise shimmers off the snow in rainbows of colors. It's my favorite time of year here. I jog with my boyfriend first thing in the morning, so we're among the few who can see this."

"I would love to see that. I love the snow. Back home, everybody complains about it, but I love the quiet after a fresh storm, when my trees are frosted white. We used to make snowmen in the backyard, my kids and my boyfrie—" She cut herself off, the word catching in her throat. "Yeah. Some of my favorite times." Pain bloomed in her chest. The happy memory had popped into her head for a moment, and then the realization that it would never happen again crashed down on her. She had to take a moment to catch her breath and hold back the tears.

When Laci glanced up, Vanessa faced the bar with wide eyes. Laci turned to see Charlie watching her, his eyebrows furrowed. He could clearly see her distress and her desperate grasp to regain control. Vanessa turned back to Laci, looking at her questioningly. "You have kids?"

Oh, thank goodness, Vanessa had offered Laci a life raft. Laci smiled. "Yes, I have two, a daughter, Alie, and a son, Mason, both in their early twenties."

When Laci looked up, she laughed at Vanessa's look of disbelief. "I can't believe you have two kids that old. I would have guessed you're in your late twenties. But that couldn't be right since I know Charlie is in his forties, even though he also looks like he's in his twenties. Is there some magic youth water where you're from?"

Laci smiled at Vanessa. "Not that I'm aware of, but maybe I should test it whenever I return."

Vanessa asked, "Did Charlie tell you we invited you to join our game and movie night group?"

"Yes, he did. I need some time to settle, but it sounds like it would be a lot of fun. Thank you for inviting me."

Vanessa smiled from ear to ear. "That's fantastic! We'll keep it down a little for you, especially on the first night, but we'll all be happy for you to join us. Oh, here comes Mr. Berkley. Ever since he lost his wife, I sit with him while he eats. I hope you don't mind."

Laci waved her hands to shoo Vanessa off, and the other woman jumped up to greet the man who stepped in the door. He had his gray pea coat buttoned and tied around his frail frame, and a worn black trilby was lifted from thin white hair as he stepped inside and headed straight for a table Vanessa was preparing for him. Laci watched his gruff face break into a genuine smile the moment he saw Vanessa.

After finishing her meal, Laci watched as the tables filled with patrons. Her sense of unease grew, and when she looked over to the bar, she caught Charlie looking right at her, a worried expression on his face. He could read her unease from a mile away. Smiling to try to reassure him, she didn't think she could convince him, or herself, that she was okay. Carefully, Laci packed up her new camera equipment and prepared to leave for home.

Waving goodbye to Charlie, she stepped out into the late evening light. Taking a moment to orient herself from their tour earlier, Laci paused at the corner of the building and mentally mapped out the path. Just as she was about to step off toward the end of the street, a hand grabbed her wrist.

Her heart jumped. Laci's gaze dropped to the curb, her mind already plotting an escape route. Buttery suede boots entered her peripheral vision. He used to buy two pairs at a time, afraid to scuff one. Loro Pianas. Her stomach dropped. As she looked up, adrenaline surged, her heart flailing against her ribs. Khaki pants. A polo shirt and sweater over a well-muscled body. The smile held the same chilling arrogance, and for a terrifying moment, her mind short-circuited. Only the blond hair, instead of black, offered a sliver of relief. Not him. But the guy had a similar possessive confidence.

The man leaned in closer, the stench of whisky on his breath making her stomach turn. "I noticed you dining alone in there. I was hoping you would consider going back in and grabbing a drink with me."

Shaking her head vigorously, she struggled to form the words. "No, thank you. I need to be going now."

Now she didn't want to lead him to Charlie's house, but she was afraid of getting lost if she strayed from the familiar path. As her panic increased, her breathing ramped up, and her vision dimmed.

When she tried to pull her arm from his grip, he tightened it, pain shooting up her arm. "Aw, come on. It's a Saturday night. One drink won't hurt."

Trying to pull away again, she was no longer able to form words. All she knew was she needed to get away and fast.

The space next to her shifted. A larger, warmer hand covered hers, effortlessly prying the man's fingers from her wrist. A deep, baritone voice cut through the fog. "She's not alone." *Tai.*

"Oh yeah? You her keeper? A pretty lady like her shouldn't be kept on a leash." The man tried to shuffle around Tai, still focused on Laci and dismissing Tai's presence.

"I'm the owner of this establishment, and I can assure you she's not available to talk to you. Now, I would appreciate it if you would leave." There was a more commanding tone to Tai's voice now.

The more this guy tried to reach her, the more panic set in, not only for her safety but for Tai's as well. Laci stood there, trying to calm her breathing. She was losing the battle. Everything tunneled further away from her.

"I want the pretty lady, not you. I don't care who you are. She was alone, and I wanted to talk to her." He practically yelled at Tai when he attempted to lean toward Laci again.

She noticed two men heading their way from inside. Where did they come from? Who were they? She glanced at the bar, seeing Charlie on the phone, watching what was happening. Everything seemed farther away than before. Darkness crept in on the sides of her vision.

Tai angled his body, watching Laci out of the corner of his eye while dealing with the other man. Because he was still holding her hand, he noticed hers go limp. Squeezing it to get her attention didn't seem to work. When he saw her head wobble, he stepped closer and placed a hand on her shoulder, wrapping an arm around her for support.

"You need to leave now. I'm giving you one more chance to do so." Tai said in a calm, commanding tone.

The man didn't give up. He tried to get to Laci again, so Tai used his free hand to stop him. The security team stepped out and tried to coax the guy back. Charlie was inside and on the phone, presumably with the police. When he had started his rounds in the main dining area, Tai had seen the man corner Laci. The stark terror on her face had been immediate, the color draining from her cheeks. There was no way Charlie could have made it in time to help her, so Tai jumped into action.

Even surrounded, the man still did not give up. When two police cars pulled up to the curb, the guy lashed out. Tai turned, shielding Laci with his body, knowing his security team could handle it.

Sergeant Jack Mathison pulled up behind the other officers and stepped out. "Tai, what's going on?"

Motioning to him to wait a moment, Tai turned Laci to face him so he could assess her situation. Her bags lay on the sidewalk. She wasn't responding to anything. Her head wobbled again, and Tai placed a hand around the back of her neck to support her. Leaning in closer to her ear, he slowly spoke, "Laci, please grab your bags and come with me."

It took two tries, but eventually, she leaned down and picked up her belongings. Gently placing a hand on her lower back, Tai guided her back inside.

As they walked behind the bar, she went right into Charlie's open arms. "Are you alright?" His arms wrapped tightly around her, and she put her face into his shoulder.

Tai spoke quietly. "Charlie, I'm going to take her back to my office. She'll be fine. Keep an eye on things out here for me."

"Yeah, I can do that." Before Charlie released her, he whispered something. She slowly nodded in response. Tai tucked her into his side, wrapping an arm around her.

With Jack following, the trio stepped through the doorway to the kitchen. Benji turned to ask, but Tai shook his head, and he returned to the flattop. Tai guided her to the seating area in the front corner of his office and helped her sit on the couch. Then, he walked to the fridge and grabbed two bottles of water. She placed her bags on the floor beside the couch, keeping them within her visual space. The men both noticed her examining the red handprint surrounding her wrist.

He noted the tremor in her hands as she fumbled with the cap on the water bottle he offered. After she took a sip, Tai introduced her. "Sergeant Jack Mathison, this is Laci. She's a friend of Charlie's and will be staying with him for a while. Laci, Jack is a friend of mine. He needs you to tell your side of what happened." Tai moved to the chair behind his desk, giving them space, but remaining there for Laci.

Jack pulled out a notebook and cleared his throat. "Laci, I need you to go through what happened step by step so we can record it."

Laci explained in detail from the moment she knew there was trouble. During her story, Jack looked over at Tai several times, his features etched with unease.

When she finished, Jack looked at her with some concern. "Laci, have you had issues in the past with this guy?"

Laci froze. She glanced over to Tai, and he braced himself for what could be coming. Laci turned back to Jack. "Not him. He reminded me of my ex-husband, who nearly killed me. Twice."

Jack gave a slight, almost imperceptible nod, turning to take Tai's statement on what happened. Tai appreciated the gesture. Jack wasn't going to push her and instead gave her space. He'd always had good instincts. Once their conversation finished, Tai said his goodbyes to Jack.

Tai crouched in front of Laci, his voice quiet. He retook her hand, his thumb gently stroking over her knuckles. "Laci, were you going to walk home after eating?"

Laci gave him a slight nod.

"You don't have to walk home. I can drive you right now. Or, if you'd feel safer, you can stay here. I'll set up a seat for you right behind the bar with Charlie."

Looking down at his hand, she whispered, "If I can stay here with Charlie, I would like to do that."

Tai stood and helped her from the couch. They walked out front. Leaving her at the kitchen door for a moment, he grabbed a chair from the front of the bar, moving it to a spot behind the bar with Charlie. He brought her to "Laci's spot" and instructed her to sit by Charlie's side for the rest of the night.

The picture became clearer as to why Charlie was so protective. Laci had come here for a respite, and a guy who wouldn't accept her rejection had just ruined it. Tai felt a jolt of anger toward himself. *I should have been on the floor sooner to stop him.*

Tai didn't expect her to move from that chair. He kept his circle small, a shield between her and the door. When he looked up and saw her washing glasses for Charlie, he had to stop and watch for a moment. Her movements were fluid as if she'd worked there for years. She knew exactly where to put the glasses back, and at times, even where to re-shelve the bottles. The two moved in perfect synchrony, a silent ballet of support. Tai watched as Charlie's service picked up speed and efficiency, his subtle gestures of comfort for Laci now woven into their rhythm.

It bothered Tai that for the rest of the night, Laci never smiled. He watched her from a distance, noting how she rarely lifted her eyes from the glasses she was washing. Every once in a while, she would scan the room, but it was a peculiar, empty scan, like a security camera panning back and forth. It pained him to know that the little joy he had seen from her earlier had been completely wiped out.

After closing, he drove home, went to his bedroom, and changed into his workout clothes. Tai needed to burn off this excessive amount of agitated energy before he could sleep. As he started his routine, his mind ran through the possibilities of seeing Laci more often and helping her feel safer in his restaurant. Both times she had been there, he could see she was scared. That didn't sit right with him. He knew this town, and she should feel safe here. It was time for a plan.

FIVE

A QUICK KNOCK ON the door woke Laci the next morning. "You up?"

She rolled over, groggily answering, "This morning thing is total bullshit."

The door opened, and her best friend's face peeked in. He gave a wry smile. "Preaching to the choir."

Charlie crossed to the bed and sat on the edge. Laci rolled and stretched, a futile attempt to wake herself, before giving up and burying her head under the pillow. He just lifted the edge to talk to her. "On days like this, I usually start with a workout before breakfast. Want to join me?"

Pushing the hair from her face, she slowly sat up and leaned back on one arm, her expression confused. "What time do you need to be at work?"

Reaching out to help control one massive tangle in her hair, he smiled. "Tai doesn't open Blackwood on Sunday or Monday. There isn't enough traffic to justify having us all stand around bored out of our minds. So, these days are ours."

"Well, that's pretty awesome. Give me a few minutes to get moving, and I'll work out with you."

Charlie got up and left her room, going down to the main floor. She pulled her hair into a bun, slipped on leggings and a worn-out t-shirt, and headed downstairs to meet him.

Starting her warm-up, Laci's muscles protested with a dull ache she hadn't felt in months. She picked up a pair of ten-pound dumbbells, a fraction of what she used to lift, and let out a soft, frustrated sigh. *Ten pounds. Six months ago, I never would have touched these smaller weights.*

From the corner of her eye, Laci could see Charlie watching her. His grip on the pulleys tightened, and she knew exactly why. It was only a matter of time before he mentioned it, so she braced herself for the conversation.

"How much weight did you lose?" he asked, his voice soft.

"I knew you noticed when you hugged me the day I arrived. I think I've lost about twenty pounds."

His face fell. "You gave up. I knew I shouldn't have left you." He sighed, the sound heavy with guilt. "I should have known."

Laci shrugged. "It just wasn't worth it. Waking, show-ering, eating...I didn't see the reason for it. When the kids moved home, I tried to function. But I still couldn't do it."

She set the dumbbell on the floor and walked over to him, meeting his gaze directly. "Look, I know it's bad."

He huffed in frustration. "I just..."

"I know," she soothed. "That's why I came here so that I can work on my recovery. I can trust you to help me, and you already are. I'm down here working out with you, right? I want to take steps to get back into life, figure out what this new life is for me, and learn how to navigate it on my own. But for now, I'm leaning on you."

"You're not completely alone, you know." His mellow tone told her how much he was hurting, too.

"I have you as my friend, yes. But you know as well as I do you can't fill that hole." The ache in her chest spread, and tears she thought she'd cried dry burned, tracing hot paths down her cheeks. "Nobody can replace Leo. I have to figure out every day, hour by hour, how I'll keep living with that gap."

Charlie slowly let go of the pulleys in his hands, then wrapped her in his arms. "If I could wave a magic wand and take this from you, I would."

Laci let out a stuttering sob.

He kissed the top of her head. "I guess I have to do what I can. We navigate from there."

She sniffled.

"All right, then, no more dwelling on it. Operation Return the Joy starts now."

She felt her heart lighten a bit. "Great, but Charlie?"

"Yeah?"

"Can it not start with you pressing my face into your disgusting, sweaty chest?"

As Laci dressed after her shower, she heard Charlie's phone ring downstairs. He answered it. She couldn't make out the words, but Charlie's tone was friendly. With leggings and a hoodie on, she opted not to spend an hour drying her hair. Instead, she brushed it back, creating a braided headband with the hair around her face. She grabbed a pair of fluffy socks, went downstairs, and flopped on the couch.

"I'll ask her, then I'll let you know...Blah, blah, blah, you're wasting time. If you'd hush up, I could ask her!" He pulled the phone from his ear, looking at it with amusement. "She hung up on me!"

He turned to her as Laci leaned over to put on her socks. "That was Vanessa. She wants to know if we'll join her and Brent for an afternoon movie at the theater. It's fine if you'd rather stay in. We can chill here, and I can kick your butt at gaming."

Laci rolled her eyes. Charlie knew she would whip his butt as she usually did when they gamed online together. Going out to the movie took some consideration, though. Her gaze fell to the bruise circling her wrist. The last time she'd ventured out hadn't ended well. But she couldn't get better if she didn't keep trying. "I think a movie sounds good," she replied. "I'll have plenty of time to hang out at home while you work, so let's go out today. I can kick your butt at gaming tomorrow."

"Are you sure you want to go out? I don't want to push you. Especially after last night..."

"I can't move forward if I don't take steps in that direction. The officer said the guy wouldn't be a problem anymore. I'll be with you the entire time we're out. I can do this."

He gave her a thumbs up, sent a quick "yes" to Vanessa, then turned to the kitchen to make brunch. While they ate, Laci tried to prepare herself for the outing. "I've kinda gotten to know Vanessa, but can you tell me more about Brent?"

"Sure, he's a lawyer, although I'm not sure what kind. Vanessa keeps trying to explain it, but I never remember. He's calm compared to Vanessa's high energy. They met at Blackwood a few years ago. Seemed to be perfect timing since she was going through a rough patch, and he made her happy again." Charlie reached for the bowl of fruit, adding more to his yogurt. "He doesn't talk much when we hang out, so I don't know a whole lot more than that."

She raised an eyebrow at him, scrutinizing what he said. "You, of all people, spend how much time hanging out with them, and you don't know much about the man? You practically know the entire life story of everybody you meet within the first five minutes you talk to them."

"Hey! That's not fair. He's a lawyer, and he knows how to keep information locked up." Charlie muttered under his breath at his plate. "And it's not five minutes. It usually takes at least ten."

Getting up to take her plates to the sink, Laci started laughing, then went upstairs to get ready to leave.

On the walk to the theater, Laci wrapped her arms around herself, her heavy hoodie just barely enough. The skies were overcast, but the wind was a calm breeze. Nothing terrible. It wasn't cold enough to see her breath in the air yet. Winter wasn't far off, but fall wasn't quite ready to give up the battle.

Charlie wasn't kidding. Sunday traffic was dead. They saw maybe fifteen, twenty people wandering the town. Most of the shops were closed. Laci's nerves calmed, not having to navigate around strangers. The theater was another loca-tion to add to her mental map of the town. On the smaller side, with only two screens, the theater was perfectly placed among the larger shops at the corner of the town square.

They spotted Vanessa and a man Laci assumed to be her boyfriend, Brent. Laci wrapped her arm around Charlie's as they approached. At five-foot-nine, Brent was on the shorter side, but then, most people were shorter than Laci. *Except Tai. Now, why did that just pop into my head?*

With spiky blond hair and blue eyes, Brent was the other half of a matched set with Vanessa. It was clear how their future children would look.

Vanessa's huge grin was infectious. "You made it! I've been dying to see this movie since it came out a week ago."

It was the latest in a superhero movie empire, which Laci was a big fan of, so she was also looking forward to it. "Did you see the previews? It looks like the main characters don't survive!"

Vanessa jumped up and down excitedly. "Yes! Oh my god, I can't wait to get in there!"

Brent held out his hand to Laci. *Here we go. Hold out your hand. He's not going to hurt you. Don't yank it back.*

"Hi there, since my girlfriend has a one-track mind now, let me introduce myself. I'm Brent, and you must be Laci."

Her hand dropped from his, and the frantic commands in her brain quieted. She managed a small smile. "Hi, I'm Laci. It's nice to meet you."

She wasn't sure if it was because of Vanessa or that, in general, Brent didn't look like a threat, but Laci could relax with him.

They purchased their tickets from a computer kiosk in the front lobby and walked in. Laci was charmed by the interior's design, which resembled an old 1950s theater, complete with vintage lights and a concession stand. Some posters from classic movies hung alongside modern movie posters. An older letter marquee above the hallway to the theaters directed customers to the correct title. Vanessa and Brent went to pick good seats, while Charlie and Laci opted to grab snacks for all four of them.

Laci was admiring the old black-and-white TV, which showed an episode of *Leave It to Beaver*, when the man behind the counter turned and grinned at Charlie as they approached. "Hi, Charlie! I haven't seen you in a while. What's been happening? Oh, who is your new companion here?"

Charlie's arm wrapped around Laci's waist as he gave the curt introduction. "Mark, this is my friend. She's staying with me." The omission of her name and the clipped, unfamiliar tone in Charlie's voice pulled Laci's attention from the TV.

Mark turned in Laci's direction. "Well, it's nice to meet Charlie's friend."

Laci felt Charlie's change in mood. He gave her a quick squeeze of his fingers, an indication she shouldn't provide any information. Her guard immediately went up. Charlie said he would tell her whom to trust and whom not to trust. Mark was a person not to trust. Pinned up against Charlie, Laci's fear stayed in check.

Mark looked to be in his mid-to-late fifties, with a goatee and dark hair streaked with gray, but it wasn't his age that caught her attention. It was the way his eyes slid down her body and back up, slow and deliberate, and then did it again. The hairs on her arms and the back of her neck rose in alarm. Charlie's hand on her tightened.

She kept her voice even to match Charlie's tone. "Hi."

As Mark moved around to serve their snacks, Laci noticed that Charlie only responded to Mark's constant babble with one-word answers, and his body shifted her away from the counter. Her nervousness grew with Charlie's lack of candid conversation. Whenever Mark asked a question about Laci, Charlie refused to answer, and she felt Charlie's squeeze on her side to stay quiet.

They found Vanessa and Brent in the theater, handed out snacks and beverages, then got comfortable. Laci leaned over and whispered in Charlie's ear, "You want to fill me in?"

Charlie's jaw tightened. "I had no idea the jerk was still in town." He blew out a breath. "When I first moved here, I lived in one of the small apartment buildings closer to the main roads. It was a three-story building with two apartments on each floor, and it was friendly enough that everybody in the building would hang out in our shared lawn area, grilling and chatting."

"I remember you telling me about it."

He tilted his head, indicating to Laci that he was getting uncomfortable. "It was mostly single people. Mark was on the first floor, and Nicole, Jack's girlfriend at the time, had the apartment across from mine."

Charlie quickly glanced at Vanessa and Brent, ensuring they weren't overhearing his conversation. She saw the hesitation in his eyes before the words came out, low and grim. "Mark hurt her. I called the police, but Nicole wouldn't talk. Mark vanished right after it happened. I honestly thought he was gone for good, that he had left town. When Nicole got out of the hospital, she moved out of our building."

Laci's hand, holding popcorn, froze halfway to her mouth. The lurch of her heart brought a familiar ache. "What happened?" she whispered.

"I moved out when I bought my house. I have no idea where he lives now, but clearly, he's still in town."

Laci needed clarification, however. "Wait, she was dating a cop, and nothing happened? I find it hard to believe he would've let that be."

"Jack was in the Army Reserves at the time and deployed. He'd finished at the police academy when the Army pulled him back in. Mark got to her days after Jack left."

Now she understood why Charlie had hesitated to tell her. *This wasn't the first time he'd witnessed an attack like this.*

"Nicole made me promise not to tell anybody anything, especially Jack. He was frantic when he returned months later, and she was no longer there. It killed me not to be able to tell him what happened. I have no idea where she moved. I thought it was back to her parents' house, but no, she left town completely."

Laci's breathing hitched, a wave of sympathetic understanding so sharp it stung her eyes. *She ran. She did the only thing she could, and she ran.*

Charlie turned to Laci, his eyes filled with deep concern. "Please be careful to keep your distance from Mark. I only know of that one incident, but I don't want to take any chances."

She patted his hand as the lights dimmed, and the movie began.

SIX

LACI SAT CROSS-LEGGED ON her bed, her laptop in front of her. It was time to take the next big step in her plan of recovery and get professional help. She had made an appointment with Dr. Tafelski before she left home to come here. He was a highly regarded psychologist, and she wanted to connect with him as soon as possible after arriving.

Her mind wandered a bit while watching the animations in the virtual waiting room. She worried about how far the doctor would go on this first visit. The office staff had sent electronic paperwork for completion after Laci booked the appointment. The forms asked if anything significant had triggered the need for an appointment. Laci had cried while filling out that section. Now her heart raced, wondering if that would be the topic of this visit.

A ping sounded, and the screen changed. A charming male face appeared, set against a backdrop of hanging plants and bookshelves. The man's gray eyes were soft and kind, immediately putting Laci at ease. She could see her own image on the other half of the screen, so she knew what he was seeing.

The soft lilt of his southern accent was the first to break the silence. "Hello, I assume you are Laci?"

Laci gave a small smile. "Yes, I'm Laci, and are you Dr. Tafelski?"

He gave a soft grin in response. "Yes, but you can call me Dr. T. Most people do since it's easier than the tongue twister. I reviewed the initial paperwork that my office had you complete before the appointment. I will not ask you to dig into your history on this first visit. We will get to that eventually. Today is more for evaluation and for us to get to know each other. If you are comfortable continuing treatment, I will schedule future appointments with you at the end of the call. How does that sound?"

She took a deep breath and released the tension building in her. "I appreciate that. I wasn't sure how fast you would want to review, and I admit, I wasn't prepared to lay it all out on the line this visit."

Dr. T smiled at her. "Can you tell me your number one priority for our sessions?"

Laci didn't need to think too deeply about this one. "I want to function as a human again. I don't want to be this shell anymore. I don't want to freak out at the smallest things. I want to be able to have a conversation with my kids without them sounding like they're walking on eggshells. I want to be present and navigate the world again without depending on my friend, Charlie."

As they spoke, Dr. T guided her through a series of diagnostic questions. Laci found herself relaxing as they went on. They weren't about her past, but about the present. They were specific, helping her untangle the knots in her mind and pinpoint individual struggles rather than feeling overwhelmed by one sweeping problem.

As he took a moment to finish the evaluations on his computer, she took a breath and prepared herself for his answers. "Laci, your inability to fully function in public without depending on Charlie is concerning. Your fear is a complex puzzle we will work on, piece by piece. Occasionally, it will get tough. As I get to know you, I will learn your limits and not push you past a breaking point."

Laci agreed with him as he continued, "I'd like to see you twice weekly for at least ten weeks. We can schedule a repeating time, and there may be one or two we must shuffle to a different time slot." Once they had it scheduled, he had a couple of more items to add.

"At the end of each session, I will give you a homework assignment. These are small tasks that, over time, will lead to bigger changes. This week, I would like you to go outside when the weather permits and walk one full lap up and down the street without Charlie. For the first two weeks, I suggest you only do it when Charlie is home. You don't have to talk to anybody. Still, I recommend that if anyone passes by or says hello, you respond with at least a hello in return. Do you think you can do that much?"

"I believe I can." She glanced out the window. "The weather is supposed to be nicer this week. Maybe after a few days, I'll try it when he's not home."

Dr. T smiled. "That is entirely up to you. Don't push too far past your boundaries. Going too far can cause a bad rebound, setting you back further than where you started. I will see you again in a few days." After they said their goodbyes, the screen went out.

Rolling off the bed, Laci stood and swung her arms overhead, and stretched her body back as far as possible.

Straightening up, she opened her bedroom door and went downstairs to Charlie. He was sitting on the couch watching TV. Laci sat and leaned against him, and he put his arm around her, pulling her close to his side.

Charlie muted the TV and looked down at her. "Well, does this doctor work for you? Is he somebody you think you can trust? Or do we need to find somebody else?"

She tilted her head up to look at him. "I like him. He conducted evaluations today, and I think he nailed everything perfectly. I have to see him twice a week for a long time. Plus, he gave me homework. I have to walk up and down your street without you once a day. I want to start this now. Would you mind sitting on your front step this time?"

When they stepped outside, Laci looked down the length of the street. She started walking, her entire focus on a single boulder marking the end of the road, trying not to look back at Charlie. Once she reached the end and made her way back, the endorphins kicked in a little, and her mind calmed. It was quiet. Instead of a running monologue of problems, there was silence. On her way, she noticed some of the residents had cute little decorations like garden gnomes in their flower beds. The unique choices made her smile. She finished and was looking forward to tomorrow's walk.

⩗

Tai picked up the ringing phone. The name on the display wasn't what he was expecting. "Jack, to what do I owe the pleasure of your call?"

"Tai." His tone sounded uncomfortable. "I did some digging and made calls after talking to Laci."

Tai felt a chill down his spine. Jack continued, "It's bad, Tai, beyond what she told us. She didn't do anything wrong. I'm honestly shocked this poor woman can keep moving forward. I have seen others give up over a lot less than what she's been through. The woman is unbelievably strong."

Tai's knuckles whitened around the phone. A part of him wanted to demand every detail, but he knew it wasn't his place to find out until she told him. "Don't give me details, but tell me, would it be safe for me to hire her at my restaurant?"

There was a long pause on the line. "A job?" Jack finally asked, his voice laced with confusion. "Her background is clean, but there are outside factors that may be risky. You don't think she's going to see it as odd that you randomly offer a stranger a job out of the blue?"

As he replayed the images of her behind the bar, Tai couldn't help but smile. "No. That night after you left, I intended for her to sit behind the bar with Charlie and stay put. Instead, she jumped in, seeming to know what she could do to help him. She only watched, then knew exactly how to insert herself. I admire that type of work ethic." *And I can keep her close.*

"That's probably a good idea. I was going to have a car patrol Charlie's street while he's at work and she's home alone. But, I'll have them patrol around Blackwood if she's there instead."

Tai got a bad feeling in the pit of his stomach. "It's that bad?"

"It's that bad. Tai, I've known you for a long time, so I'm saying this as a friend. Tread lightly, and don't get involved with her until you know her past." Jack saw right through him.

"Can you keep your men from being seen too much?" Tai asked. "I'll ask my security guys to come in a bit earlier each night and hope Charlie doesn't notice the change in their schedule."

"A few of my guys already patrol in street clothes, so tourists don't know they are officers. What's the worry about Charlie noticing?"

Tai turned to look out the window and saw the sun setting. The calming blues and purples provided a beautiful backdrop to the clouds rolling in. "Look, I get the feeling it's been the two of them against the world for most of their lives. How would you react if a group of people suddenly stormed in, trying to protect the most important person in your life when it's been your job for years?"

"I get it. I'd probably go apeshit and try to chase anybody off. I've been doing it, and I'll keep doing it. Are you at all worried about what could happen at your restaurant?"

"No, at the end of the day, it's a business I can rebuild. The people are irreplaceable, which extends to whomever they consider family."

"Can you text me to let me know when she's there with you? That will help me direct coverage as needed."

"I can do that. Thanks for calling me."

As Tai hung up, his mind churned through horrific possibilities of what else Laci could have endured. That night, she had gone so pale and unresponsive that it scared him a bit. All he could do was give her time. She trusted him, but she didn't know him well enough yet.

Since that night, Charlie had come in without Laci. When Vanessa asked Charlie about it, he said Laci was staying home and working on things. Tai felt responsible because she didn't feel safe in his restaurant, so she was now avoiding it.

His unfolding plan served a dual purpose. Hiring Laci would give her a reason to come back each night. She could stay with Charlie while he worked. Having her around would also provide them with the opportunity to get to know each other.

Charlie and Laci were getting in a little more gaming before he left for work. While he was away, she planned to stay home again and read a new book she'd purchased. The weather had turned nasty that morning, and they woke to thunder shaking the house. It had calmed from a deluge to a steady rain, but it was still bad enough that Charlie decided to drive instead of walking.

"Shit! How do I keep forgetting you do that damn sneak attack?" Charlie's growl of frustration echoed through the gaming room as Laci once again beat him in their favorite PvP game. "You're on the same damn screen as me!"

"Because you get so wrapped up in your next move," she snickered, "you tunnel vision and don't see mine!"

She playfully stuck her tongue out at him, and he returned the same.

Charlie's phone rang from the kitchen. "I give up!" he groaned, tossing the gaming controller onto the chair with a theatrical thud.

"Baby." Laci chuckled at his tantrum. She shut every-thing off, then followed him down the hallway.

He picked up his cell phone from the counter, and his eyebrows scrunched together. "Hey, Tai. Is everything okay?"

Laci guessed it was unusual for Tai to call Charlie, espe-cially since they would see each other in about two hours. She perused the fridge for a drink. Charlie turned, looking at her with one eyebrow raised. "Yeah, she's here with me...No, she didn't have plans...Sure, not a problem. See you soon." He hung up the phone, then turned to her. "Tai asked if you could come in with me. He wanted to talk to us both before I started my shift."

"Do you think it has something to do with what hap-pened last time I was in there?" She was done rehashing the incident and didn't want to discuss it again.

"No, I didn't get that sense. Tai would have gone over that with us sooner. It has to be something else."

The only way to find out was to go. Within twenty minutes, they headed into the storm in Charlie's car. Even though it was late morning, the sky was nearly black. As they pulled into the parking lot behind Blackwood, the rain eased. They thought they could run for the door. Unfor-tunately, when the two of them rounded the front of the building, the rain picked up again. Tai swung the door open for them when they approached.

As they stood on the mat inside the door, dripping water from their clothes, skin, and hair, Tai went behind the bar and grabbed two clean towels for them to dry off what they could. The darkened restaurant, with its faint aroma of the grill, wiped away the cold, ozone-laced smell from the storm outside. Laci patted her face, hair, and arms. She was glad she didn't regularly wear makeup. Otherwise, she would look like a clown from a nightmare movie.

Charlie looked outside. "Hey, boss, it's gonna be dead today."

Tai chuckled. "Yes, I suspect the storm will hold back the crowds. I was hoping I could have some time to chat with the two of you before we get things started here."

Charlie and Laci looked at each other. "Sure," they said in unison. Since they weren't due to open for another hour, Tai led them back to his office. He gestured to the couch in his seating area and offered them bottled water.

When Tai sat in the chair facing them, Laci noticed something she hadn't seen the last time she was in here. The chairs and couch were deeper than usual, designed to accommodate Tai's larger frame. It occurred to her that all of the seating out front was also deeper and the tables wider. Tai had designed every aspect of his restaurant, featuring high ceilings, wider tables, and larger chairs, while maintaining a cozy atmosphere that provided comfort for taller patrons. It was a subtle detail, but one that conveyed his thoughtfulness.

Tai began, "I asked both of you to come in because I have a couple of questions I thought would be better to ask in person, not over the phone."

Laci's body involuntarily tightened, and Charlie must have felt it. He placed his hand on her knee and spoke for both of them. "Go ahead and shoot. We'll answer what we can."

Tai took this in stride and moved forward. "First, Laci, I noticed you jumped in behind the bar the other night to help."

"Yeah, sorry about that. I felt useless sitting there. I wanted to help things move along a little more smoothly. It was my way of contributing after you helped with the guy who grabbed me."

He gave her a reassuring smile. "Nothing to be sorry about. I was quite impressed. I assume you have experience in the food service industry? It typically takes a good bit of time for somebody new to jump in effortlessly and not get in the way."

Charlie jumped in, happy to respond on Laci's behalf. "She doesn't have food service experience." Laci squeezed his hand to try to stop him from continuing, but he kept going. "She does have experience in improving workflows and streamlining processes. Plus, she and I have worked together in the past. We can quickly sync with one another's needs. It felt awesome to have that back again."

Tai smiled. "I'm glad the dynamic duo could reunite for my benefit. I don't know if you're working somewhere else while you're here with Charlie..."

"No, I'm not. I, uh, I stepped away from my job a while back." Laci looked at Charlie, and he gave her a reassuring smile.

Steepling his fingers in front of his face, Tai studied them both. "Well, I would like to propose something. Would you be interested in working here alongside Charlie? You can do whatever tasks make you most comfortable. That seemed to be your flow the other night."

From the corner of her eye, Laci could see Charlie light up. But her stomach turned, and her hands went clammy cold. She couldn't meet the demands of a job she knew inside and out. How could she commit to a position in the public eye night after night? There was no way she could interact with customers every night. She could barely interact with strangers one-on-one on rare occasions. What if she couldn't do it and disappointed Charlie? What if she disappointed Tai?

Charlie squeezed her hand and murmured in her ear, "No worries. You know I talk enough for both of us."

A smile touched Tai's lips at Charlie's comment, and he leaned forward. "I won't push you to work past your boundaries. I'm offering you a position that allows you to contribute in a manner that suits you best. You can do what you want. If that means no customer interaction, then that's fine with me. I saw this as an opportunity for you to stay with Charlie instead of staying home alone while he works. I'll also pay you for your time behind the bar the other night."

Laci took the chance and looked directly at Tai. His dark eyes stayed locked on her, conveying his sincerity. She realized then why he hadn't made the offer over the phone. He knew she had to see him, to see the honesty, *to trust.*

"Okay," she said, her voice barely a whisper. "If I don't have to talk to customers, then I think I can do it."

Charlie kissed her cheek. "Dynamic duo is back again!"

With a broad smile, Tai chuckled. "How about you and I complete the paperwork while Charlie starts opening?"

Charlie turned to Laci to confirm her comfort with him leaving. She nodded, growing comfortable enough with Tai to be alone with him briefly. With that, Charlie jumped up and headed out the door to the kitchen.

Tai leaned back and looked toward the door. "Charlie."

"Yes, my sugar…"

"Charlie." Tai's warning tone was a deep rumble.

Charlie chuckled. "Yeah, boss?"

"Leave the door open so she knows you're there while we wrap this up."

As Charlie left the room, Tai moved to his desk. Laci moved to the chair on the other side of his desk to make the paperwork more manageable and gave Tai a shy smile. "Thank you for that. I know you don't know why, but I appreciate it."

Tai stopped, looked directly into her eyes, and she felt something she hadn't felt in a long time. There was a tiny flicker of a flame inside of her that had long ago gone out. It was barely there, a little bit, but she sensed it. Laci blinked, the pieces falling into place. It wasn't just the open door. It wasn't just the job offer. He was doing all of this to make her feel safe, to take some of the burden off of Charlie.

Lowering his voice so only Laci could hear, Tai said, "Whatever the reason you came here to stay with Charlie, I don't need to know. I've come to realize Charlie would lay his life on the line for you. If anything happened to you, he would die with you. If I can provide something to help alleviate some of the burden for both of you, regardless of the situation, then I'm happy to do my part. I just want you to know, I'm in your corner, too."

Blankly staring at him, she blinked. "Thank you, Tai."

With the paperwork complete, Tai led Laci to the bar area, where they joined the others. Since Vanessa and Benji had arrived, Tai announced, "Laci is now part of our team. She'll be a bar runner for us. I've seen enough to know she'll be an exceptional addition to our group."

Vanessa cheered, throwing her hands in the air, then ran up to hug Laci. Benji gave her a quick, firm high-five.

Charlie pulled her into a big hug, his arms a familiar shield, and whispered, "Having you here with me will be amazing."

Now that she was officially part of the crew, Laci observed everyone's habits to move as efficiently as possible. Starting again behind the bar with Charlie, Laci then added the task of filling drink orders for Vanessa. Tai showed her how to buss tables. She also learned how to use the commercial dishwasher to clean dishes. As long as customer interactions were minimal, Laci was happy to help with whatever was needed.

Laci was also aware that when she moved out from behind the bar and away from Charlie, Tai would move to within a couple of tables' distance. He did this while making his rounds, talking to customers. Soon, she adjusted to his presence near her and even built some comfort in being able to step away from Charlie under Tai's watch.

After several nights, she had her routines down. The customers became a background to her, and she hardly even noticed them. Each night, however, Laci became increasingly aware of Tai. Eventually, she could sense his exact location in the space without even needing to look for him.

It had been so long since she could do that with someone other than Charlie and her kids that she wasn't even aware of it happening until one night when she felt Tai approach. The moment she detected him moving, she knew she had to get back behind the bar. He approached at a speed that told her he was coming to shield her. It wasn't until she was by Charlie's side that she looked up and saw she was right. Tai had moved to within feet of where she had been standing. He spoke with a guy near the door, blocking him from getting to her.

Charlie whispered in her ear, "I saw that. You're coming back to yourself."

For a moment or two, Laci watched Tai before heading into the kitchen. Just as she turned away, she saw him look back, a slow grin spreading across his face.

SEVEN

A FURIOUS, STINGING PRESENCE, like a swarm of angry bees, ripped Laci from sleep. He was here. Her mind, still attuned to his rage, ticked through the defenses she'd performed in her nightly, compulsive ritual. She knew every lock was fastened, every window secured, and the alarm was set. So how did he get in? How could he possibly know she was alone?

The floor creaked in that spot only she knew how to avoid. Confirmation that he was climbing the stairs. She didn't have much time. Laci quietly rolled off her bed to the floor. She reached up, grabbed her cell phone from the nightstand, and unplugged it. She crept to the bathroom, shutting and locking the door behind her. Hitting the emergency button on her phone, she heard the operator and whispered her need for help. Opening the door to the cabinet under the sink, she reached in, groping around in the dark for the weapon she knew she had hidden. Laci had known this day would come. Every room had a weapon, such as a baseball bat or tactical pen, hidden and ready to grab at any moment. Now, she could only wait. And hope the police were fast enough.

He was at her bedroom door. The lock would provide little resistance. She had seen him kick in a door so many times, and she knew how fast he could do it. This time, though, the doors were solid wood with reinforced frames. A change she insisted on when remodeling this home.

Laci crawled to the other side of the bathroom and into the walk-in closet, closing the door behind her. Creeping on all fours behind the table in the middle of the space, she snuck into a rack of clothing that hung low enough but missed hitting the floor. As she situated herself against the wall and pushed the clothes back in place, she heard him yell for her. The emergency operator's voice barely registered in the muffled space. Laci whispered her reply that he was right there. The operator tried to assure Laci that the police were nearly at her home, but Laci couldn't help but feel it was too late. She wouldn't survive this time.

The boom of him finally kicking in her bedroom door reverberated through the room, but she held in her scream. A crash echoed as her nightstand lamp shattered. Then came the shuddering impact of her bed being flipped, sending vibrations through the floor. At any moment, he would see the closed bathroom door. Any moment, he would have her.

Her body recoiled, every muscle tight. The memory, a raw and brutal flash, of his fists, the searing pain, it all slammed into her. He always took her to the precipice, to the edge of death, but never over. This time, she hoped he would. She hoped it would be fast.

Charlie would take care of her babies. He would tell them about her. As she covered her head, she sent them a silent message of love.

A kick to the bathroom door. Another. One more, and he was in. The lock gave a final groan. Laci held her breath. The door flew open.

The scream ripped from her lungs, and Laci sat up, thrashing against an invisible attacker. Her heart frantically hammered against her ribs. The air was thick and thin all at once, making her head dizzy.

"Laci! It's me! It's just me!" Charlie's voice broke through the panic.

A form moved into the room, and she saw not a monster, but Charlie. He held his hands up, a silent, patient plea, not daring to approach until she gave the signal. She raised her left arm, her hand shaking. He swooped in, pulling her into his lap, holding her tight against him as the sobs finally broke free.

Charlie rocked Laci back and forth, holding her and kissing the top of her head. "It's me. He can't get you. It was a nightmare, and he wasn't here. I promise you." His hand gently ran over her head and down her hair in a repeated, soothing path. "I've got you."

Laci had heard words like that before, not from Charlie, but from Leo. They'd turned out not to be true. Leo couldn't have known, but it was a lesson learned too late when they thought they were safe and let their guard down.

⛰

Laci sat on the couch, staring into the backyard, where fresh snow lay. The early morning sun shimmered across it like diamonds. Grabbing her camera, she opened the door enough to get a clear shot. She was locking the door when she heard Charlie come down the stairs behind her.

"Please tell me you got that shot."

"Yes, I did indeed, good sir." Laci lifted the camera to show him the screen.

"Seriously, you should start selling your photos again. They're beautiful."

On the wall hung one of her more recent pictures. Carla had been so helpful in getting the print and framing done in time for Laci to gift it to Charlie on his birthday. The two of them were in the woods, where they found a massive pile of leaves blown into a nook. Laci set up her camera with a rapid shot, and they sat in the bank, repeatedly throwing leaves over their heads. Their eyes were fixed directly on the camera, their smiles tamed after they regained control of their laughter. The leaves in the air formed a perfect combination of in-focus ones flying over their heads and blurry ones closer to the camera.

He stepped away to the kitchen. "I'll see you at work after your appointment, right?"

"Yeah, Dr. T will be an hour, and then I'll leave right after."

"Alright, text me when you leave the house so I know when to expect you."

"I will, I promise."

Laci watched him step out the front door, hearing the deadbolt slide into place. The nightmares had returned full force since she'd started counseling with Dr. T. Every night before bed, Charlie made it a point to show her he checked every lock on every window and door, and he always locked them before leaving.

Despite Charlie's reassurances that it was okay and he could make up for his sleep in the morning, she felt horrible about constantly waking him with her nightmares. Plus, she needed rest, too. It was wearing her down, so hopefully, Dr. T could offer a solution.

Today was the first time Laci's appointment clashed with her start time at work, so it would be the first time she walked to work alone. She was a little nervous, but the two of them had walked the path enough times that she knew it well.

Laci booted up her laptop at the kitchen table to prepare for her appointment. Over several visits, she noticed other changes as well, positive and subtle ones, but they were there.

The screen changed, and Dr. T was on her right. "Good morning, Laci. Did you get snow in your area?"

Smiling back at him, she replied, "We did. It's beautiful."

"I got some too, but probably not nearly as much as you since I'm located in Denver." He gave a brief nod, ready to get down to work. "Alright, Laci. Why don't we start where we left off? How has the homework been going for you?"

"They are going well. I've done each one every day I could, weather permitting. Even if I can't get outside, I walk on the treadmill downstairs. I know it's not the same thing, but the walking helps to clear my head."

"Excellent, the fact that you keep moving is good. Are there any other positive changes you have noticed?"

She stopped to think about it. "I noticed I've opened up a little more. I can now detect other people, not just Charlie or my kids. You know, that thing where I told you I can sense their movements without looking at them?"

"I remember."

"I can do that with somebody else now. Tai, who owns Blackwood, moved between me and a customer. I was at a table and didn't see any of it. I sensed his mood change and felt him shift, so I picked up and returned to Charlie's side. When I looked up, I saw Tai standing close to where I'd been, and he was in front of a customer."

Dr. T stopped taking notes and looked at her through the camera. "Why do you think Tai moved to get between you and the customer?"

Laci hadn't even really thought about it. "I assumed it was because he knew I didn't want to interact with anybody while working, so he stopped the guy from talking to me."

This answer satisfied his question, so he moved on. "Now, let's tackle the tough one. What's been the biggest struggle for you since we last spoke?"

She took a deep breath. "My nightmares. They've gotten worse. I had a bad one last night, reliving the night my ex tried to kill me the second time. Some are mostly accurate with pieces of actual events. Others are a mosh pit of pieces and parts. I'm not sleeping, and Charlie isn't sleeping because he comes to help me when I scream out. They've been happening almost every night now."

Dr. T started typing on his computer. "I'm messaging a colleague of mine. She is one of two psychiatrists here in our practice. In our case review, I mentioned your nightmares picked up, so she is familiar with your situation. She said she could prescribe something if you would like to try that. Be aware that it has some side effects that can be concerning. They don't happen to everyone and should dissipate with time, but be aware they can happen."

Laci noted everything.

Now, he looked concerned. "Let's go back, and I'd like you to tell me what happened that night."

A little under an hour later, Laci texted Charlie that she was leaving the house but had one stop to make before work. There was no response, but she also didn't expect one. If he had customers, he wouldn't be looking at his phone. Now, she had to figure out where the pharmacy was in relation to the walkway. Laci zipped up her coat, stepped out the front door, and locked it. After pulling it three times to check it was tight, she was satisfied and headed to the end of the street. Her appointment had flayed her nerves raw. Every detail of the attack, spoken aloud, now echoed in her mind as she navigated the quiet street. She was listening to every noise around her on her walk, trying to pick up on anybody approaching too fast so she could be ready to defend herself.

Laci navigated with the map on her phone. She got to the walkway, went straight through, and came out into town as always. According to her map, the pharmacy was to her left. As she approached the town square, the movie theater came into view.

Once again, she stopped, checked her map, turned, and noted the pharmacy should be down the street in front of her. She crossed over, and sure enough, four doors down, she found the pharmacy. They had her prescription ready, so she picked it up, paid, and stepped back onto the street. She knew she had to turn back to the theater, so she walked toward that point.

Then she felt it. Sharp, stinging prickles ran down the back of her neck.

Someone was watching her. Laci kept her head up and let her eyes move in all directions, but she couldn't see anything. The sunglasses she had on hid her eyes from everyone. It might have been her imagination since she was already on edge from her call with Dr. T, but she had to be sure. Looking around, she sought out shelter, but not one where many people would see her. Quickly, she stepped into the theater's front door, figuring no one would be in the lobby. The last time they came in, the lobby had a computer kiosk, no humans working, and she was right. She needed to know if she could catch what was causing the feeling. Looking through the glass, she could only see other residents going about their day.

"Laci, is that you?"

Laci almost jumped and screamed, but she stood solid. Her brain redirected resources, forcing a calm response. Turning smoothly so he wouldn't pick up on her fear, she replied, "It's Mark, right?"

"Yeah, that's me! Is everything okay? I saw you come in and not move." He had a smile on his face, but for some reason, Laci felt the smile wasn't right. Mark had his eyes intensely focused on her. Laci turned back to the door and looked out. Mark stepped closer behind her, and she could hear his breathing too close. Her skin crawled, and her mind screamed to run.

Think Laci. "Oh, all is good. It's my first time walking around town without Charlie, and I think I got turned around. When I saw the theater, I figured I could reorient myself starting from here."

"Are you enjoying living with Charlie again? I bet you missed him after he moved out of your place to come here. Are you heading to work at Blackwood?" *Wait, how did he know all of that? Don't confirm anything. Get out of here.*

Now, she needed to escape without looking like a lunatic. "I realize now I need to turn right out of here, go down three blocks, and then turn left."

"That's it. Did you need help with anything else?" She detected him taking another step closer to her. Now he was in her personal space. Charlie's warning rang in her head. A primal need to escape seized her. She was alone with him. Charlie had no idea where she was.

"No, thank you. Charlie is expecting me, so I'll be on my way."

Laci stepped out onto the street and turned right. She did her best to walk briskly, but not so much that she looked like a maniac. The unwelcome, yet familiar symptoms of a panic attack crept in. Counting out the blocks until she found the familiar street of Blackwood, she turned and made her way up the storefronts.

Laci stopped just short of the restaurant windows, out of sight of the bar. She leaned against the brick, forcing herself to take long, slow breaths. The feeling of being watched was gone, but the interaction with Mark had left a lingering chill. If she walked in now, Charlie would see it all over her face. Sinking onto a nearby bench, Laci tried to find a single point of focus, just as Dr. T had taught her. A crack in the pavement. An orange leaf caught in the sidewalk, shuddering in the breeze. But the images of Mark's predatory smile and his creepy eyes broke through.

The door to Blackwood opened, and Tai stepped out. A fresh wave of panic hit her. *He's going to wonder why I'm just sitting here when I'm already late for work.* She frantically tried to school her features before he got to her. There was no way she could let him or Charlie see the mess she was in.

Tai made his way over during her internal argument and stood before her. Now, it was apparent he had come out to find her. Charlie must be having a heart attack because she took so long.

"Before you ask," Tai began, "No, Charlie isn't upset. He did get your text, told me something delayed you a bit more, and he has gone on to take care of his customers."

The relief hit Laci, and she took a breath. "Then you came out here by chance?" *Please say yes.*

"No," He motioned to the restaurant. "I was in my office and saw you on the security cameras."

Laci looked up and saw the one at the top corner of the building pointing this way down the street. *Damn.*

So much for going in looking like everything was okay. Laci glanced at Tai, and she could see compassion on his face. "Sorry, I'm running late. I had an appointment, and then I made one more stop. I got a little turned around on my way back. I stepped into the theater to reorient myself, but Mark saw me and started talking to me."

Something flickered across his eyes that she didn't quite catch. "So, you ran into Mark?"

"I met him the other night when Charlie, Vanessa, and I saw a movie. I got the memo that I should watch what I say around him. Charlie didn't even introduce me to him."

Tai took a moment before answering, "Will you take a walk with me? I'll text Charlie and tell him I ran into you and asked you to join me on my errand."

Laci's mind battled a wave of guilt. Being close to Tai would only make it worse. But she wasn't settled enough to face Charlie and didn't want to burden him.

Dealing with the guilt was easier than placing the responsibility for her emotions on Charlie. Laci stood, so Tai took out his phone to text Charlie. At least this would give her an excuse to take more time to calm down. Her nerves were glowing embers, and she needed to recover. They walked back the way she came but turned left at the end of the street. She had no idea where they were going, but she still trusted Tai enough.

He smiled. "I told him I had to run to the store around the corner, so we don't have long. I'm also trying to move out of the perimeter of my security cameras in case he gets any ideas to go to my office. We'll walk back that way shortly."

Laci couldn't help but smile. "He would run back there to watch, ensuring you're not abducting me."

Tai chuckled. "He trusts me, but only to a certain point with you. I respect those limits and make sure I never cross them. I've never had somebody I was so fiercely protective of, but I've seen it happen enough times with friends to know better than to cross that line."

As they walked, she thought about how Tai had treated her over the past several weeks. "I appreciate the extra effort you've put into respecting my boundaries, too. Even though I'm sure they aren't crystal clear, I've noticed you've given me the space I need."

There was a pause, and Laci could tell he was working out how to respond. "I try to keep my restaurant a safe environment for anybody who walks in. When it comes to my staff and their loved ones, I'm extra vigilant and do what I can. It still bothers me that an incident occurred with you."

Tai took another moment and continued, "When you stopped coming in with Charlie, I really hoped you weren't avoiding the place for fear it could happen again. I could tell Charlie was worried about you being home alone while he was at work, and I see how much more relaxed he is with you by his side. I hope you know I'll do everything I can to ensure you feel safe when I'm around."

Laci felt he didn't mean only at Blackwood.

"Mark is somebody you should do your best to avoid giving information to." Laci could tell by the tone of his voice that he was reigning in some anger. "Unfortunately, Charlie learned that the hard way during his first year living here. I'm asking you to steer clear of Mark if you can."

She took a moment to respond, then said, "Tai, he knew my name. He knew things about my past with Charlie, things I'm sure Charlie's never told any of you. He asked about my work here, and I realized we haven't crossed paths since I was hired. I didn't confirm anything, but I can't believe Charlie would have told him those things."

Tai stopped and turned to face Laci. "It's a small town, so it's easy to find out you now work for me. Knowing about your friendship with Charlie, I can tell you with certainty that Charlie wouldn't have told him. Always operate with extreme caution around him, okay?"

Great, just what she needed. Another person to be concerned about. At this point, she may as well roll out a naughty list like Santa. She looked into his eyes. "I promise I'll be careful."

Tai didn't move right away. He stared at Laci, and she felt the heat in his gaze. Then, the moment passed, and they resumed their path. "I can ask somebody to find out how Mark possibly knew those details about you." They walked around the block and back to Blackwood's front door.

"I appreciate that."

Tai waved in the door just before opening it. "You'd better get in there before Charlie thinks I kidnapped you."

They laughed as they walked in, and when she could smile at Charlie, she realized what Tai had done. He'd seen her on the cameras, unable to control her fear, so he'd walked with her until it was gone. His calm presence had cooled her internal chaos.

Laci got behind the bar and stowed her belongings as usual.

Charlie had several customers at the bar, but still stopped to give her his full attention and whisper, "Everything good? Did the appointment go well?"

She whispered in his ear, "Yeah, I had to stop at the pharmacy. Dr. T got me something to stop the nightmares, and hopefully, we can both get some sleep."

His eyebrows knitted as he lowered his voice to say, "It's okay. If you don't want to take anything, I'm not upset. We get our sleep later."

A gruff voice from the other side of the bar slurred at them, "Heeeeeyyy lovebirds. If you twoooo are done sayin' sweet nothins in each other's ears, I'd like my beeeer."

Charlie grinned, dropping his head on Laci's shoulder. "I'm coming, Huey. Keep your pants on!"

After closing that night, Charlie and Laci said goodnight to everyone and started walking home. Senses scanning the area, there was no feeling of the presence that had been there earlier. Laci now believed her morning therapy session had skewed her perceptions.

Laci got ready for bed and pulled out the prescription Dr. T had ordered. After the day she'd had, she was sure the nightmares would come tonight. She hoped this would work.

A soft knock came at her door. "Do you want me in here in case the meds don't work?"

A simple nod was all she could manage, knowing that if she had a bad reaction, she didn't want Charlie vaulting across the hall for her.

He came around and flopped on top of the duvet. "How did your appointment go today?"

Laci rolled over, her gaze finding his. "We talked about that night... when you and the kids were on your adventure weekend." Her voice was quiet, hollow. "I just keep going over it, trying to find a way I could have fought him off. But there was no way. It took three huge cops just to pull him off me and pin him down."

Charlie reached out and grabbed her hand. "You did the one thing you could. You held on and survived. I know how hard that was, but you were still there to raise your kids, and that was how you won." He kissed her hand. "Let's get some sleep, and tomorrow, we can kill zombies to make ourselves feel better."

EIGHT

Charlie and Laci walked a few streets over to the whitewashed brick ranch. The houses here sat farther apart with sprawling lawns, a contrast to Charlie's more condensed street.

Soon after Charlie rang the bell, a petite older woman with graying hair in an ear-length bob opened the door. "Oh, Charlie! You made it. Come on in. Vanessa and Brent arrived a minute or two ago, so they haven't started anything yet."

Charlie stepped in and held Laci's hand as she crossed the door's threshold. "Marie, this is my friend Laci, who's staying with me. Laci, this is Benji's wife, Marie. Don't let her innocent look fool you. She's mean and cunning when playing games."

Marie chuckled, playfully smacking Charlie on the arm, then opened her arms to Laci for a hug. For a fleeting second, Laci tensed, the instinct to shrink away still strong. But Marie's expression was so open and warm, Laci found herself leaning down, accepting the hug before she could overthink it. The scent of nutmeg surrounded her, and when she stood again, Charlie squeezed her hand in silent support. They handed their jackets to Marie, set their shoes by the door, and headed toward the back of the house.

Marie walked with them. "Laci, it's nice to meet you. We enjoy having everybody here to talk and have fun, so please, make yourself at home."

Laci gave a timid smile to the other woman. As they followed Marie to the back of the house, Laci held onto Charlie's arm, a slight tremor running through her. She was still nervous about being in a small enclosed space with a group of people. But knowing everyone here helped her take this step into something she wouldn't have even considered a few short weeks ago.

Once past the enclosed foyer, they walked into a vast space with vaulted ceilings. Everything looked newer and brighter than she expected. Vanessa, Brent, and Benji were sitting around the table. Charlie guided Laci toward the open kitchen, where Benji had drinks and food laid out for them.

Benji called over, "You two help yourselves to whatever you want, and come on over."

Laci looked at the spread of food, including tiny skewers of caprese salad, a platter of smoked salmon, and a bowl of fresh fruit. "Benji," she teased, "don't you get enough of making food at work? Why are you doing it at home, too?"

He grinned, adjusting a plate on the table. "Food is a passion, not a job for me. The best part is seeing people enjoy what I've created." He paused, his smile softening. "That's why Tai and I clicked. When he was opening Blackwood, he told me he didn't want to micromanage. He wanted to be out front, among the customers, and he needed somebody to handle the food. I knew right then I'd found my place. I've been there since day one."

Vanessa snickered. "I'm pretty sure Benji was there first and Tai had to build Blackwood around him."

Laci realized then that Tai had formed a fantastic team with these three people who worked with her. Each had a passion for their area of work. Benji loved creating the food, Vanessa loved chatting with the customers at their tables, and Charlie loved being behind the bar, mixing drinks and talking with everyone there. Then Tai was at the top, loving what he had worked hard to put together and seeing each of his components work in tandem. A faint smile crossed her lips as she remembered when she, too, had been the head of a well-oiled machine.

Charlie nudged Laci with his elbow and pointed at a few platters. "Here, carb monster, you'll like these."

Marie walked behind the two of them as they grabbed plates. "I found a man who can cook and didn't let go. That's partly why our marriage has lasted over thirty years."

Thirty years. Thirty years of marriage seemed like a lifetime. Watching the easy affection between Benji and Marie caused a pang of regret. She had once dreamed of a marriage like that. Her own had become a living nightmare.

As they sat down, Vanessa gave Laci a high-five in greeting. Laci couldn't contribute much to the conversation since it revolved around local topics, but she still enjoyed listening and observing how everyone interacted outside of work.

Her gaze swept across the room, lingering on the high, vaulted ceilings and the warm glow from the fireplace. Decorations still hung from the Thanksgiving holiday, giving the home a warm, amber hue.

Benji must have noticed her admiration. "We remodeled and expanded the back of the house about eight years ago," his cheerful voice piped up from across the table. "It worked for us while raising our boys, but we wanted a space where, when we have grandkids, they come over, hang out, and we can all spend time together instead of being separated into different rooms. So we bumped out the back, tore down the walls, and created a family space for us all."

Laci glanced at Benji and Marie. "How many kids do you have?"

Marie beamed and walked over to the fireplace on the far side, bringing back a framed photo to show her. "This is Matt and Kyle. They are twins and both are serving in the Navy. And this is William. He lives an hour from here and works for a publishing company." Laci smiled at the men in the photo, who looked like younger, taller, thinner versions of Benji.

Charlie chimed in from his seat, "Laci has two kids. Alie and Mason. They are freaking awesome. I'm fairly certain they are geniuses like their mom, too."

When Marie returned, she asked to see a photo. Laci scrolled through her phone and found a recent picture of her, Alie, Mason, and Leo at a wedding reception for one of Alie's friends. They were all dressed up, smiling, looking like they had no cares in the world. A wave of sadness washed over her. It had been one of the last, perfect moments before reality crashed down. Charlie looked over her shoulder and put his arm around her. Laci showed her phone to the others.

"These are my kids. Alie is a programmer, and Mason works in video game design."

Marie took her phone to look closer, and Laci knew the question was coming. She braced herself. "Oh, your kids look exactly like you! You all look absolutely stunning, all dressed up. Who is this handsome man with you three? Is that their father?" It wasn't her fault for being curious. None of them knew what had happened.

How could she answer this without losing her mind? She took a deep breath. Another. Charlie's arm tightened around her. "That was Leo, a man I was seeing until he recently passed away."

Breathe Laci. Breathe. She focused on the heat of Charlie's arm around her, the gentle bump of his head against hers. She kept her eyes fixed on her hands, unable to meet their gazes. If she saw the sorrow there, she knew she would crumble.

"That's why she came to live with me," Charlie jumped in smoothly. "So I can be a daily pain in her ass about not spending enough time with me while she was off dating somebody." When everyone laughed, Laci gave him a thankful smile. *Charlie to the rescue.*

"Laci, will your kids be coming to visit you for Christmas?" Vanessa was also trying to move the conversation along for Laci's benefit.

"Yes, they'll arrive next week and plan to spend the entire month here. Alie's boyfriend has to work, so he'll stay home and watch over the house. The kids will be here through the new year." She was excited to see them.

Benji smiled. "We're hoping the boys can visit soon. William will be here for sure. He never passes up on holiday meals. Vanessa and Brent usually stop in, so you should come too."

"I think the kids would love that. They will quickly tire of hanging out with Charlie and me, so getting out with others will make them happy."

Charlie grumbled. "What do you mean, they will get tired of us? I'm a freaking delight to hang out with."

Laci patted his cheek and, in a mocking tone, consoled him. "Of course you are. You're the center of entertainment for anybody that meets you."

The entire group laughed.

As they wrapped up their visit in the movie room, outfitted with oversized, comfy recliners, a snack stand, and surround sound, Laci leaned into Charlie's side, and he patted her arm. Thanks to him, she was emerging from that shell again. She was starting to thrive more each day, little steps at a time.

Laci turned her head on the pillow to watch the snowflakes float down past the small gap of the window where the blinds didn't quite meet the sill. Charlie's quiet footsteps approached her door, followed by a soft knock.

"Come in," she said softly.

The door opened, and Charlie walked in behind her, sitting down on the side of her bed and placing a hand on her shoulder. "You doing okay?"

Laci blew out a shuddering breath, trying to hold back the tears from falling again as they had last night. "I'm not sure."

"Well, I came to the realization this morning, it's now December, and I seem to be seriously lacking in Christmas decorations," he said, squeezing her shoulder. "I know how absolutely disappointed you must be since you're the queen of Christmas and all. I was thinking maybe you could help me correct my mistake and join me for some shopping. I'll even let you get whatever you want to make it look as if Christmas puked all over my house."

That elicited a snort from Laci. She rolled over just enough to squint her eyes at him. "How dare you use my most sacred favorite activity, shopping for Christmas decorations, against me and my melancholy?"

"Well, the kids will be here this afternoon, and I think it's important for all of us to keep Christmas this year. It's not going to be easy, but they need to see how well you're doing, and that will help all of you get through this first Christmas without Leo." He stood. "Now get up and move. You have a lot of my money to spend."

Charlie was right. The moment Laci walked into the store, with its pine scent, blinking lights, animatronic characters, and shimmering ornaments, she couldn't help but smile and begin to sing along to the Christmas music. Charlie laughed as he watched Laci work her magic, fitting three carts' worth of decorations and food into the back of her Yukon after a full hour of shopping.

As she prepared the last of the sandwiches for lunch, the front door opened, and she heard her daughter yell, "The celebrations can begin!"

Laci practically ran to the foyer to hug Alie and Mason. Charlie wrapped his arms around everyone, and in that moment, Laci almost felt whole again. The three people she loved most were right there with her.

When she leaned back, she saw her own features mirrored in their faces. Both were tall and slim, with her hair color, though it was darker due to their father, and they shared her light caramel skin tone. The kids dropped their bags in the foyer and came in for lunch.

That evening, the boys worked outside to put up lights around the windows and a lighted sleigh with reindeer on the lawn. Inside, the girls wrapped pine garland around everything they could, set up a tiny lit village of shoppers and ice skaters along the breakfast bar, and scattered fake snow on every surface possible.

Together, they decorated the Christmas tree, and Alie carried down a small box from upstairs. "I brought the ornaments Leo gave you. I thought you would want them here with you."

Tears ran down both of their faces as they hung the ornaments. Mason and Charlie linked arms and then wrapped their arms around Laci and Alie from behind. Looking up at the beautiful new tree, at the ornaments from a past life and this new one, a peace settled in her chest. She wasn't erasing the past. She was weaving it into her future.

One evening, the kids came to Blackwood for dinner and sat at a high table, allowing Laci and Charlie to talk to them from the bar.

Vanessa stopped to see them. "It's so great to meet you! I was so excited when your mom said you two were going to come visit."

"Well, now she works someplace awesome." Mason beamed.

"That's because you're always eating." Alie rolled her eyes.

"Exactly!" Mason laughed at his sister.

When Tai came out of his office, Laci happened to be standing by the table, so she introduced them. After the introduction and their exchange of "Nice to meet you," Laci watched Tai's face turn to her with a raised eyebrow.

She grinned. "Oh, did I forget to mention to you I have kids?"

Both kids tried to cover their mouths to hide their laughter. Tai walked off, shaking his head and smiling.

Then Charlie called out from behind the bar, "Don't worry, boss! They're both mine!"

Laci and the kids burst into laughter. They caught Tai running his hand down his face, trying to hide the fact that Charlie had gotten the better of him.

Benji and Marie hosted everyone over for a holiday meal. Happy chatter and joyful music floated to them as they stepped into the house. Charlie's surprised shout startled Laci and the kids. When he stepped aside, she saw not only William there but also the twins, who had somehow managed to secure a few days of leave to come home and celebrate with their family. Their parents were beaming. It was heartwarming to witness her friends having their entire family together, and Laci felt a warmth spread through her chest that had nothing to do with the glowing fireplace.

As they ate, Benji, wearing a Santa hat with a bell that jingled from the top every time he moved, regaled them with the story of how the twins had surprised their parents. "William had called to say he would be arriving late due to a problem at the office. Marie and I were watching TV back here when he came in. Since it was late, we decided to shut everything down and head to bed. We turned the corner into the hall, and I nearly had a heart attack when I saw movement in the dark at the other end. Then William flipped on the light, and there stood our boys with huge smiles. William went to the airport to pick them up and snuck them into the house."

Marie grinned at the memory. "I was so happy to see them!"

"Mom, you nearly blew out our eardrums. You screamed so loud," Matt said, deadpan, smirking at Marie.

"That pretty much matches how our mom came running at us when we arrived here two weeks ago," Mason added. "Must be a mom thing."

"Nah, that's how she always greets me when I come home," Charlie replied, laughing as Laci dramatically sighed and rolled her eyes.

At one point during the evening, Laci sat back and watched her children effortlessly engage in discussions. She had once worried her anxiety might rub off on them, but she realized she had raised them to be independent, and that's precisely what they were doing. Mason, William, and Benji delved into a deep discussion about the merits and flaws of story plots in books and video games, frequently rotating through the kitchen for more snacks. Meanwhile, on the couch near the fireplace, Alie and Kyle shared an intimate conversation.

Laci felt Charlie's hand slip into hers under the table, drawing her into the conversation he was having with Marie, Vanessa, and Matt. During a lull, she asked something that had been bothering her.

"I noticed, despite decorating the space and giving gifts to the kids that come into Blackwood, Tai seems somewhat withdrawn lately." Her heart sank as most of the faces around her turned sad.

"Christmas is his favorite holiday," Charlie began. "But it's a tough time for him."

Benji chimed in. "A few years after opening Blackwood, his parents passed away, one right after the other. And his brother isn't around."

"Tai usually goes away this time of year. It's hard for him to be home alone now," Vanessa added. "I'm not really sure why he's home this year."

Laci looked at Charlie and her kids. Their faces reflected the same concern they had for her when she was alone after Leo died. "Okay, then, how about we invite him to join us? Even if he doesn't accept, at least he'll know somebody cares about him."

"I'll ask him," Charlie said. "I'm sure he'll appreciate it."

On Christmas Day, the four of them kept up their traditions, with Laci and Charlie going downstairs first while Alie and Mason waited upstairs for her signal to come down. She started this when they were toddlers, so she could set up the video camera to capture their shocked faces when they saw the gifts Santa had brought. Even though they were adults now, they continued the tradition. It was a special ritual between them, and the kids even made exaggerated faces of shock when they saw the packages beneath the tree.

After opening gifts and enjoying pancakes Charlie made for breakfast, the boys went off to play games. As Alie and Laci prepped dinner, Alie asked, "Mom, have you set a time for coming back?"

Laci thought about it before responding. "No, I've been focusing on counseling and working through things. I haven't thought about it."

Laci watched Alie, sensing the weight of the words to come as her daughter took a deep, steadying breath.

"Mason and I... we talked," Alie began, her voice soft but firm. "We think it would be better for you to stay here longer. The house is fine. We're taking care of it. We just... we can't give you what you're getting here. We've seen your progress, and we don't want you to lose that momentum. You are building a life here."

Laci's gaze drifted to the Christmas tree, now glowing with lights and ornaments. A life here. Was she building a life here?

"At home," Alie continued, "you barely left the house. You never had a social life, even before... everything. You put your life on hold for us. Here, you're thriving and safe. We want you to consider staying long-term. Charlie agrees." The finality of her words hung in the air, a mix of love and painful truth.

Laci paused, looking down at the counter. Alie was right. Even before everything happened, it was rare for her to go out. Now, she visited with Vanessa and Benji.

"I'll consider it. But...I miss being at home with you both. I missed you while you were away at school, and then the moment you came back, I was gone again."

"I understand, and we miss you too." Alie stepped closer and wrapped her arm around Laci for a side hug, resting her head on Laci's shoulder. "But we both know it's better for you here. At home, memories of Leo were in every corner of the house, and you rarely left. Here, it's a blank slate, a way for you to start fresh. Plus, I think it's helped Mason and me learn responsibility for the house."

Smiling, Laci hugged Alie back and whispered, "I'm so proud of the people you two have grown up to be."

Later, Tai arrived to join them for dinner, and Laci found it strange to see him away from Blackwood, dressed in jeans and a sweater instead of his usual business casual attire.

He handed her a tall gift bag. "Since I know you and Charlie don't drink, I brought a sparkling cider from an orchard in upstate New York. I visited them often when I lived in the city and got to know the owner well."

Admiring the bottle, Laci smiled up at him. "Thank you! I can't wait to try it."

During dinner, Laci noticed the way Tai looked at her across the table. He was engaged in conversations with her kids and Charlie, but she couldn't ignore the intensity of his gaze. *You can't let him in. You have to keep him away.*

Somehow, Charlie managed to say goodbye to Tai and disappear, leaving Laci to walk Tai out at the end of the night. Internally grousing at Charlie, she walked out to the front step with Tai.

He turned to her and lifted his hand to her cheek. As he spoke, he rubbed his thumb gently on her skin. "Charlie told me it was your idea to invite me. I want you to know I appreciate it."

Gently removing his hand from her face, Laci held it for a moment and then let it go. "I couldn't stand the thought of somebody who loves Christmas being alone today. I know how much it means to me to celebrate with my family, and you're welcome to join us for any celebration."

"Thank you." He stepped away and disappeared around the corner of the garage.

Laci closed the door behind her and needed a moment to catch her breath, feeling the heat from Tai's touch lingering on her skin.

"You have feelings for him," Alie said just above a whisper.

Startled because she hadn't realized Alie was there, Laci jumped and then rested her forehead against the door. "I don't know."

Alie placed her hand on Laci's arm to make her look up. "He's a great guy, but we both know the risks..." She trailed off.

A leaden ball of dread formed in the pit of her stomach, but Laci tamped it down. Wrapping an arm around Alie's waist and leading her to the living room, she put a happy note into her voice. "Come on, it's still the holiday, and we have old Christmas movies to watch."

NINE

"Laci, can you tell me why you stopped Tai from touching you?" Dr. T asked, his pen scratching against his notepad.

With the kids and Charlie out on a grocery run for their New Year's celebration, the house was quiet enough for her call.

The memory surfaced, pulling her back to that moment on the step. She could still feel the heat from Tai's gaze, a warmth she couldn't allow herself to feel. "Because I can't let him."

There was a pause, and then the follow-up questions. "Are you not interested in pursuing anything more with Tai? Is he pushing you past a point you don't want?"

Taking a breath, Laci looked off to the side for a moment. She couldn't even make virtual eye contact with the doctor. "If the circumstances were much different, I would accept the advances. I would be open to trying to take things further. But they aren't different. This is my reality. I can't. I can't do it again. I can't put his life at risk."

The doctor stopped writing again. Laci learned it was his way of pausing to fully concentrate on her face and read her reaction to a challenging question before she covered it up.

"You are certain the end scenario would be he ends up dead like Leo?"

She nodded, slow and heavy. A hot prickle stung the back of her eyes.

"So, when you deny yourself this, is it like retreating to the box you use to lock out everybody? Does it feel safer in there, not just for you, but for everyone else?"

She couldn't speak, only able to manage another jerky nod, a silent admission of the truth.

"What will you do if Tai won't accept sitting in the box you try to put him in? What will you do if he comes and pulls you out of your box?"

The thought terrified her. Her body, heart, and mind would never recover if she allowed another man into her life only to see him murdered in front of her again. *Never again.* The thought was a shard of ice in her chest. She shook her head, unable to speak.

Dr. T brought her back. "Laci, not today, but soon, you will need to step out of that box, flatten it, and toss it out. Denying yourself even the possibility of happiness is not going to help you move forward. I'm speaking about everything around you. You need to be open to positive happenings. You have come so far to this point, and it's about time you work to pull down the barriers you have up between you and everyone else."

Laci stared straight ahead at the screen, anger and frustration bubbling to the surface. "Dr. T, every time I've tried to find happiness, it has been ripped away from me violently and painfully. I can't stop it. I can't see when it will strike. All I know is that eventually, it will strike with a speed and precision that leaves me hollow. I can't let it take another life. And I sure as hell can't watch it happen again."

He gave her a gentle acknowledgment. "Laci, tell me what happened the night of Leo's murder."

Her body locked up. She didn't want to relive it. But some small part of her knew that to move forward, she had to do this. Dr. T always pushed her, but never too far.

She took a breath. "We went out to dinner at a neighborhood restaurant. It was a place we loved to visit because it had good food and a comfortable atmosphere. There was a small band playing on the street nearby, and it was the first warm evening after a long winter, so we sat on the patio to listen while we ate."

Her mind took her back to that moment. They were discussing taking a vacation. She remembered sitting there, watching Leo's eyes light up as he listed all the places they could go. At that moment, she felt her life was complete. She had a man she cared for, her kids were thriving, and she was happy.

"After dinner, we decided to walk down to see the band playing. A crowd gathered to watch, and Leo walked up and tipped them. He always gave as much as he could to others." She felt the fear slide down her spine again. "We continued to walk through the park for a bit while heading home. Other people were walking the path, so we didn't even notice the men until they were on us. They looked like everybody else out for the evening."

Dr. T was observing her. "What happened, Laci? Walk me through what you remember."

The tears fell from her face as the sobs ripped through her. "A hand clamped over my mouth. It smelled like cigarettes. I was yanked backward, my arms pinned behind me. I heard a choked gasp from Leo, then a flurry of movement as he tried to fight them off. He was trying to get to me. But there were too many. Two men grabbed him, and then three, arms were flying in every direction."

Her breath hiccupped, and she swallowed hard. "The man holding me pressed me against his body, forcing me to watch as they beat Leo. I saw the flash of fists, heard the sickening thud against his body. Then, a pair of hands were around his throat, and I watched, helpless, as they choked the life out of him. I tried to scream, but the hand muffled it, forcing me to watch as they let his body fall to the ground. They held me there, their grip unbreakable, for what felt like an eternity, long enough to make sure no one would help. Long enough to make sure I couldn't."

She would have tried to bring him back. Had they dropped her sooner, she would have done anything to get him back. But they wouldn't let her.

"As I blacked out, I heard one of them say my ex sent them, a lesson that I can't replace him. I can't be happy without him. The next thing I knew, paramedics were over me, pumping air into my lungs as I lay on the pavement. People surrounding us were watching. Police were everywhere. Leo was dead."

There was a moment when Dr. T let her try to catch her breath before softly asking his next question. "And you believe if you try to find happiness like that again, it will be taken from you just as violently."

She could barely whisper a response. "Yes."

Charlie and Laci were eating breakfast together at the table when his phone rang with a sound she had never heard before. His lips pressed into a thin, hard line, and a mask of anger settled over his features as he slowly rose from the table and picked it up.

He took a deep breath before answering. "Travis, what is it?"

It was his stepfather. Laci froze, the spoon halfway to her mouth. She stared at Charlie, hoping it was Travis at worst, calling to berate Charlie, and nothing more. She listened to Charlie's side of the conversation. He had long ago trained himself to have no emotion when talking to Travis, so hearing the monotone voice was like nails on a chalkboard to her.

"What hospital? What are they saying? I'll see what I can do." He pinched the bridge of his nose and took another deep breath. "Travis, I have a job and a home to manage. I'll be there as soon as I can. Keep me updated, and I'll let you know when I arrive."

He hung up the phone and took two deep, steadying breaths. He looked toward Laci with more anger than concern. "It seems as if my mother is very sick and is in the hospital. Travis claims it's really serious, and they worry she won't make it."

He groaned while running his hands over his head and gripping his hair. "I don't know how I should feel about this."

It had been many years since Laci had any encounters with Charlie's mom and stepfather. They were the reason

Charlie had moved out of their house and into her home be-fore they both graduated from high school. Rising from the table, Laci walked over to him, wrapping her arms around his waist and holding on. After a moment, his arms came around her, and he rested his face next to hers.

"I think I should go. If it's bad and my mother dies without me there, I'll hate myself for the rest of my life for it."

Laci looked into his eyes. "I can go with you."

"No. Absolutely not. I don't want to leave you home alone here, but you're not ready to face everything there again. I love you, and I know you want to be there to support me. I just can't take the chance of you backsliding in your progress because you're trying to be there for me."

"I get it. Things have been good here. With the meds, I can sleep. You go, and I'll have Vanessa or Benji to call on if I need company."

He kissed the top of her head and then released her. "I have to get a flight, plus tell Tai I can't come in for a while. Will you continue working without me? I want to let him know."

"I'll keep going. Without you there, Tai might appreci-ate my help." *Plus, I won't be home alone the entire time you're gone.*

He agreed and made calls. Within a short time, he had a flight booked for that evening. Laci overheard him call Tai as they were eating lunch before he had to leave.

"Hey Tai, I've gotta leave town for a family matter. I honestly don't know when I'll return, but I hope no more than two weeks...No, I can't take her with me. She's better off here...Yeah, she said she would still work even without me, even though it's the slow season, she feels she could help since you'll be down a bartender…Yeah, I'll give her your number…Man, you know that's not necessary…Yeah, okay, I'll let her know."

There was a long pause, and Charlie looked up at Laci, his eyes broadcasting his worry. Then he clenched his jaw and looked out the window. *This is killing him not to be here to protect me and lean on somebody else.*

"Look, man. I seriously appreciate you saying that. You can't even begin to fathom what she means to me, and if anything happened to her, yeah…All right, thaaaaaank you-uuuu." A quick glint of mischief crossed his eyes. "Yeah, I'll miss you, sugar da…" He huffed and held up his phone. "He hung up on me."

They laughed because they knew Tai had to be smiling on the other end. "So, what was that long conversation about?"

Charlie grabbed her phone, pulled up the contacts, and added a new contact for Tai. "Tai has a couple of requests while I'm gone." He set her phone down on the table between them. "First, please call him if anything goes wrong. No matter the time of day or night." He tapped on her phone for emphasis. "Second, he's offered to pick you up and bring you home for every shift."

Laci stared at him. "Tai does know I own a car, right? I can drive myself if I want."

Charlie reached across the table, his hand wrapping around hers. The warmth of his grip was a stark contrast to the cold fear he couldn't hide. "Yes, but I'm asking you to go along with it for my peace of mind. Please, Laci. I don't want to imagine what could happen if you're walking out there alone in the middle of the night. I know this town is safe, but still…"

She squeezed his hand in return, the fight leaving her. "Okay. For your peace of mind."

"He also offered to have you stay in one of the spare rooms at his place."

Laci's resolve returned, stiffening her shoulders. She pulled her hand back, a defiant look on her face. "And that's where I draw the line. Not a chance."

Charlie quickly packed and put his bags in the car. They stood in the garage together, and he hugged her as tightly as he could. "I don't want to leave you like this. Please be safe. I'll call you every day."

She squeezed him back, not actually ready to let him go. "Charlie, everything has been quiet here with no issues. I'm safe here, being so far from home. Go, and know I'm with you, sending you as much love and strength as possible."

He kissed her temple and let go. Laci stepped back into the doorway to the kitchen and watched him open the garage, pull out, and drive off. Watching until the garage door rumbled shut, plunging the space into near darkness, she then stepped out and slid the security lock with a solid thunk. Reaching up, she gave the red cord a sharp tug, disconnecting the opener. *No chances.*

Laci stepped back in and closed the kitchen door. There were about thirty minutes of daylight left to move around and feel as safe as possible before sunset. Running up to her room, Laci pulled out one box from her closet. Charlie didn't know this, but she'd packed all her security gear just in case. She picked up the box and took it downstairs with her.

The first metal brace bar felt cold and heavy in her hands, a promise of security as she wedged it under the handle of the front door. She adjusted it until the fit was perfect, then gave it a hard tug. It didn't give an inch, a solid, immovable barrier. She did the same for the door leading from the kitchen to the garage. Then came the back door. Laci stepped out into the freezing January winds to put a lockbox around the handle, preventing anybody from turning it. Then, like the other two doors, there was another brace on the inside.

Next were the windows. Laci couldn't prevent someone from breaking the glass, but she could prevent them from sliding open or quickly climbing through by installing braces on each one. Gathering up all her cameras, she got to work placing them. Adjusting with her phone, she could get coverage over the entire first floor. She tested them by walking through the space, and each one was quickly alerted with a notification on her phone. Then she played a glass-breaking sound and watched as multiple alerts popped up. She set up a camera in the basement to cover the windows and main workout area. It, too, alerted her.

The sun was setting, and it was getting too dark outside, so she ran around and closed every blind and curtain. Laci couldn't handle the thought of someone being able to see her when she couldn't see them. She put the last of her items in play, motion sensors on several steps, Charlie's bedroom door, the hallway, and her bedroom door. Of course, she would trip these as she moved around, but Laci would know the speed and time she had left if anybody approached her.

After placing and testing the last motion sensor, she returned to her closet. She moved the fire ladder under the window on the opposite side of her bed. Never again would she be trapped with no escape from the second floor. With one last box from the closet, Laci moved methodically from room to room, stashing a defense weapon in each. Finally, she felt as if she was as safe as she could be.

Realizing she hadn't connected with Tai, she quickly texted him that Charlie had left and she was settling in to make dinner for herself. Moments after she hit send, her phone started ringing.

"Hello?"

The deep timbre of his calm voice came over the line, and Laci felt herself relax a tiny bit. "Laci, I was starting to become concerned when I didn't hear from you right after Charlie had to leave."

That's because I felt utterly freaked out about being home alone, even though I'm safe here. I ran around like a crazy person putting security in place. "I'm sorry about that. I decided to get some things done around the house, but I lost track of time. I'm good. I'm going to get dinner and then watch a movie or something."

"Alright, you know I'm here. Anytime, for anything. I'll be there around ten tomorrow to pick you up for work."

Laci felt a small, reluctant wave of gratitude. "Sounds like a plan. I promised Charlie I wouldn't argue about the ride, so thank you for doing that, Tai. I appreciate it."

"Don't mention it," he said, his voice dropping to a lower, more serious register. "Just sleep well. I'll see you tomorrow."

Now, Laci was conflicted. The nightmares had lessened with Dr. T's help, but her fear was spiked again, and her stomach clenched at the thought of them returning. The meds could stop them, but the side effects made her feel vulnerable and unable to defend herself. She wasn't sure what was worse, the terror of the dreams or the disorientation of the pills. She'd decide when bedtime came.

And I won't think about what Dr. T would say about all this, she told herself, glancing around the fortress she'd built.

Tai picked up his phone and flipped through his contacts. He tapped the one he needed.

"Tai, what can I do for you?"

He tried to temper his frustration, but after talking to Laci, Tai knew it was imperative to involve his friend. "Hey, Jack, listen. Charlie had to go out of town for family reasons, leaving Laci home alone. I spoke with her and can tell she's scared."

"Do you know when he'll be back?"

"No. Charlie hoped it wouldn't be more than two weeks, but he couldn't say. Could you keep an eye on his house for a bit while he's away? I'll pick her up and drop her off for her time at work, but I know she won't let me get any closer."

"Yeah, no problem." Jack paused. "Do you know how well she's gotten to know locals?"

Tai thought for a moment. "Charlie has introduced her to a few people so she's more comfortable, and I've seen her start to chat with the people she knows when they come into Blackwood."

Jack blew out a breath. "I happened to be talking to Mr. Berkeley recently. He mentioned there was a stranger in town asking about Laci. A guy and his wife said they were passing through town on their way to a lodge up north. Mentioned a friend of theirs had recently been here and told them all about how wonderful it was, and to get in touch with Laci."

Fuck. "Did he say how much info these people got?"

There was a light chuckle. "I asked Mr. B that same question. Pretty sure the old man wanted to slug me for asking. He said, and I quote, 'Ain't nobody be telling anybody bout that poor girl. All you gotta do is look at her to know she's had troubles and ain't nobody here gonna lead it back to her.'"

Tai sat up in his chair. "Except, if this couple ran into Mark, then all bets are off."

"That's what I'm worried about, too. Based on the description Mr. B gave me, I'm trying to pull together security footage from around town."

"I can scan through my security recordings, too. If he was after her, then he likely stopped into the restaurant." Tai offered.

"Tai, she shouldn't be left alone," Jack said, his voice dropping. "I'm afraid she's in real danger, and I don't want to see her hurt."

Tai shot to his feet. He paced in his home office. "I know, Jack. You know I'd do anything to keep her safe." He ran a hand through his hair. "I offered her a room here. She refused. I'm doing everything I can, but I'm flying blind. I don't even know what I'm up against."

A pause stretched between them, thick with unspoken words. "Tai," Jack said softly, "I'm sure she's choosing the lesser of two evils now. There's a reason I have officers around your restaurant. I've already warned you that outside forces are a concern. She's well aware of that fact, and she'd rather face it alone than risk anyone else."

The frustration was a hot, sharp coil in his gut. He wanted to be there for her, especially with Charlie gone, but she kept pushing him away. Now, Jack was confirming what he already suspected. She was in danger. But what kind? What the hell were they not telling him? The questions clawed at him. Why was it a risk for him to get closer to her, but not for Charlie?

"Alright. I promised Charlie I would do everything I could to help while he was gone. If anything happens, I'll need to do something about it."

"I get it. I have an idea on how to help, but I have to make some calls. Tai, I don't want to see this destroy you personally. Take extreme care around her, or she'll likely react to put herself in even greater danger."

Tai hung up the phone, realizing his effort to respect her boundaries would fall apart if he didn't do this right. All he wanted right now was to have her here with him, where he could support her and help her feel safe.

TEN

Laci survived the night nightmare-free. *One down, many more to go.* She rolled over to check her phone, but the screen was dark. There were no missed alerts. While getting ready for work, the phone dinged relentlessly as she walked around the house. At least she knew the cameras and sensors were still active.

After she'd made breakfast, Charlie called.

"Hey," he said, his voice heavy with exhaustion. "How'd you sleep?"

"I did well, no nightmares," she answered, trying to sound more confident than she felt. "It's weird being here without you, but I'll adjust. How are things there?"

"Travis is still a jerk. He's got a whole new list of names for me now. And my mother doesn't appreciate my lack of pity for her. Honestly, I barely recognized her. It looks like the smoking and drinking are finally taking their toll."

"How are you feeling about all that?"

There was a heavy pause before he answered. "I care... a little. She's my mother. But I feel guilty that I don't care more. You know what I mean?"

"I do." Picturing him in his old room, she decided to lighten the mood. "Are you at least enjoying time with the kids without my supervision?"

He chuckled, "Oh yeah. They welcomed me with open arms. They're doing a good job of caring for the house."

"Good. Tai will be here shortly, so I need to finish getting ready. Take care of yourself."

"Got it. Love you."

"Love you too."

Laci cleaned her dishes and ran upstairs, triggering the motion sensors again, to grab one more device before Tai arrived. Since she couldn't leave the security brace on the front door when she left, she placed the new sensor on the doorframe, setting it to notify her if the door was opened. Just then, Tai's text pinged through the foyer, a message that he was five minutes away. She quickly slipped on her boots and coat, grabbed her bag, and pulled the brace off the door.

A large, all-black Yukon pulled into the driveway. Laci locked both the handle and the deadbolt, testing them twice before walking to the SUV. Tai got out to open the passenger door for her. As she settled in, she watched him circle the front and slide behind the wheel.

He smiled. "Good morning. Ready to get this day started?"

"As ready as I'll ever be."

As he pulled out of the driveway, Laci scanned the outside of the house for anything unusual. Seeing nothing, she opened her phone and cleared the notifications she had caused. Now she would know if anything was triggered, it wasn't her. Not that she expected anything. Trouble stayed near her home, and she was too far from there to have any issues.

The ride was quiet until they reached the main road.

"Laci, can I ask you a question?" Tai's voice was low.

The list of possible questions was endless. "Only if you're okay with me possibly not answering."

"Charlie's incredibly protective of you. How did that start?"

So many answers came to mind, but given how close he and Charlie were, she opted for the extended version. "Charlie and I have been attached at the hip since third grade. He spent most of his time at my house because his mom was a single parent and had to work long hours. My parents had grown accustomed to having him around. We were a package deal. We rarely hung out at his house. Charlie was never comfortable with me there."

"Why not?" Tai asked, his eyes fixed on the road.

"His mom always had a new boyfriend moving in every few months. I was too young to understand that she depended on them to support her and Charlie. I just knew I was there to hang out with my best friend." She turned to look out the window, watching the town wake up. "In school, other kids picked on him. He was small and scrawny, so I was the one who stood up to the bullies. By middle school, he'd started working out and hit a major growth spurt."

"And that's when the tables turned and he became your protector?"

"Yes and no. Around that same time, his mom married Travis. Charlie and Travis never got along. It all came to a head one summer when I went over to his house to work on a class assignment. Charlie was mowing the lawn, and Travis was on the front porch, drinking. I was just close enough to hear Travis crudely ask why Charlie hadn't 'tapped that' yet."

Tai's hands tightened on the steering wheel.

"Charlie stopped the mower and asked him to repeat it. Travis, being drunk, did. Charlie just growled at him for talking about me that way. Travis got in his face and started yelling about how Charlie must be gay, because no straight man would 'just be friends' with me. Then Travis jumped him, punching him and calling him every awful name in the book. I was trying to get him to stop when Travis swung back and hit me by accident. I fell and hit the pavement hard. That's when Charlie just... snapped."

Tai's voice was dangerously level. "What happened?"

"The neighbors pulled Charlie off Travis, telling him I needed him more than Travis needed a beating. By the time the police arrived, Charlie was holding me in his lap. An officer tried to cuff him, but all the witnesses jumped to his defense. Then his mom came running out of the house screaming, defending Travis."

"Son of a..."

"Yeah. The police arrested his stepfather, and his mom threw Charlie out, tossing his stuff onto the front lawn. The neighbors helped pack his things and moved him into my parents' house. He told me later he would have just let Travis beat him, but when I got hurt, everything changed."

Tai pulled into the parking lot behind Blackwood but made no move to shut off the engine. He stared at something in the distance, taking several deep, measured breaths before turning to her. "Look, I promised him I would be here for you while he's gone. I'm asking you to let me do that."

Laci could feel his gaze on her as she watched the first light snowflakes of the day land on the windshield. How could she tell him that no matter what he did, she would never be completely safe? Only Charlie knew the whole story, the complete danger, and he was immune to it.

When she finally turned her head to face him, she realized how small the space was, how close he was. The moment their eyes met, that familiar intensity sparked between them, now amplified by the proximity. He was wholly focused on her.

This had to stop before it went any further. "Tai, I appreciate the offer. But Charlie knows exactly what level of hell he's stepped into with me. I can't let you do the same. I accepted rides because it eased Charlie's mind to know I wasn't walking alone, especially at night. I promise I won't take risks, but I can't let you get any closer. It's too dangerous. I won't let you risk your life for me."

Breaking eye contact, Laci opened the door and stepped out. The bustle of the town seemed to vanish, muffled by the falling snow. She closed the door and waited, forcing herself to focus on a single snowflake melting on her gloved hand, an anchor to hold her in place until Tai shut off the engine and came around to her side. By the time he reached her, she'd squared her shoulders, her expression carefully neutral. It was a sharp, painful act of self-preservation to avoid his gaze, but it was necessary. She was starting to have feelings for him, too. And that was the most dangerous part of all.

Inside Blackwood, Laci fell into the routine of opening the bar. She would work with Tai, just as she would have with Charlie. Benji and Vanessa rolled in, asking where Charlie was. Unsure how much he'd told them, Laci just said he had to deal with family issues back home.

As customers arrived, it became clear she and Tai had no rhythm. They kept clashing behind the bar, running into each other, fumbling orders, and causing spills.

Now aggravated, she grabbed his arm, stepping directly in front of him. "Tai. Stop. You have to stop adjusting for me. I can't learn your routine if you keep changing it. This is your bar. I need you to move like you normally would, and I'll adapt to you."

Too late, she realized how close they were. The smell of beer and food faded, replaced by something warmer, something that was just him. Her hand was still on his arm, the muscle beneath her fingers tensing. An intense, heated look passed over his features as he gave a slow nod, his gaze dropping to her lips for a fraction of a second. Laci was the one to break the spell, stepping away quickly. They needed space.

She turned to grab plates from the service window for Vanessa, who met her with a massive grin.

"Girl, you and Charlie have a flow, no doubt," Vanessa whispered, giving her an exaggerated wink. "But what just happened there? That was pure fire."

"Hush. You have tables to serve." Laci heard her giggle as she walked away.

To put even more distance between herself and Tai, Laci moved to the kitchen to wash dishes. A knowing grin was already on Benji's face as she stepped through the door.

"Not you too," She groaned. "Don't you start."

"I'm not saying anything..." he said, flipping something on the grill with a sizzle. "But I think that says it all."

She rolled her eyes at him. Right now, scrubbing dishes by hand sounded like a fantastic idea.

From the kitchen doorway, Laci watched Tai find his rhythm. He moved with a fluidity she was beginning to understand. She saw him reach for the shaker and, without thinking, stepped forward to clear the space on the counter where she knew he would set it down. He glanced at her, a flicker of surprise in his eyes, quickly turned to a small, appreciative smile. From then on, they moved as one. The restaurant wasn't as busy as usual, given New Year's resolutions were still holding on, but it was steady until dinner picked up.

Then Mark walked in and sat at a table near the bar.

Laci averted her eyes, feeling the familiar, sickening crawl of her skin as his gaze drilled into her. Beside her, Tai stiffened, his movements faltering. When she saw the flex in Tai's jaw, her heart raced. His eyes flicked between her and Mark, gauging her fear. With every minute Mark stared while she and Tai tried to continue working, a tremor grew deep inside. Tai's repeated attempts to position himself to block Mark's view of Laci only made it worse, causing them to bump and fumble again.

Laci moved close and stood on her toes to whisper in his ear, "I'm going to the kitchen."

Before she could step away, he wrapped an arm around her waist and pulled her flush against him. The move was so unexpected that her hands landed flat on his chest, a rock-solid wall of muscle. Against all logic, her body instantly calmed. He leaned in, his deep voice a low rumble in her ear that sent goosebumps racing down her arms.

"It's not just me watching out for you," he murmured. "There are others here to help."

She gave a tiny nod of acknowledgment.

When she pulled her head back, he didn't release her. He held on a moment longer, his eyes searching hers, assessing her fear. She forced her expression to remain calm. After he finally let her go, she escaped to the kitchen.

A wave of heat washed through her as she stepped up to the sink. Tai's voice in her ear had melted everything inside her. Being pressed fully against him made her mind flash to a similar scenario, but with far less clothing. Her face burned, and she had to hide it from Benji before he commented. She took a deep breath. Laci had to get back on track. There was a potential threat just on the other side of that wall.

After Laci disappeared into the kitchen, Tai felt as if a piece of himself was missing. Pulling her against him had been a fatal error. Now he wanted her even more. The almond scent of her hair was imprinted in his brain.

Tai did his best to move normally, trying not to raise Mark's suspicions. The off-duty officer at the end of the bar gave Tai a subtle look. Each time he passed the kitchen, he glanced in, reassured to see Laci safely at the sink. When Tai looked up again, he saw Mark head toward the bathrooms.

As he approached the officer's end of the bar, Tai served him another glass of ice water.

"He's not gonna try anything in here," the officer said quietly. "Relax."

Tai just smiled like he would for any other patron.

Mark returned to his table, adjusted his seat twice to get a better view into the kitchen, then finally paid his bill and left. Tai watched Mark disappear from view and relaxed, certain Laci would reappear soon.

He was wiping down the counter when the door swung open with a rush of freezing air. Jack walked in, a broad smile on his face, with another man following behind.

"Jack, how are you?" Tai greeted, shaking his friend's hand.

The two men settled into seats at the bar.

"Doing good. Tai, this is Vincent Stonebrook. He grew up near here and just moved back."

Tai held out a hand. "Vincent, nice to meet you. Can I get you anything? One of Benji's burgers?"

"Seriously, man, you have to try one," Jack urged, nudging Vincent. The nudge did nothing. It was as if Jack had tried to push his elbow into a brick wall.

Vincent was observant, his eyes constantly scanning the room. Tai noted the man's high cheekbones and the stark line of his short black hair. There was a stoic quality to his features that, along with his powerful build, gave him an undeniable presence. But there was something else, a certain way he held himself that Tai had also seen in Jack.

"I guess I'll have to try a burger then. Surprise me," Vincent said, his voice just loud enough to be heard over the crowd.

As Tai put their orders in, Laci's laugh drifted from the kitchen, making his heart lighten. He glanced up and saw her in an animated conversation with Benji. She had changed so much from the woman who had first arrived here months ago.

When Tai turned back, a knowing smirk was on Jack's face. Tai shot him a warning glare. Just then, Laci peeked her head out, scanning the bar. The visible sigh of relief she let out when she saw Mark was gone tightened something in Tai's gut. He held out an arm, beckoning her over.

"Laci, you remember Jack. And this is his friend, Vincent."

"Nice to see you again, Jack. And nice to meet you, Vincent," she said with a gentle smile.

"How have you been, Laci?" Jack asked, his voice full of charm. "Still enjoying it here? I know Tai can be a stubborn pain in the ass."

Tai had to walk to the other end to serve a new customer, ignoring his best friend's purposeful goading. Watching as Laci leaned on the bar to talk more intimately with Jack and Vincent, he became agitated when she let out another small laugh for Jack, not him.

"You know he's not interested in her," Vanessa's quiet voice broke through his thoughts.

Tai looked down at her, seeing the familiar pain in her eyes. "I know. It's just hard to remember when he turns on that charm."

The corner of Vanessa's mouth ticked up. "He's not looking at Laci the way he used to look at Nikki. He's not interested in anyone else as long as he knows she's still out there somewhere."

Tai wrapped an arm around Vanessa in a quick side hug. "I'm sure she is. We would've heard otherwise."

"That's what keeps me hopeful," she said with a sad smile. "Now, if you want to get anywhere with Laci, you should figure out something for the two of you to do while Charlie's gone. It's the only chance you'll have to get her alone without him tagging along." She grabbed her tray, plastered on a happy mask, and walked toward her table.

By the time Tai returned, the men had their food.

"Do you think I should tell Jack about my encounter with Mark?" Laci asked him.

Not indicating he had already talked to Jack about it, Tai agreed. "Absolutely. It can't hurt to keep him in the loop."

Laci turned back and described the incident at the theater in detail.

Jack's brow furrowed. "How many people here could have known Charlie lived with you?"

Laci glanced at Tai. "As far as I know, no one. Charlie never told anyone here about me. Tai didn't even know Charlie lived with me until I told him on the way to work today."

Tai confirmed with a nod.

"Well, he could have found your address online," Jack suggested.

Laci shook her head. "You won't find my address by searching my name. Same for Charlie."

For a moment, confusion clouded Jack's features before clearing into recognition. "I can't exactly go interrogate Mark about where he got his information," Jack said, a hint of frustration in his voice. "But now that I know, I'll keep an ear out."

"Thanks, Jack. I really appreciate it." Laci looked relieved. Grabbing a bin of dirty dishes, she headed back to the kitchen.

Jack wiped his face with a napkin and looked back at Tai. "Now, we should discuss why Vincent and I are really here."

ELEVEN

"Mom, there's a letter here about a recall on your car," Mason's voice cut through Laci's call with Charlie.

"What's the recall for?" Laci asked.

"Uh, something in the engine. It has a lot of red boxes with exclamation points and says it's urgent."

"Give me that," she heard Charlie grumble in the background. "Crap. Yeah, it's the ABS Module. You need to get that done right away."

Fantastic. "I'll just wait until you get home. It made it across the country. It should be fine for a little longer."

"No, get this done now," Charlie scolded. "Who knows how long I'll be here? According to this, it can catch fire while sitting in the garage."

Laci let out a frustrated grumble. "Fine. I'll figure out where to take it."

Glancing up at the clock, she realized Tai would be arriving any minute. "I gotta go."

After saying their goodbyes, she had just enough time to get her coat and boots on before she saw Tai pull into the driveway. As usual, he held the door for her.

After clearing her security notifications, Laci started searching for a local dealership. She must have groaned out loud, because Tai turned to her with a raised eyebrow.

"Problem?"

"There's an urgent recall on my car, and I'm trying to figure out where to take it." She looked up from her phone. "Do you know a good place?"

"What do you drive?"

Laci bit back a grin. "A Yukon."

Tai's laughter filled the SUV. He pushed a button on his steering wheel. "Call Alan."

A gruff voice answered. "Service Department, Alan speaking."

"Alan, it's Tai. I have somebody here with a recall notice for her Yukon, and I'm guessing mine is on the list too."

"Tai! Haven't seen you in a while. Yeah, it's a serious one, major fire risk. Yours is on the list. If you can bring both in today, I can get them done before the rush. Shouldn't take more than an hour or two." They heard typing. "I can fit you in around lunchtime."

"We'll be there. Thanks." Tai hung up. "The shop is closer to the city. Let me run into Blackwood and tell Benji and Vanessa we'll be gone for a bit. Then we'll come back here to get your car, and you can follow me." He glanced over to her. "Do you have snow tires on yours?"

"Snow tires? No. I drive just fine in the snow with my all-season tires."

He gave a slight grimace. "Snow where you are from is different than up here. It's critical to have real snow tires because our snow compacts to ice on the roads, or you may need to navigate over high drifts."

"Oh. Didn't realize it was different." She took a moment to consider. It seemed ridiculous to buy snow tires if she was going back home at some point. But if something happened and she needed to drive before leaving, it was better to be safe. "Okay. Do you think the shop can put them on while we are in there?"

"If not, I know another place we can take it to get them done."

A couple of hours later, Laci pulled into the dealership's service department on the outskirts of the city. The area was a chaotic mess of construction and traffic, putting her on edge. She lost count of the cars that cut into the safe space between her Yukon and Tai's. With each swerve, she pictured herself sliding on ice, sandwiching a smaller car between their two massive vehicles. In a moment of panic after one close call, she missed a light Tai had just made, almost leaving her stranded and unsure of the way, but Tai had pulled over to wait for her. She had no idea where she was going without him. Tai pulled into one bay, and an attendant motioned for her to pull into the next.

Laci parked and sat for a moment, trying to compose herself, but the mechanic politely opened her door, disrupting her reset.

"Ma'am, we'll take it from here. If you can leave your keys, the waiting area is right around the corner."

Laci barely registered his words or the hand he held out for her keys. The loud clang of a wrench hitting concrete made her flinch. When the chatter of an impact wrench went off, little sparks of light danced across her vision. Every noise was now amplified. The traffic outside, the closing of the metal garage doors, and shouts across the garage all felt like an attack.

As she tried to control the overwhelming sensation with breathing exercises, she was instead assaulted by the thick scent of fuel and oil, heavy in her lungs. Her focus narrowed to the waiting room door, as blackness crept in from the edges of her vision, blocking out everything else. She had to make it to that door. Except now it felt as if she were on a ship at sea, the ground rolling in waves.

A warm hand spanned her back, a solid support in the chaos. "I'm here." She looked up to find Tai smiling down at her and instinctively leaned into his strength.

Inside, a clerk was firing questions at her, and Laci was still struggling to comprehend. Tai took over, answering what he could and giving her a light squeeze when she needed to respond. She assumed they'd sit in the waiting room, but instead, Tai guided her out the front door, his hand a steady presence on her back as he led her across the street. He stopped at a small coffee shop with an ornate emerald door and a beautiful stained-glass insert. It was a cozy shop, its glass counter filled with a variety of pastries.

Tai ordered for both of them and handed her a coffee before leading her to the small café table by the window. He pulled two blueberry muffins from the paper bag. The muffin practically melted in her mouth, the comforting sweetness immediately calming her frayed nerves.

"I thought for sure we'd need to get back right away," Laci said quietly.

"Benji and Vanessa can hold down the fort," Tai replied, taking a sip of his coffee. "Vanessa will run the bar."

"I didn't know she had that experience."

"Can she make every drink Charlie or I can? No. But the locals know her limits." Tai's lips twitched. "And if anyone gets mouthy, that woman can deliver a verbal beatdown with the sweetest smile on her face."

Laci laughed. "I seriously love her."

"They run the place whenever I take a vacation. It's nice knowing it's in good hands."

"When do you take vacations? You haven't taken one since I started." She scanned the people on the street out of habit.

He turned his coffee cup on the table. "Usually over Christmas or around the end of this month. Find a nice tropical place to lie on a beach."

"My parents loved to travel. We took a big trip every summer. The beach trips were always my favorite. But my ex hated leaving home, so that part of my life just...stopped." She traced the top of the cup, her gaze distant. "And when it was just me, Charlie, and the kids, we couldn't afford it. It wasn't until later in my career that we could finally go out and explore."

"Alie and Mason really impressed me. They're remarkably mature for their age. Watching you and Charlie, I assume you raised them as a team."

"Thanks." She gave him a half grin. "The early days were rough. He would take care of the kids during the day while I was at work, then he'd head out the door to bartend while I was home getting dinner on the table and then our nightly routine of baths, books, and bed. When they started school, then Charlie could work later into the night because he could sleep while they were gone." Laci glanced up at him.

"Did you want kids? I figured a guy like you would have been married and a football team of boys."

Tai met her eyes, smiling widely. "Nah. I love interacting with the kids who come into the restaurant. But I know my limits, and diaper duty is beyond them. Parenting is not a responsibility I'm cut out for."

Something deep within her seemed to settle. "I always wanted a big family, but it just wasn't in the cards. I have my two, and I'm happy to see them thriving on their own now."

When they finished, Tai cleaned up their trash and took her hand. He guided her through a small alcove that opened into the coziest bookstore she had ever seen. Shadows seemed to cling to the walls, absorbed by the rich, emerald green flocked wallpaper. Its repeating fleur-de-lis pattern was soft as moss, a velvety texture that muted both sound and light, giving the room an intimate, Gothic feel. Dark mahogany shelves were packed with books, and live plants hung from the ceiling. The scent of aging paper and leather filled the air. She just wanted to curl up in one of the plush maroon chairs and read every book in the store.

As she looked closer, Laci realized they were all used books. "Wow. I haven't seen some of these titles on shelves in years."

"A friend of mine has a business a few blocks away," Tai said, his voice a low rumble behind her. "We stumbled on this place one day. Now I come in here whenever I'm looking for a new-to-me read."

Laci looked over her shoulder, meeting Tai's gaze. "And you brought me here because...?"

"Because Charlie mentioned you liked to read," he said, squeezing her hand. Only then did Laci realize he was still holding it. "I figured since we both like to relax with a good book, maybe you'd enjoy this."

She froze, caught by the genuine softness in his eyes. He'd remembered a small detail about her and acted on it. The realization rattled her, and she quickly turned back to the shelves to hide her reaction.

"Welcome!" A woman about the same age as Laci, with purple hair, greeted them. "Please, take your time and look around. If you're looking for a specific genre, I can point you in the right direction. You're also welcome just to sit and read if you'd like."

"It's like you read my mind," Laci whispered.

The clerk grinned. "Would I prefer people buy the books and take them home? Of course. But, I also know that in this area, libraries are pretty much non-existent, so if I can provide a quiet escape for somebody who maybe can't afford to buy, then that's what I'll do."

"Appreciate the help," Tai responded on their behalf. "We have some time on our hands, so we'll likely be looking around for a bit."

When the clerk walked into the office, Tai leaned down to Laci's ear. "They have a donation jar at the register or an option to upcharge your purchase to help out." His warm breath caused goosebumps on her neck.

When she turned her head slightly, their lips were only inches apart. She was close enough to see that his deep brown eyes had golden flecks. "Thanks. I'm definitely going to do that."

The genres were pretty easy to figure out based on the titles of the books. Then she caught one that made her snort.

"*The Secret Life of Inanimate Objects (And Why Your Stapler Hates You),*" she read out loud.

Tai picked up a book and showed it to her. On the cover was a mostly naked man with ripped abs. "Is this your style? *Stop, Drop, and Roll Won't Work on My Heart.*" He flipped it over to read the back. "Can their scorching passion survive as the town burns around them?"

"Oh my god, shut up!" Laci was laughing hard now. "That can't be real."

Tai looked at the cover again. "I mean, clearly the book is real, but I'm pretty sure this guy's abs are not. I think that's a third nipple." The broad smile on his face as he enjoyed torturing her with funnier titles made him look younger and so much more relaxed than the carefully controlled business owner she knew. The sound of her own laughter felt freeing.

They moved together down a cramped aisle, their shoulders occasionally brushing. Laci's fingers drifted over the spines until they stopped on a handsome maroon volume with gold lettering. *The Silent Curator.* She pulled it from the shelf, feeling its solid weight in her hands as she read the description.

"Find one?" Tai's voice came from beside her. He'd been browsing the same section, and now he paused to see what she'd chosen. He held a book of his own, the cover an abstract swirl of blue and gold.

"I think so," Laci said, showing him the cover. "A portrait goes missing from a private gallery in a remote castle. The theft is just a cover for a much older, darker secret."

"A mystery," he nodded, his expression curious. "What is it about them that pulls you in?"

She hesitated a moment. "Life has been...chaotic." She ran a finger along the worn spine. "In these, I get lost in following the clues with the characters, knowing that in the end there is a solution. Order is always restored."

The confession hung in the air, feeling more vulnerable than she'd intended. Tai was quiet for a moment, just absorbing her words.

"What about you?" she asked, gesturing to the book in his hand to shift the focus. "I didn't peg you for a sci-fi buff."

He looked down at the book, a faint smile touching his lips. "Don't let the spaceships fool you. World-building fascinates me." He met her gaze, his eyes thoughtful. "Somebody imagines a complete society from scratch, the politics, the economy, everything. Reading them as I grew up gave me perspectives my college business classes never could. College taught me the management, these taught me to see the potential."

They paused, watching each other carefully.

"Huh," he said after a beat, a look of quiet discovery on his face. "Restoring order versus building it from scratch. Two sides of the same coin, I guess."

A small smile touched her lips. "I guess so," she said softly.

Tai gave a slight nod and turned back to the shelf. "Well, this one's a classic. I think I'll get it."

They both picked out a few books, and at the register, added generous amounts to the donation jar. He carried their bags back to the dealership.

"Let's drop your car off at the house, and I'll drive you to Blackwood."

Laci was ready to protest, but when she looked up at him, she saw that the easy humor in his eyes was gone, replaced by a quiet intensity. It was a promise he'd made to Charlie, and his steady gaze asked her not to make him break it.

"Alright," she agreed, her voice steadier than she felt. "I'll follow you."

⩕

That night, after closing, Tai took Laci home. He held the bags of books she'd bought while she unlocked the door. Inside, she slipped off her boots and hung up her coat. Tai stepped in behind her, closing the door.

"Thank you for the surprise today," she said, smiling up at him.

Tai chuckled, holding up the bags. "I'm not sure you left anything in the store for them to sell."

Playfully grabbing the bags from him, she laughed. "I only got enough to last a week or so." She turned to place the bags on the bottom step of the staircase.

When she turned back to say goodnight, the look on his face stopped her short. The air in the foyer crackled. He took a slow step forward, closing the distance between them.

His hand slid around the small of her back, pulling her in as he lowered his head. His lips were soft, tentative at first, pressing gently against hers. Laci's hands seemed to move on their own, sliding up his chest until they rested on his solid shoulders. His scent surrounded her. There was an underlying clean smell of his warmed cotton shirt, but also a hint of the sweet, oaky bourbon that had splashed on him earlier. The kiss deepened, a gentle pressure becoming a firm, searching heat. The faint roughness of his evening stubble grazed her skin, and a low sound rumbled in his chest, vibrating through her hands. All rational thought dissolved. The world outside the foyer ceased to exist. All that was left was the dizzying sensation of Tai's mouth on hers and the warm, melting feeling that started in her belly and spread like wildfire.

He pulled away, their foreheads touching as they both caught their breath.

"I'll be here in the morning," he murmured, giving her another soft peck on her lips. "Good night, Laci."

It took Laci a full five minutes before she locked the door and slid the brace back in place. She stood for a long moment, one hand pressed to the cold wood of the door, the other against her racing heart. The ghost of his kiss still lingered on her lips. She picked up her books and walked up the stairs. Sitting on the edge of her bed, the war inside her began. Her body vibrated, desperate for more. Her heart pounded with a searing guilt. And her mind, the logical part that had kept her safe for so long, was screaming in a cold panic. *This is dangerous.*

TWELVE

THE SLOW DRIP OF coffee was the only sound in the quiet kitchen. It had taken every ounce of Tai's self-control not to kiss Laci in the bookstore yesterday. The memory of it, the surprised delight in her eyes, the sound of her laugh, replayed in his head. That kiss had been inevitable, and he already wanted to do it again.

Once the pot stopped dripping, Tai poured himself a mug and made his way down the hall to his office. Calls had to be made, and that included Charlie. There was something else Tai had seen with Laci the previous day, and he needed more information on how to handle it.

An exhausted voice answered. "Hey, boss man."

"Charlie, how are things there?"

"Aggravating," Charlie growled, a rare moment of anger. "I know my mother is dragging this out to keep me here, but I can't figure out what the deal is. Even my stepfather is acting differently. How is Laci?"

"She's okay. She's at your house. But Mark is aware of your absence." Tai blew out a silent breath, hoping Charlie trusted him enough to keep Laci safe.

"Damnit. I knew he would be a problem. I just didn't know when or if he would try something."

Running a finger along his brow, Tai continued. "Well, your absence seems to have pushed him to try something. He came in and sat near the bar, and while she knew not to look his way, she didn't see him watching her every move. I tried to block his line of sight, to show him she wasn't alone, but that just made her notice how agitated I was getting."

A slight smile touched Tai's lips as he remembered how beautiful she looked, even though she was pissed off. "She scolded me earlier for trying to adapt to her, telling me to move the way I wanted, and she would learn to move around me. I didn't realize that's how you two operated. My mistake was trying to move more like you."

Charlie chuckled before he responded, his mood clearly lifted by talking about Laci. "No, Laci's a chameleon. She'll change to the people and the environment, at least when she's doing well. Laci was reading you so she could adapt. Trying to work around her pisses her off."

"That must be what happened. She stormed off to the kitchen, and when she returned, she stood still for only a moment before moving in perfect sync with me."

Charlie's smile was audible. "You need to be aware that means she can also read your emotions. She can sense you in the same space. It's also how she detects somebody with bad mojo."

"Ah, got it. When Mark walked in, she must have sensed my agitation. She stopped me again and said she was moving to the kitchen, staying in there until Mark left." Tai still remembered the relief on her face when she saw that Mark was gone.

Charlie hesitated. "Do you think Mark is going to be a bigger problem?"

"No. I'm with Laci anytime she's out of the house, and starting tonight, another layer of protection is in place. You have nothing to worry about." Tai cleared his throat. "But, there is something else. Twice now, I've noticed Laci seems to have a negative reaction when her stress levels rise. The night that guy grabbed her, I was positive she was going to pass out. Then, yesterday, at the service shop, it was as if she completely checked out and swayed. Is there something I should know?"

"Tai." Charlie let out an exasperated breath. "I know she told you her ex tried to kill her. Both times, he did it in a way that inflicted a maximum amount of pain before she blacked out. She's been through so much. Her body now protects itself with an automatic emergency shutdown. If she gets into a situation where she feels overwhelmed or threatened, the clock starts ticking to help her before she just... turns off."

"Charlie." There was now a tight knot in Tai's chest.

"That's the one thing that scared me about leaving her. If she has a nightmare, I'm not there to help."

Tai wasn't sure he heard right. "What do you mean, nightmares?"

"Part of the reason she's staying with me is that she needed professional help and didn't want to be alone after dredging everything up. The therapy sessions triggered epic-level nightmares. I have to be alert because if one is bad enough, it could trigger her mind to interpret it as a real threat, causing a reaction. Feeling horrible about waking me every night, she asked her doctor for something to help. The prescription worked, but the side effect was extreme dizziness."

The combination was not good, given that Mark knew Charlie was gone. Tai's mind spun with the dangerous possibilities. "You should know that she's installed security around the house. I saw a brace by the front door."

"Exactly like her house. She must have brought it all with her and hidden it from me. That means despite everything, she's still terrified." Charlie blew out a breath. "And she won't tell me because she doesn't want me to feel bad."

"Then she's putting on a good front, because I haven't seen any indication she's scared to be alone when I drop her off. My offer for her to stay here still stands." Tai really hoped she would accept.

"I'll remind her, but I doubt she'll take you up on it."

After ending the call, Tai moved on to his other tasks before driving to Laci's.

Not falling asleep was a battle Laci was losing. A nightmare had been triggered last night after a noise on the back deck startled her while she was getting ready for bed. Heavy clouds obscured the moonlight, obliterating any chance of seeing what was out there. From her bedroom window, she stared into the darkness, her heart racing for what seemed like hours, until a huge form stepped into view. Then the deer knocked its antlers into the railing, repeating the sound.

Breathing a sigh of relief, she sat on the edge of her bed. The incident, however, had spiked her fear level enough to spark a nightmare. Taking her meds was a necessity, but the nightmare came anyway, waking her. Getting out of bed was too dangerous with the drugs in her system. The last time she'd tried, she tripped and hit her shoulder on a door frame. Instead, she sat up and waited for her body to calm before trying to sleep again.

Once the meds wore off, Laci checked for notifications, but there were none. A short workout and shower did little to wake her up. An extra-large cup of coffee was in her hand when Charlie called.

"Hey, Charlie," she answered sleepily.

"Oh, you sound exhausted. Did you take your meds?"

"I did, but I had a nightmare anyway."

"Tai called me. He told me you've turned my house into Fort Knox." Charlie's soft and comforting voice almost made her cry.

She cringed a little. "Oh."

"Why didn't you tell me you brought the security equipment? And how much did you bring?"

Thinking of a good excuse was pointless. She knew she'd get a talking to from Dr. T if she lied to Charlie. "Everything. And I didn't want to tell you because you have enough on your plate. Just think of it as my extra set of eyes while you're away."

Charlie let out a frustrated sigh. "If you're that scared, why don't you stay at Tai's house?"

"And bring trouble right to his door? Hell no!" The response was harsher than intended, but exhaustion had frayed her nerves. "Sorry. No, I can't do that to him. What's going on there?"

"Something isn't right. Travis is acting weirder than usual, and my mother is doing everything she can to stay in the hospital. You know my mom. There is no way she can afford this."

"Could something be wrong that they can't find?"

"No, they've run every scan, every test. Her symptoms keep changing. I think she's looking up illnesses on the internet and then listing them off to the doctors. It makes no sense. I'm taking a break today to hang out with the kids."

"Give them hugs and kisses for me. Tai texted that he's ten minutes out, so I have to go."

"Alright. Laci, I love you."

"Love you too."

By the time Tai pulled up, Laci was ready. She removed the brace, stepped outside, locked both the handle and the deadbolt, and walked to the car, where he held the passenger door open for her. Inside, she enjoyed the blast of heat he had cranked up on her side.

He walked around and climbed in. "Good morning. How did you sleep?"

A yawn escaped before Laci could stifle it. "Unfortunately, not very well. I'll be okay."

Tai didn't press. He let the space remain quiet as they drove. Before they reached the end of the street, her eyes fought to stay open. She was out before they made the turn.

Light tapping sounds filtered into Laci's dreamless sleep. She remembered falling asleep in the car, but now there was a pillow under her head. Opening her eyes, she saw the chairs in Tai's office. Pushing up on an elbow, she saw Tai working at his desk, typing something on his computer. "Okay, how did I get here? I haven't sleep-teleported since I was six."

Tai chuckled as he walked around the desk and sat next to her. "I called Benji to open the back door. I pulled into the alley and carried you in."

"How long have I been out? Who's working the bar?"

"Vanessa and Benji have it handled. You've been out for about three hours. You needed it."

"Did I....I mean...I didn't scream, did I?" Embarrassment washed over her, but not knowing would be worse.

"No, you were silent the entire time, I promise." Standing, he crossed the room and retrieved a bottle of water from his mini-fridge. He handed it to her. "I take it you scream in your sleep?"

Laci paused, sipping water. "Yes, for the past several months. Poor Charlie gets his sleep interrupted. Sometimes, when we know one is coming, he'll sleep next to me so all he has to do is roll over instead of sprinting across the hall."

"He mentioned you might not have taken your meds last night."

"My doctor prescribed them to stop the screaming. The only issue is the dizziness. It's like being drunk. If something happened, I couldn't defend myself. I took them last night, but the nightmares won."

Putting her face in her hands, she sighed. The nap had taken the edge off her exhaustion, but a familiar dread still coiled in her stomach at the thought of another night.

The warmth of Tai's hand rubbing her back in a comforting gesture seeped in through her shirt. "Did Charlie tell you what I offered?"

She pushed her hair back and glanced towards him. "Yes, and I have to think about it. I appreciate the offer, but the last thing I want is to disrupt somebody else's sleep."

Leaning closer, he murmured in her ear, "You wouldn't."

His lips brushed against her temple. As good as it felt, showing affection in front of others was a risk to his life. That conversation needed to happen soon.

Laci stood and took off her coat. "I'm ready to get to work, if you don't have any objections."

If her abrupt reaction shocked him, he didn't show it. He stood and ran his fingers through her hair. "You had a little bedhead. All good now."

Rolling her eyes, Laci huffed. "Oh, great. I'm a functioning adult, I promise."

He chuckled as they walked out together. On the way through the kitchen, Benji stopped her for a hug. "Hey, if you need to stay with us, you can. You don't have to be alone."

She smiled back. "I know, Benji. I appreciate it."

Stepping out behind the bar, Vanessa practically launched herself into Laci's arms. "I don't have space for you, but Brent and I can stay with you while Charlie is gone."

"I appreciate it, but I think I'm good for now."

"Okay." Vanessa turned to grab orders.

Tai stood behind Laci. "I hope you see you're part of this family now. Any one of us is here for you." He moved around her and opened the stations behind the bar.

"I do see that, and I appreciate it. I just have to weigh certain decisions carefully." Laci wished she could erase the look of concern on his face.

Another person walked in behind Laci, and she spun to see who had joined them. It took a moment to recognize the man. "Vincent, right?"

As before, Vincent's features were unreadable, except for the fractional rise of one dark eyebrow. He held out his hand, and Laci shook it, surprised at his gentle grip.

"Nice to see you again, Laci." His voice was so quiet she doubted anyone else heard him, but its gentle tone immediately put her at ease.

Tai's hand settled on Laci's shoulder. "Vincent will be working here now. He'll handle the heavy lifting, bringing in stock and generally helping me keep an eye on things."

Her gaze caught Vanessa fanning her face and mouthing, "Oooo girl!" The gesture caused Laci to look at the two formidable men now sandwiching her, and she burst out laughing.

The dinner rush returned to normal. Tai moved with an effortless rhythm that was easy to follow, a welcome change from the chaos of the previous night. Vincent somehow blended into their routine, moving to keep up with the demands.

On the way home, Tai tried to lighten the mood. "So, where did Charlie's 'Baby-girl' nickname come from?"

Laci smiled. "In high school, we were hanging out with friends when one commented to Charlie how he's not obviously gay like other people we knew. He knew he was gay from an early age, but learned to hide it because of his home life. He uses his charm on everybody, making it unclear to outsiders. Plus, he would use me as a decoy."

Tai raised an eyebrow. "A decoy?"

She laughed. "If he needed a female partner for anything, I'd play the part. In response to our friends, he flipped his imaginary hair, tilted his head, and asked me in this very feminine voice, 'Oh Baby-girl, did you want to go shoe shopping this weekend?'"

Tai laughed, and she knew he could picture it perfectly. "Charlie was being sarcastic, but he started using it to get a laugh out of me, and it stuck. When he says it now, it feels like home."

Turning the tables, she asked, "What about you? Who do you have in your life?"

He cocked his head slightly. "My brother and I grew up around here. My parents are gone. The house I grew up in is on the eastern side of town. I still own it and rent it out."

"Where is your brother?"

He sighed. "Honestly, I don't know. Felix was always in trouble. Our parents were older and couldn't keep bailing him out. With so many alcohol-related charges, he couldn't find a decent job."

"Did he come to you for help?"

"Not then. I moved to the East Coast to learn the trade and save up to open my own place here. My brother couldn't find me, but I knew what was happening from my parents." A small smile touched his face. "They were my first customers. Seeing their smiles made me feel like I'd finally accomplished my dream." The smile faded. "They must have bragged about it, because Felix showed up shortly after. He needed cash, and I had nothing to give. Everything was tied up in the restaurant."

"I bet that didn't go over well."

"No. I had to remove him. About four years later, my parents passed within a month of each other. My brother showed up again for his share of the inheritance, not knowing they had nothing. They held middle-class jobs and struggled to make ends meet. I'd bought the house from them in the last year, so they could live without worrying about bills. Felix lost his shit and demanded money from me again. When I told him no, he left and never came back. That was six years ago."

"So you lost your entire family in a matter of months."

"Yes. But my parents died in love and at peace, and I was able to provide that for them. So that helped me through it. My brother was an idiot for years, so it was no great loss."

When they arrived, Tai walked her into the house. The click of the door closing behind her made her heart skip a beat. After putting her things away, Laci took a deep breath and turned to face him.

Tai's jaw clenched, a clear signal of his unhappiness about leaving. Lifting a palm to her cheek, he ran his thumb along her temple. "Are you sure you want to stay here alone? I have no issue with you staying at my place. Or with you waking me if you have a nightmare."

"I know, but I'm so exhausted, I'm sure I'll sleep through the night." Laci offered a smile she hoped was convincing.

Stepping forward, he wrapped her in his arms and leaned down to kiss her. This time, his jacket was open, allowing her to run her hands across his abs and around his waist. As the kiss deepened, he pulled her tighter.

His warmth seeped into her, a feeling she had long forgotten. So long. For so long, she had been ice cold. Empty. Now, as his mouth explored hers, her muscles uncoiled, surrendering to the heat. His hands moved to cup her ass, pulling her tighter until she could feel the rock-hard length of his arousal against her belly. Her own body responded, a deep ache waking from the depths.

Laci could tell the moment he reined himself in. Little by little, the grip on her loosened, the kisses pulling back to light pecks on her lips. Their breathing was rapid, something neither could control.

Their foreheads touched. "I can sleep in the other spare room tonight."

The war within her mind took off. Part of her didn't want Tai to go, but she couldn't risk going any further. "No, you need to go home. I'll be fine."

A low growl seemed to rumble in his chest. "Promise me you'll call if you need me."

Laci met his eyes. "I promise."

He nodded against her forehead, stepped back, opened the door, and was gone. The sudden rush of cold winter air was a shock against her heated skin. For a moment, she just stood there, catching her breath. *Is this really happening?* Turning, she locked the door, placing the brace in its spot, and headed upstairs. When she climbed into bed, pulling the heavy blankets over her, the exhaustion set in. *Maybe tonight I'll get a whole night of sleep.*

THIRTEEN

Laci wasn't looking forward to rehashing what had happened in the shop and her nightmare, but she knew Dr. T would see that something was wrong. Once she gave him the rundown, they agreed to focus on tactics to counteract her body's shutdown response when her fear crossed a certain threshold.

There was one piece she hadn't told him, and the guilt was eating at her. She had to be honest. "Tai kissed me goodnight the last two nights. He keeps offering for me to stay at his place and, last night, he offered to sleep in the other guest room instead of going home. All so I would feel safe and not be alone."

There was barely any reaction from Dr. T. He tilted his head slightly. "Not to sound like every therapist in movies and TV, but how did you feel about that?"

She offered a weak smile. "It scares me that he has deeper feelings for me than I can give him. It scares me that somebody will kill him if I open up to the possibility of those feelings. Also, it worries me to have those feelings again, especially so soon after losing Leo. I feel like some part of me is cheating on him, that I haven't mourned his loss long enough."

This time, Dr. T kept writing as he spoke. "Tell me about this feeling of cheating on him. What does long enough look like to you? What does it feel like to keep your life on hold for someone who can no longer live it with you?"

She didn't have an answer this time.

He stopped and looked at her. "Laci, have you been upfront with Tai and told him no?"

She slowly shook her head.

Now, he was sternly staring at her through the camera. "Why do you think you won't tell him no? Why do you keep doing this back and forth, where he pursues you, and you back off? Each time, you let him in a little further. From what you have told me about him, I understand that if you flat-out told him no, he would stop. He would respect that line in the sand. And yet, you haven't drawn it."

The week fell into a dangerous rhythm. Rides to work were filled with childhood stories that complicated Laci's feelings for Tai, and shifts behind the bar passed with flawless teamwork that sharpened her ability to read him. Each night ended with a goodnight kiss that felt like a double-edged sword. A part of her was hopeful because it was a return to her old self, but it was also deeply concerning because she was getting too close. Her two days off provided a much-needed escape, giving her the time she desperately needed to finally decide if, and where, she would draw that line in the sand.

There was an impending snowstorm, so Laci had to get to the grocery store and back before that hit. She gathered everything she needed, then stood at the closed door and stared at it. It would be her first time going out alone since Charlie had left. She could take her car to the store. It would be way out and around, but it would work. She could call Tai to take her, but then he would have to drive all the way down here, which seemed excessive for a quick trip to the store.

I can do this. Laci stepped outside, her hand steady as she turned the key in the lock. With a deep breath, she set off down the street to the walkway.

The store manager waved hello to her and stopped to chat as she walked in. Charlie had introduced them on one of their trips here, so she was comfortable talking to him. The store was quite busy since many other residents were also preparing. Laci took her time and gathered everything she would need for the next week or so. An hour later, she checked out, packed everything in Charlie's wheeled bin, and then headed home, pulling the cart behind her.

Being snowed in was something she usually enjoyed, a familiar comfort from her life back home. When she returned, she noticed the neighbor next door on her front step. Laci hadn't spoken much with the neighbors, mostly waving to them in passing. Today, the neighbor waved Laci over.

Laci walked up her drive and then noticed the concern on her face. "How are you, Kathy?"

Kathy, a retired teacher in her sixties, and her husband, Henry, a former factory worker, had moved here soon after Charlie bought his house to escape the city. "Hi, Laci. How are things with Charlie away?"

"Oh, I've been managing. Being home alone is weird when you're so used to having another person around. Especially when it's the other person's house." Laci smiled at the oddity of that situation.

Kathy glanced over to Charlie's house and then back at Laci. "I wanted to let you know I noticed a man looking around the house today, right after you left. He only went to the front and this side between our houses, but I knew something wasn't right. He dressed like a repairman, but I knew you wouldn't have scheduled any repairs while Charlie is gone."

Laci fought to contain her panic. Her phone was in her pocket, but with the noise of the store and the walk home, any notification would have been missed. "How long was he here?"

"Only for about five minutes, I came out to see who he was. Now, I've had enough teenagers try to lie to me that I can spot it a mile away. This man dared try to tell me he had an appointment for a repair." She put her hand on her hip and popped it out to the side. "First, any repairman around here has identification hanging around their neck, clearly displaying which company they are with. Second, he never knocked on the front door. I caught his tall, blond head walking right around the house. Third, there were no markings on the pick-up he drove off in after I told him Charlie was due home any minute."

Laci kept her demeanor calm, but inside, she was screaming. "I appreciate it, Kathy. I hope he just had the wrong house, but I'm thankful for neighbors like you who watch out for others. You'd better get back to your house. You're going to freeze to death out here!"

"Oh, I'm good, but if you need anything, you can come over here. Got it?"

"I got it, thanks." Laci hustled home, got in the front door, parked the bin, turned, locked, and braced the door.

She pulled out her phone. There was a notification that she had opened the front door to come home, but that was all. She breathed a small sigh of relief.

She gathered everything back up and took it to the kitchen to put away. Charlie called for their morning chat as she took care of the last of it.

"Hey, Laci, how's it going?"

"Good, Blackwood is hopping again. Nobody wants healthy food at home anymore."

"Are you still in sync with Tai behind the bar?"

"Yeah, he's relaxed now and does his thing while I work around him. Also, the new guy, Vincent, is a huge help."

"New guy?" Charlie's voice was laced with uncertainty.

Laci giggled. "Don't worry, Tai isn't replacing you. Vincent helps by carrying crates and stuff from the cooler. He doesn't say much, but from what little I've talked to him, he's really nice."

"What does he look like?" Laci could almost imagine Charlie bobbing his eyebrows up and down.

"Uh, well, he's like six three, dark hair and eyes, dude is built, but he's really gentle and quiet."

"Well, maybe I should get home sooner." They both chuckled. "What are you going to do today with your day off?" Charlie asked.

"I got groceries, and I'm ready to be snowed in. We're expecting a major storm to move in this afternoon. The skies here are already ominously dark."

"Oh, that will be fun. Stay in, watch movies, read books, or play games."

"Exactly. I talked to Kathy next door, too."

"Wow, chatting with my neighbors!"

Laci paused momentarily, wondering if she should tell him what Kathy said. "Charlie, she said she caught some tall, blond guy dressed as a cable repairman snooping around the house."

"What happened?" The easygoing warmth vanished from Charlie's voice.

Laci took the time to explain everything that Kathy told her. "I don't think he meant any harm. I checked the security, and there were no alerts. He probably got the wrong house."

"Laci, why don't you go to Tai's? You can relax up there and not worry about anything. He wants to help."

It was obvious to her that Tai hadn't been filling Charlie in on how he said goodnight to her each time he dropped her off, and she wasn't ready to tell Charlie either. "I've had no nightmares and full nights of sleep after that one night. I feel safe here with the storm coming in. I'll be fine tonight. Besides, I don't think there is time to reach Tai's house safely. As we've been talking, the snow has started to fall. How are things there? Will you be coming home soon?"

Charlie blew out a long sigh over the phone. "I think the doctors are fed up and will kick my mother out of the hospital today. She took her symptoms too far and tried to convince them that her prostate was keeping her from peeing."

"Um, I guess she doesn't know..."

"No, she doesn't know that women don't have a prostate. I can't confront her in the hospital, so I have to wait until she's home to find out why she put up the charade."

Laci cringed at hearing him explode in anger like that. It was so out of character for him. "I'm sorry you're dealing with all of this."

"Hopefully, by the end of next week, you and I will be curled up on the couch eating popcorn and watching movies together."

"Can't wait. Give everybody at my house love and hugs for me."

"Will do. Bye, Laci."

Laci hung up and watched the giant snowflakes fall, a peaceful sight that wouldn't last. Knowing the calm was temporary, she began preparing for the loss of water and electricity.

Tai placed the pot on top of the other freshly washed dishes in the draining rack. Thick snow piled up on the kitchen windowsill, obscuring the dark world outside. Grabbing the towel to dry his hands, he felt the vibration of his phone in his pocket. Checking the screen, he quickly answered the call.

"Charlie, it's late there. Everything okay?"

There was a ragged breath on the other end of the line. "No. No, it's not okay. Tai... I had a really rough day, and I need your help."

"Sure, anything. How can I help?" Tai turned from the kitchen and walked briskly to his office, ready to take notes.

"Laci is in more danger than I thought," Charlie's voice broke. "I don't want to call her and freak her out, but you have to get her to your house. Don't take no for an answer. I need to know she isn't alone."

Tai froze, his hand tightening on the phone. "How bad is the danger, Charlie? Tell me what's going on."

He heard footsteps and the click of a door closing in the background. "To understand," Charlie began, his voice strained, "you need the whole story. Laci will be livid with me for telling you, but I'll deal with that later. It started in college, after she met her ex-husband."

Tai sank into the chair behind his desk. A grim sense of relief settled over him. The vague pieces Jack had hinted at were finally clicking into place. But relief was immediately chased by a wave of guilt. This was a story he should have heard from Laci. "Go on."

"She tried to convince me he was a great guy, but I never really liked him." Charlie cleared his throat. "Soon after Alie was born, I noticed changes. Laci had bruises she tried to explain away. She'd call me in tears at night when she was left alone with the baby. Then she admitted that she found drugs in his car."

Leaning forward, Tai ran a hand down his face. "And she stayed."

"You know how stubborn she is," Charlie said, the frustration raw in his voice. "She wanted to try to get him help. She wanted to fix things. Instead, it got worse. Mason was only a month old when the cops showed up at my door with the kids."

Tai's heart dropped. "What happened?"

"They said they'd arrested her ex and that she was in the hospital. A neighbor found her...damnit, Tai...she was unresponsive, curled in a ball on the kitchen floor with the babies wrapped up in her arms."

"Were they hurt? The kids?" Tai asked, his voice tight.

"No. Not a scratch on them. They were in their beds when he hurt her. She was trying to gather them up and get out when she passed out." There was a heavy pause. "He did a few years in jail. When he was released, he found her again despite my moving them to another house with me."

"The second attempt to kill her," Tai concluded grimly.

"The cops got there just in time. We moved again, found the house she owns now. Then she met Leo. Leo was...safe. He was good to her, and I thought this was all finally over. That's when I traveled the country and landed there."

Tai remembered that day that Charlie happened to be eating at Blackwood and stopped him to ask about bartending.

"Then, last spring, I got a call and you helped me get back home," Charlie continued.

"I remember. I didn't know why, but I knew you were in too much of a panicked state to book tickets and drive."

There was a heavy pause now. "Professional hitmen were hired to kill Leo. They forced Laci to watch."

The line went silent as Tai struggled to process the words, the air stolen from his chest. "Was it..."

"It was him," Charlie confirmed, his voice thick with anger. "The hitmen told Laci her ex sent them. But because of the condition she was in, needing the paramedics to revive her, the cops couldn't use her testimony. Because he was in prison, and his family is dripping with money, the prosecutor wouldn't touch it."

Tai gave Charlie a moment. He could hear the unshed tears in his voice. "Is that why she came here?"

Charlie sniffled. "She disappeared. Physically, she was here, but mentally, she disappeared. She would wake at three every night, when Leo would get up and ready to be at work by five, only to realize he was gone and give up. Night after night. I was finally able to convince her to come here and stay with me."

Tai stood, pacing his office. The helplessness was suffocating. "So what's happening now? What's changed?"

"My mother," Charlie spat the word. "A man came to their door and offered them cash to tell him where Laci was. He already knew she hadn't been home in months."

"Wait, how would they know she was with you? Was it her ex?"

The raw anger in Charlie's voice was palpable. "I have no idea how they knew! By the description, it wasn't her ex. But it gets worse. After hours of arguments, they finally confessed that he came back, offered them *more* money to get me out of town and away from her. The whole 'emergency' and hospital stay with my mother was a setup to leave Laci unprotected."

The pieces clicked together in Tai's mind. "Then she would be walking to and from work alone," he said aloud. "My being there....it was messing up their plans."

"Exactly! And now she's alone, with a storm rolling in, and they've had somebody watching her for months. I'm stuck here, the airports are a mess, and I can't get a flight." Charlie's voice cracked with desperation. "Look, I know she does this yo-yo thing with you, pushing you away and then letting you get closer. It's because she's scared of this. She's trying to protect you from him. I've always thought you'd be good for her, and I've been trying to get her to see that, too."

It all pulled into place. Her flinching at loud noises, the way she avoided crowds, and the haunted look that shadowed her eyes when she was stressed. Her constant retreat whenever he got close wasn't a rejection. It was protection. She was trying to keep them both safe. A weight lifted from Tai's conscience, knowing Charlie was in his corner. "I can take care of myself. Laci is what matters."

"Her ex still has several years left to serve on his sentence, but with all of this happening, I'm worried something has gone wrong. I can't get answers about him tonight. Please, Tai. Get to her."

"As soon as the snow lets up enough for me to drive, I will. You have my word." Tai said, his voice deadly calm.

After they hung up, Tai opened his contacts and dialed a number.

"Jack, I need your help."

FOURTEEN

A DEEP, MUFFLING SILENCE woke Laci. Outside her window, the world was buried in a thick, pristine blanket of white. Seeing the time on the clock gave her some relief that she had not lost power. Mother Nature was taking a breath before round two later today. For now, there was peace. The perfect, majestic scene had Laci grabbing for her camera. From her bedroom window, the angle was perfect. Trees in the distance stood painted in white. After snapping several shots, she put her camera back in its bag and dressed.

The coffee maker was gurgling away when her phone rang. Glancing at the screen, she paused for a moment before answering it. These two days without contact were supposed to be a reboot for her body and mind. But she also knew he and Charlie would send the National Guard to check on her if she didn't answer.

"Hi, Tai."

His deep voice now caused her insides to melt each time she heard it, especially over the phone, directly in her ear. "Hi, Laci. Did you get through the storm alright?"

"I'm good," she said, her nod useless over the phone. "I still have power and water, so I'm making breakfast and lying around gaming today."

"I was going to come into town, maybe stop by and see how you were doing, but I'm snowed in."

She knew there was no good reason for him to risk coming into town on their day off. "Tai, I'm good. I assume Charlie told you what happened yesterday."

"He did, which is why I wanted to come and see you."

Laci pulled a plate from the cupboard. "My security is still in place, and I'll be fine."

"Please, Laci, call me if you need me. Or better yet, call the police. They can get to you faster."

"I promise."

As she hung up, a strange tension in Tai's tone prickled at her. She'd checked all her braces this morning, and they were solid. The snowplows were struggling to keep up with the volume of precipitation, which made car travel a mess.

With round two arriving in a few hours, she felt safe. The snow in the backyard was an undisturbed blanket, so she moved to the gaming room to check the front. Still nothing. No movement, no tracks, just a quiet stillness. Giant drifts of snow looked like waves in a vast white ocean. There was a massive pile of what little she could see of the driveway. It almost looked as if the house was in the early stages of becoming a small snow fort.

Walking back to the kitchen, Laci grabbed her breakfast and sat at the table with her notebooks, Dr. T's homework that had become her daily ritual. Now that she had only one appointment every other week, it was up to her to make sure she completed these daily tasks to keep her mental health in control.

One by one, she worked through them until she reached the last book, where she could write with a single stream of consciousness.

I was actually looking forward to the snow. I wanted the peace of it, the quiet, a real, official excuse to be locked in here and feel safe from the world.

What I forgot about, until the coffee kicked in, was the driveway. It's completely buried, and I know I have to handle it before the next storm comes this afternoon, which will make it impossible.

I can hear Charlie's voice in my head, telling me I can leave it. But I can't. I can't be the only house on the street buried in snow. I hate the thought of the neighbors thinking I'm lazy or, even worse, helpless. The thought of Mr. Henderson coming over to do it for me... that feeling of being pitied would be so much worse.

Being out there feels scarier than usual, though. Especially after what happened yesterday. The idea of being so exposed, with nowhere to go...

So, I'll wait a little while. When I hear the other snowblowers start up, that's when I'll go out. Hopefully, everybody will be too preoccupied with their own driveways to try to talk to me. But at least there will be other people around, other eyes to watch out for me, just in case.

After capping the pen, she stared at the page. A cold knot tightened in her stomach. Without Charlie here to talk about her entry for the day, she could now see the fear and isolation creeping back in. This looked more like her entries when she had first started these homework assignments. Slowly, she closed the notebook.

After going outside to snowblow the front walk and driveway while the neighbors were out doing the same, Laci tucked herself up on the couch in her sweats and hoodie, sipping a mug of hot chocolate and watching a movie under a cozy blanket. She tried to convince herself that being alone today was helping, that she could form a plan to improve without the influence of the two protective men in her life. But the words from her journal echoed in her mind. Without someone to talk to, she was turning in on herself again.

She watched as the snow fell in the second round of storms, the afternoon sky looking rather ominous. Today was the first time in a long time that she felt safe and locked away from the world. The storm was her protector. It wanted nothing from her, demanded nothing of her. For a few hours, at least, she could simply be.

⟁

The distinctive ring of his cell phone woke Tai from a deep sleep. Who was calling at this hour?

Groggily, he rolled over to look at the screen. Adrenaline jolted him fully awake. "Laci, what's wrong?"

Her voice barely whispered over the line. "Tai, I'm sorry to wake you." The fear in her voice had him sitting up and swinging his legs over the side of his bed. "I had a nightmare, and I can't shake it off. I just have this eerie feeling, and it won't go away."

"I'm right here. I'm not going to hang up." Tai put great effort into keeping his voice calm. He got out of bed, pacing the floor with the frustration of being unable to get to her. If she were here, he could have her in his arms to hold and reassure her. But instead, she was far from him, alone and scared. "Please check your security right now and make sure everything is clear. That will at least give you the knowledge that nobody is there."

He heard her shift, and taps came over the line before she came back on. "There are no alerts. I'm probably just overreacting to my dream. I feel horrible now for waking you."

He tried to regulate his voice to keep his frustration at the space between them from coming out. "Laci-baby, did you take your meds tonight?

"No, I felt safe with the storm, so I didn't take them. In a way, I think I would feel worse now if I had because I wouldn't be able to defend myself, and that would ramp up my fear even more."

With Charlie's warnings in mind, Tai's concern sharpened. He listened to her gentle, yet even breathing, ensuring she kept it steady throughout. What else could he do or say to help her feel better?

"How about you check outside through all of the upstairs windows. I'm sure if you can see that nobody is around, then that will help."

"Okay, I can do that. But I'm taking you with me." He heard her shuffle again, followed by movement. "Nobody in the back yard, for what I can see. With the snow coming down, I can't see too far."

He listened to the change in her breathing as she walked through the house. "Nothing on Charlie's bedroom side of the house. And the plow is coming down the street now. I can see with its headlights that there are no cars in the street, and nobody outside in the front. I feel like an idiot now. I totally overreacted and got you involved in this. I'm so sorry."

"Don't be sorry, and don't doubt your instincts." He sat down on the side of his bed. "I'm glad you thought to call me. I told you I have no problem with it."

"Well, I didn't want to call Charlie and add to his problems back home. He would freak out about not being here with me. And I didn't want to be completely alone, so I called you."

Warmth bloomed in his chest to know that she had turned to him for help. Yeah, he was second after Charlie, but that was understandable right now. "Do you feel safer now after checking everything and talking to me?"

Another pause. "I think so, but can you stay on the phone with me a little longer?"

"Of course. Laci lay back down, and I'll stay with you." Tai listened for any noise in the background, for a ping from her security. Then, he listened to her breathing steady and eventually deepen into the rhythm of sleep. He wouldn't be sleeping the rest of the night.

Tai muted his phone so he could hear Laci, but she couldn't listen to him. He made his way downstairs to his kitchen to start making coffee. He would stay awake, listening to her and the noises in her room, to ensure she was safe.

He grabbed his mug and walked down the hall to his office to make some plans. He sat and booted up his computer, the sound of her soft, even breathing easing his worry. Even though she didn't want to admit it, she needed his support, and he was prepared to show her that he was ready for it.

The brightness of the sun woke Laci. She looked down and saw her phone on her pillow, still on a call with Tai. She picked it up. "Tai?" she asked.

His deep voice came over the line, wide awake. "Good morning, Laci."

Had she slept with the phone on all night? She'd fallen asleep and forgotten to shut it off. Laci must have groaned out loud. She heard his deep chuckle through the line, "We're not opening Blackwood, but as soon as I can, I'll be driving down there to check it over. Did you still want to be alone? My offer to stay here is still open. I can stop by, and you can follow me back."

She gave up the fight. Even her mind was messing with her now, and she couldn't stay alone anymore. "I'd like to stay at your house. Let me know when you're coming, and I'll pack up my car while I wait."

"Good. The roads are a bit worse up here, so it will be a while, but I'll get there as soon as possible."

She needed to get moving if she was going to take all she wanted. As she pulled her suitcase from the closet and started dropping clothes into it, her mind battled again. On the one hand, she was relieved not to be alone anymore. On the other hand, this could put Tai in greater danger.

She went downstairs for a late breakfast, and as she was cleaning up, there was a knock on the front door. Laci froze, and her heart jumped up into her throat.

Another knock on the door, then a male voice called out, "Laci, it's Jack. Can we talk?"

Rounding the corner to the front door, Laci saw that Jack had his badge plastered against the glass so she could confirm it was him. She removed the brace, unlocked the door, and allowed him to step inside with another officer behind him.

Laci took their coats, and they removed their boots. "Can I offer you two coffees? It won't take long to make."

They both nodded, and Jack responded, "That would be great. We need something to warm us up after all that snow."

As Laci moved around the kitchen, they stood on the other side of the breakfast bar. "Laci, this is Officer Fischer. We were hoping to talk to you a bit this morning."

"Is something wrong? I mean, the worst thing to happen since Charlie left was Kathy next door saw a guy dressed as a cable repairman looking at this house, but he left when she stepped outside." She handed them the mugs and motioned for them to take a seat at the dining table.

Jack took a sip and set his mug down. "Can you tell me about what happened?"

Laci gave him the short story and caught Jack and Officer Fischer sharing a look.

"Were you able to confirm that this guy didn't get into the house?" Officer Fischer asked.

Laci pointed to the back door, the windows, and above the cabinets, where her cameras sat. "As you can see, I set up a lot of security measures after Charlie left. If anything moves in the house, it alerts my phone. I had no alerts yesterday besides me opening the front door."

Jack then looked her in the eye. "Laci, have you had any contact from your ex-husband?"

The world spun, and she grabbed the table. Jack was around the table in a heartbeat. *He was still in prison. He had to be in prison. Nobody had called to say otherwise.*

Jack was kneeling next to her, trying to get her attention. She turned to face him. "Jack, do you know…"

Concern etched lines around his eyes, but his voice was honest when he spoke. "I called your hometown police department after the night with the guy who grabbed you. When you said your ex-husband tried to kill you twice, I wanted to know the details. I had to determine the level of threat he posed to you. I needed to know that my guys were there to watch out for you if necessary."

Her panic rose. "Tai?"

"No. I did talk to Tai, but he insisted I not tell him anything. You needed to tell him whatever it was because it would break your trust if he asked me for the details."

Laci agreed. Today was the day she had to tell him. Too many times, she'd weaseled out of it, but now it was unavoidable. They were getting too close, and if her ex found out, Tai's life would be in danger.

After a moment of contemplation, she looked at Jack. "It wouldn't be like my ex to hire somebody to try to get to me. Yes, he likes to spend his money, but his focus on me means he wouldn't hire somebody to get me. He would wait until he was out of prison and then come after me. He might hire somebody to watch me, but how could he have found me? Only my kids and Charlie knew I was here."

Jack's expression turned grim. "Laci, I've done some checking." He paused, his gentle tone now scaring her. "He's not in prison anymore. He's been out for over six months."

Free? No, it's not possible. There was a sudden whooshing in her ears. He wasn't supposed to be out yet. They told her he wouldn't be eligible. How could he be out?

"N... Nobody called me," she whispered, the words barely forming.

Jack ran a hand over his mouth. "The record showed that they attempted to contact you."

Of course, because six months ago, she was a non-functioning shell that had blocked out all but her kids and Charlie.

She barely registered when Jack was talking to her again. He grabbed her hands to get her attention. "Laci, I don't think it would be a good idea for you to be alone while Charlie is gone. I know you're still relatively new to the area, but have you gotten to know anybody well enough that you could stay with them?"

"I, uh, had a bad nightmare last night and called Tai. I must have fallen asleep with Tai still on the phone. When I woke up, he told me he would come here to drive me back to his house, and I agreed. I don't want to be here alone again."

Jack smiled. "Good. Do you want us to stay with you until he can get here?"

She thought about it for a moment. "Actually, yes. I hope it won't take too long for Tai to have clear roads, but if my ex has somebody here to watch me, then I'm not taking any chances."

Jack and Officer Fischer stayed at the kitchen table while she ran upstairs to gather the last of her belongings. She brought them all down and removed the brace from the kitchen door.

Placing her bags in the back of her car, she rounded to the other side to unlock the garage door and found a problem. "Jack!"

They both came out to the garage. "What is it?"

At the lock on the outer garage door, Laci pointed. A fresh dent marred the steel plate, a clear imprint of attempted force. Then, her eyes dropped down, catching gaps along the bottom of the garage door.

Officer Fischer immediately got on his radio. Jack moved her back into the house to the living room couch. "Stay here. It's in the middle where we can see you."

Within minutes, more police cars pulled up. Her peaceful sanctuary was now filled with heavy booted footfalls, chirps of radios, and murmured discussions. Every inch of the house was checked, photographed, and examined. It was no longer providing the safety and privacy that she had this morning.

Through the window, Laci could see them making rounds outside, taking photos, and examining the lock on the back door. Even a tech guy was checking her car.

With all this happening, Laci didn't hear Tai's text that the roads were clear and he was on his way to pick her up. She listened to the low rumble of his voice as he talked to Jack at the front of the house. Since she was ordered not to move from the couch, she stayed put, curled up at one end, staring out the back door at the snow-covered trees. Tai sat at the other end, but she barely acknowledged his presence. Eventually, he laid his hand on the middle cushion, palm up, and she slid her hand into his.

When Jack, the tech, and Officer Fischer entered the room, she pulled her hand back.

Tai did the talking for her. "What did you find?"

"Somebody was able to wedge the garage door up enough to get a tracker on her car. Because she locked that door, they couldn't get the opener to work. It appears that they attempted to force it open afterward. I have to believe they had much worse plans for her vehicle, and she thwarted them. Laci, were you wearing gloves when you installed the lock on the back door?"

She turned her head to them to respond, "No, bare hands."

"Did you carry that lock in a bag of any kind?"

She shook her head. "No, a cardboard box."

"We found fabric threads snagged in the lock mechanism. Looks like somebody tried to yank it off."

Laci shrugged one shoulder. "Good luck with that. Not only did I lock it as tightly as possible, but I also glued the joints. I have the key for it and know how to break the bond."

Tai gave her a look of surprised respect, while Jack's eyebrows shot up. Officer Fisher and the tech just blinked.

Jack continued, pointing to the window by the dining table. "We spoke with Kathy and got a description of the guy who was looking around the house."

Tai broke the silence. "Is that everything, Jack? Or can I get her out of here now?"

Jack sounded somewhat defeated. "Unfortunately, the storm covered up anything else we could have found. So yes, you can go. I'll post officers here again to watch the house, and Kathy said she and Henry would keep an eye out, too."

Everyone helped her get Charlie's house back in order and locked up. As Laci started her car, she took breaths to calm herself. Things didn't add up. Who could have possibly done this? She had traveled across the country, far from his reach, believing she would be safe here. He never traveled, so she thought he would never come for her. But now...

FIFTEEN

THE KNOTS IN LACI'S shoulders loosened little by little as they drove up the hills to Tai's house, leaving the town and her nightmare behind in the valley below. Charlie had told her it was a long drive.

Soon, the modest homes of the town gave way to larger, more secluded properties, each one positioned to take advantage of the valley view. The trees grew thicker until, at the very end of the road, a single property stood alone.

Tai pulled into the driveway, the gate opened, and he drove them through a cove of trees. The house that emerged from behind the trees wasn't just a house. It was a fortress of log and stone. It looked like a secret wooded retreat meant to keep the world at bay. Tai pulled into the garage, and then Laci parked her car next to his.

As soon as the garage door closed, he was at her door, opening it for her. "Let me help you get your bags."

Through a back hallway, they stepped out into one massive, two-story great room. She had trouble taking it all in. Enormous walls of windows enclosed the space. The snow-covered trees out front were the perfect background to the stone fireplace. On the back side of the house, they looked out over a beautiful stone patio and yard, with the valley below. The mountains on the other side of the valley were evident today, completely covered in snow.

Dark wood floors and a deep maroon sectional brought warmth to the space. The kitchen and dining area were very similar to Blackwood, somehow giving Laci a feeling of familiarity.

Tai turned to her. "You have your choice of bedrooms. They're all upstairs."

She looked up and noticed the bridge overhead, which ran through the middle of the space with black iron railings. It, too, was made to take advantage of the view through the windows.

They walked across the living room and climbed the stairs to the bridge. Tai pointed to the left, at the top of the steps. "My bedroom is there in that back corner. There is another one here, in the front." He turned and pointed across the bridge to the opposite side of the house. "There are two bedrooms on that side of the bridge. All of them are pretty much the same, each with a bathroom."

Laci chose the option on the same side as his room because it was closer to the stairs, eliminating the need to cross the open bridge. They made a tiny U-turn, and he opened the door to a beautiful space. A large king-size bed sat to the right, facing the windows and door out to the snow-covered trees. She had to get photos of that outdoor scene while she was here. As she walked around to the other side of the bed, she entered a vast bathroom with even more windows overlooking the trees at the front and side of the house. Everything was stone and concrete, a huge soaker tub sitting under the windows.

"I'll let you get settled. If you'd like, I can make us dinner soon."

"Thanks, Tai."

He gave her a single nod and made his way out of her room. She sat on the edge of the bed, trying to center herself again. Too much had happened in the last twenty-four hours. Since she didn't bring everything with her, only what she would need for a few days until Charlie returned, it didn't take her long to unpack. By the time she finished, though, it was clear the sun was starting to set. She stepped onto the bridge and had to turn back to grab her camera. The view was stunning.

Tai looked up from the kitchen below. "Oh, I have a much better view of that."

He came up the stairs, took her hand, and went to his bedroom.

It was a mirror of hers, but his was decorated in dark blue and black, while hers was in lighter colors of beige and forest green. On the opposite wall were French doors leading to a balcony.

He opened the doors and motioned for her to step out. The open, unimpeded view of the sunset over the mountains took her breath away. She could not believe Tai had this view, and he spent almost every sunset in town working. She started snapping photos as the sun slowly descended.

"Tai? How come you didn't open today?" Laci was very much aware of his moving up closer behind her.

"The storms messed up my usual delivery and prep," he said, his breath warm against her ear. "No one was coming out anyway. I'll just prep everything tomorrow morning.

You're welcome to join me or sleep in and come for your regular shift."

The temperatures had dropped from cold to freezing, and the sun had disappeared entirely behind the mountains. As she turned to go back in, Tai wrapped his arms around her and gently kissed her.

Laci pulled back a little. "I have a lot to tell you." She lifted her lips into a half smile. "Plus, I'm starting to freeze my ass off out here." That got a laugh.

As they ate dinner, Tai asked her questions. "You have an ex-husband, so I know you were at least married once. Any other relationships?"

Laci felt the sadness creep in. "I had one after that, Leo. We met at a work function about six years ago. I worked in finance, and he was part of the warehouse crew. He asked me out, but I turned him down. I was a single mom with two young teens. My life was chaotic, plus I was still very much uncomfortable with the possibility of being in another relationship."

She half smiled, remembering how determined Leo was. "He never gave up. He still sat with me, chatting. Over time, we got to know each other well enough that I finally felt comfortable and agreed to go out with him. After that, we were together. He moved in with me after my kids left for college. Then, I lost him."

The familiar pain roiled up, twisting the knot in her stomach again. *He died because of me. He died because he was with me.* She should have known, but she let him in, and Leo lost his life as punishment for that decision.

Tai placed his hand on hers. "I'm sorry. I can't imagine the pain of that loss." He gave her a moment to slow her breathing. "You came here shortly after that, right?"

Laci pulled her hand back and sighed. "I wasn't functioning. I left my job, my kids were away, and I was alone. When my kids came home, I didn't want to burden them with caring for me, so I tried to appear as if I was functioning fine. Apparently, that wasn't working because the kids ratted me out to Charlie. Charlie ordered me to pack my bags and get my ass out here because he would care for me. It took a while, but I finally agreed."

Tai stood, picking up the plates. "That sounds like Charlie. I'm thankful he did that."

She sadly smiled as she stood to help clear the rest of the dinnerware. "I am too. Because of Charlie, I've been able to take the burden of day-to-day decision-making off my plate and concentrate on therapy."

Tai turned to face her when she placed the dishware on the counter. The ghost of Leo's death rose between them, cold and sharp. The memory forced her to take a step back, a stark reminder that this closeness was a danger she couldn't afford. He didn't move toward her to make up the space she created. "You said you were concentrating on therapy. How has that been going?"

Laci walked back to the table and continued clearing it. "Good, I researched to find somebody before I got here. I like Dr. T. He's gentle enough to walk me through things, but he's stern when he wants to make a point. I started with seeing him frequently, but now I'm down to one every other week."

"If you need to get to a session, I can take you. You can also go during work hours. I don't want that to get in your way." He looked at her sincerely.

"I appreciate that, but everything is virtual. I schedule appointments early, so I'm done well before the start of work. I won't see Dr. T again for a few days." She picked up the last items from the table and put them away, where she saw Tai grab them.

Once they had cleaned everything, Tai led Laci to the couch in front of the fire. Laci was practically balled up in the corner, as far from Tai as possible, because now it was time. She had to tell him. Jack said Tai refused to get the details from him. "Tai, you need to know about my past. I'm afraid you're putting yourself in danger. My ex-husband is a real threat. This morning, Jack informed me that he was out of prison."

Tai sighed and looked down at his clasped hands. "I have to admit, and don't kill him because there was a good reason, but Charlie told me two nights ago about your history. He called me because of some developments and knew you were in greater danger than you were aware. He could only make me understand if he gave me the background."

Developments? Her voice sounded like it had been chipped from ice. "What developments?"

"Charlie's mother was never ill. Somebody paid her and her husband to devise a plan to get Charlie away from you. Tai filled her in on everything Charlie had learned at his mother's house. As he spoke, Laci felt her blood drain. It had all been a setup. Her instincts were not wrong. The day she got lost making it to Blackwood alone, she picked up on someone's presence. Someone had been watching her. Her ex must have sent someone to find her.

They expected her to walk to work alone and keep to her routine, but instead, Tai picked her up each day. Occasionally, she saw cops passing by on her street, so there's no doubt that the man trying to get in saw them too. That's why he had no choice but to move when the storms hit. Tai couldn't get to her, and the police guards were gone. Whoever this was, he struck at the moment when she was utterly alone. No Charlie, no Tai, and no police. Just as her ex had done when he broke into her house years ago. Fear exploded inside Laci.

No, no, no, Tai had been there with her. If it were her ex, he would have seen Tai there. Tai would be a target. Whoever he hired to watch her would have reported how long she and Tai were together. They could have observed her working with him at the bar. Vanessa and Benji's statements on the first night, when Charlie was gone, came back to her memory. They saw the connection between her and Tai out in the open, *where anybody could see it.*

Laci jumped up, terror now taking hold. Tai stood too. He stepped in her direction, but she backed up, her hands out to stop him. "No, Tai, you don't understand. If it's him, if he was directing all of this, then he has seen you with me. I can't stay here. He'll kill you. I can't. I can't do it again."

Tears were running down her face. How could she believe she would be safe here? How could she be so stupid as to think that maybe she could be close to another man? She had to go. She didn't know where, but she had to get as far away as possible.

Laci took off running up the stairs as Tai tried to catch up with her. She heard him calling her name, but ignored him with one focus, grabbing her things and getting the hell out of there. She would start driving and figure it out along the way. She had to go. It was the only way. If her ex realized she'd left town, he might leave Tai alone. It didn't matter what Tai wanted. He'd get past it, and he would be alive to do so.

Right as Laci entered her bedroom, Tai caught up with her. His stern voice didn't stop her. "You're not leaving."

Between sobs, she turned and yelled back at him, "Yes, I am Tai. I have to go. I can't stay in this town. He'll kill you. If I leave now before he knows where I am again, maybe he'll leave too. I have to go now!"

She turned to get around the bed, and when his hand grasped her wrist, she spun and pounded her hands into his chest. In response, he wrapped his arms around her in a hug. As she tried to break free of his hold, he tightened his arms to pin hers against his chest.

Quietly in her ear, he whispered, "Laci, breathe."

She couldn't. The panic had complete control. Stars danced in her vision, and the room spun.

"Laci. Breathe." The command from him reached her brain. Laci took one huge, shaky breath.

"Again, Laci-baby. Breathe." The static and chaos calmed. She dragged in another shuddering breath. He wasn't hurting her. The arms pinning her were a support. The steady rise and fall of his chest against her cheek became her guide. She focused on it, instinctively trying to match his rhythm.

The tears still running down her face were now soaking his shirt. "I can't lose you, too. I can't have it happen again."

His breaths stayed even, but he loosened his hold on her slightly. "Why won't he go after Charlie? What is it about Charlie that gives him some level of protection?"

Before Laci could answer, he moved them to the bed and sat, bringing her into his lap. Lying her head on his shoulder, she tried desperately to stop her tears. Having his arms still around her helped lower her heart rate.

"The best guess anybody has is that his targets are not just anybody who will hurt me to lose. He only targets anybody who could fill what he sees as his role in my life. Charlie would never fill that position. I love him dearly, but not romantically. Leo filled that role. When he found out that Leo moved in and I was happy with him, he had to remove the threat to his position of power."

The image of Leo's lifeless body lying on the street flashed in her head, and she couldn't help but sob again.

"I understand. And you believe your ex will come after me now because I've been trying to get closer to you."

"Yes."

"And that is why you have been doing everything possible to stay clear of me."

"Yes."

"And you're willing to risk us losing each other if it means I'll still be alive?"

"Yes." No hesitation. She didn't even need to think about it. She'd spent so much time and energy trying to stay clear of him. Laci knew what he wanted and finally admitted that she wanted it too. But she couldn't take that chance. Tai had slowly whittled away almost every blockade she'd put up.

"Listen." Tai ran his fingers through her hair and tucked it behind her ear. "It's dark, and you don't know these mountain roads like I do, especially in the snow. I'm worried about your safety out there. Will you agree to stay here tonight? I highly doubt anybody would have time to make their way up here. If it makes you feel better, don't take your meds. I don't care if you wake me with a nightmare. I'd rather you feel safer being clear-headed."

"I understand."

He kissed her temple. "I'm going to let you go now. Are you going to try to bolt for the door?" She shook her head. "Alright." He stood and put her on her feet. "I'm going to leave you here now. Why don't you try to relax and get some sleep? I'm going to clean up downstairs and get to bed. I'll wake you to go in tomorrow, and you can see how you feel then. Deal?"

She agreed. Tai gently kissed her forehead, turned, and walked out the door, closing it behind him.

Laci stood in the middle of the room, feeling cold and terrified. Everything she knew now confirmed it was her ex. He was here. Tai's life was in danger. She would leave in the morning. Grabbing her suitcase, Laci packed almost everything into it, keeping out what she needed for tonight and the morning. Being packed and ready to run brought some calm to her mind. Tai was right. Navigating those twisting mountain roads at night, in her state, was too risky. She would wait for the light of daybreak. Then, she would run.

Trying to relax before bed, Laci walked into the bathroom and turned on the faucet in the tub. The sound of the water running somewhat soothed her chaotic mind. She kept reminding herself that once the sun rose, she would get dressed, gather her bags, get in her car, and go. She would miss everything she built here. Leaving Charlie would be excruciating. Vanessa and Benji had become such good friends. And her heart ached to know that she was walking away from Tai. She had to leave. It was the only way to keep Tai alive. She would get on the road and drive home to her kids. Then, she would never let another man in again.

A bloodcurdling scream woke him. Tai was unsure if it was something he heard or imagined. Then it happened again, and he heard something hard hit the wall in her room. Tai was out of bed and across the small distance from their doors in a split second, fearing that someone had somehow broken in and gotten to her.

She screamed again. "No! I can't!"

Tai opened the door to her room. It was dark, but he could make out her form in bed, alone. "Laci, I'm right here. It's just a nightmare."

She wasn't moving, but he could hear her whimpering. Tai went to her, sat on the bed, and cradled her upper body. "Laci-baby, it's me, Tai. I'm here, and you're safe."

A sob. "Tai?"

"Yes, I'm right here. I have you."

Her hands moved over his chest and face as if she couldn't believe he was real. "I thought he killed you. I saw it. Right in front of me."

"I'm okay. I'm right here."

Another soft sob. "I don't want to be alone."

Tai stood, getting his arm under her legs and the other behind her back to fully carry her. "Come on. You're sleeping next to me."

Her body relaxed. Tai couldn't tell if she had gone back to sleep.

He climbed back into his bed and lay her down with him, her head resting on his shoulder and her body in the crook of his arm. He reached down and pulled the covers over them. Then, he turned toward her and wrapped her up in his arms.

This is right. She belongs here, with me, in my bed. The full length of her body pressed against his made him feel like a missing piece of his life's puzzle had just snapped into place. A pang of regret hit him. He wished she had come to him willingly, not chased by nightmares. No longer would he tiptoe around Laci's resistance. It was time to show her how much he wanted her and that she knew he would not let her go. *I won't let you go,* he vowed silently. *You're mine now, and you're safe with me.*

Just as he drifted off into sleep, he felt the soft, ghost-like press of her lips against his neck.

△

Laci was pressed against a hard male body and knew it wasn't Charlie. Tai. She was in bed with Tai. He'd gotten her during her nightmare.

"Good morning," his deep, sleepy voice rumbled, and she felt it from his chest.

She tilted to see his eyes. "Morning. I'm sorry about the nightmare."

He moved his head down to kiss her. "Quite alright. Not every night do I get to rescue a damsel in distress." He kissed her again. "It's still early enough to get breakfast before heading in. Are you ready to get up and moving?"

Laci couldn't tell him that she was going to leave. There was no time for breakfast, and she would never return to Blackwood again. She was taking these last moments to treasure in her memory before she left.

He must have seen something in her because Tai rolled them both, so he was over her. His weight pushed her into the softness of the mattress, and she could feel his body tense and ready for action. She also felt how hot and hard he was against her belly. He lowered his head to kiss her again, and it felt like live energy ran through every inch of her body. His tongue made its way in, and now her temperature rose.

He moved to kissing and nipping her neck, then made his way to her ear. "I'll make a deal with you." His words, whispered directly in her ear, gave her goosebumps. "You stay with me today. Come in, work by my side."

The war inside her between heart, mind, and body was tearing her apart. She wanted to stay. Every fiber of her body wanted to stay. Her mind knew it wasn't safe for her to do so. Tai would end up dead.

She opened her eyes to look at him. Her voice was a raw whisper, laced with pain. "I can't. I can't stay here."

She expected hurt, maybe resignation in his eyes. Instead, she got six and a half feet of raw male determination. He dropped to kiss her again, then trailed kisses down her collarbone. He shifted, sliding his lower body between her legs, so his length was now rubbing against her core. Laci felt her resolve slipping little by little.

He lifted his head to look her in the eye again. "You come with me to do the prep work this morning, and we'll call and talk to Charlie on the way. If he agrees that it would be best for you to leave and get away from me, I'll bring you back here to pack your car, and then you can go. But, if he asks you to stay, you promise to stay, and we can continue this tonight."

He moved his hips, a slow, deliberate pressure against her core that sent a shockwave through her, and kissed down her neck. It took everything in her not to moan in pleasure and let him know he was starting to change her decision.

When he lifted again to look her in the eye, she agreed.

Swiftly, he was gone and out of bed. "Get up. We have work to do."

Laci turned to watch him walk to his bathroom. No shirt, loose pants. And dear god, the muscles in his back looked like someone had chiseled them from stone. "Holy hell." Crap. She must have said that out loud because she heard him laugh as he closed the bathroom door.

The longer drive to Blackwood only gave Laci time for a full-on internal battle. She stared out at the snow-covered trees, plotting out how she would leave, while the memory of Tai's body pressed against hers fought back. When Charlie called, he asked her to put him on speaker.

"I need to know you are safe with Tai." Charlie's voice filled the car. "You can't be alone at any time because that is when you are most vulnerable to attack." This wasn't helping her escape plan at all. "I booked my flights, and I'll be home soon if the weather doesn't cause more delays."

She didn't outright agree, but she also didn't argue with Charlie before ending the call. Tai stayed silent the rest of the way.

Once they arrived, it was business as usual. They walked in through the front door, and Laci went to stow her stuff where she usually did while Tai headed back to his office. As Laci was working to pull chairs down, she heard the rumble of a large truck.

Tai was opening the kitchen's back door to greet the delivery guys when she stepped into the kitchen. Tower after tower of fresh food came in the door and was stacked next to the long island of the cooking area. Once everything was in and Tai confirmed, he grabbed an apron from the wall, put it on, and then grabbed one for her. As she put it on, he explained how to prep, contain, and store each item. Laci reached for a knife and began working with him.

He stood next to her, and as he turned for a container from the counter behind them, his arm brushed hers. A moment later, he reached around her, the front of his body against her back. His hand touched hers when he placed the next item for her to cut up. Laci's body warmed with each of his clearly deliberate touches.

Vincent drifted in, silent as usual, giving a nod to each of them as a hello. Benji walked into the kitchen, hugged Laci, and said hi to Tai. Vanessa came in soon after. It was time to open up and get things rolling. The lunch crowd descended in a wave of noise and orders. Laci moved on autopilot, grabbing glasses, wiping down spills, her mind a thousand miles away.

"Need more limes," Tai's voice was a low rumble next to her ear, making her jump. He hadn't seemed to move from the other end of the bar. His arm brushed hers as he reached past her for the cutting board, a deliberate touch that sent a jolt straight through her. Every nerve ending was on high alert, cataloging each time he was near, each accidental touch that felt anything but accidental. How was she supposed to survive the day when every moment felt like a prelude to a night that terrified and thrilled her in equal measure?

Vincent passed by with his second haul of beer from the cold storage, stocking the coolers under the bar. Grabbing the basin, Laci moved out to the high-top tables to clear them off. Vanessa and her team were finally catching up as the afternoon slowed a bit. Glances among them all conveyed the same message. If lunch were this bad, then dinner would only be worse.

Sure enough, the line out the door kept them hopping. Laci was running between the kitchen and the bar, trying to keep things in order for Tai. Through the pass-through window, she watched him effortlessly handle three orders at once, his tall body moving with ease. *Would he move that easily with me?* His head turned, and his eyes caught hers for a split second, a silent reminder of his promise. The sponge falling back into the soapy water made her realize she'd stopped moving entirely.

As the last customer walked out into the darkness of the night, Vanessa turned and looked at everyone else. "What in the hell was all of that? People were insane tonight!"

Everyone nodded in agreement. Laci looked to Tai and felt the heat of his gaze.

SIXTEEN

He's watching. Laci could feel him, but she couldn't see him. The air crackled, heavy with an anger she knew was directed at her. The restaurant closed only moments ago. The only noise was hers and Tai's footsteps on the parking lot pavement, though Laci knew they were not alone. The darkness seemed to blot out the light of the street lamps. The air was thick, heavy, and ice-cold.

Laci stopped, and Tai eventually stopped, noticing she was no longer at his side. He didn't say anything and looked at her questioningly. Every nerve screamed a warning, but the direction of the danger remained elusive. She heard him move. He thought he was stealthy, but she had already picked up on him. The figure stepped out from the alley. It was him. Like she knew it would happen, he was here to kill Tai. She barely had enough time to warn Tai and jump to block the attack as he raised his arm toward them for the first strike.

A fiery pain bloomed in her chest. She saw Tai's face, a mask of horror, as she fell to her knees, the air stolen from her lungs. Looking down, she saw blood blooming on the front of her shirt. *Why can't I breathe?*

"Laci-baby, breathe." Tai. She could hear him, but his lips weren't moving.

She looked down to see her blood pooling on the ground. Her vision tunneled as darkness crept in, her brain starved for oxygen. She collapsed to the ground.

"Laci. Breathe now." The panic in Tai's voice rose. She tried to pull in the air, but it wasn't working.

Laci could feel someone against her. "Baby, open your eyes."

She tried, but they were too heavy. Lips on hers. Tai's lips on hers. He was trying to force a breath into her lungs. He pulled back. "Take one breath for me."

She inhaled, finally able to take in a breath of air. "One more baby, take another breath." Laci pulled in one more. "That's it, keep doing that."

With each breath, she came back to her body. Little by little, she realized it was a nightmare, not reality. With each breath, she realized she was up against Tai. The smell of his soap filled her lungs. His concerned face was right in front of hers in the dark, the moonlight casting enough of a glow for her to see the panic in his eyes. His hands were on either side of her head.

He lightly kissed her lips. "Are you back with me?"

"Yeah," she whispered.

He released her head, his own breath leaving him in a ragged sigh as he gathered her against him, one arm protectively across her back. He simply held her, the steady beat of his heart a comfort.

The remnant of the nightmare still clung to her. Touching her chest, there was no wetness, no blood. She ran her fingers over Tai's bare chest and saw no wounds. Relief washed through her to know that they were both safe. Then she looked around and saw Tai's room.

Wait, how did I get here? The last thing Laci remembered was falling asleep in her bed. "Did I sleep teleport again?"

A deep chuckle. "You could say that. Once I got ready for bed, I went to your room to say goodnight. I knocked, but you didn't respond, so I cracked open the door to look. I saw that you hadn't even gotten into your bed, but had fallen asleep on top of it. I carried you here to sleep next to me."

She grinned at him. "You do realize that in the time I've known you, you've carried me more times than in the past thirty-plus years of my life. I'm not a petite woman."

He smiled. "All that time in the gym was worth it to have you here next to me."

Tai rolled toward her, his mouth covering hers as gently as possible. He had to feel her breathing, alive. Waking to her nightmare-choked gasps had terrified him.

A gentle coaxing was all it took. Laci opened for him, and when his tongue swept in, her body melted against his. The need to be gentle tempered his urgency. His hand slid to her ass, pulling her tight so she could feel his want. In response, her nails raked lightly down his sides, setting his skin on fire.

He rolled her onto her back, his mouth moving from her lips to her neck, earning a soft moan. His palm slid under her top, tracing the soft skin until he felt the raised lines of scars, physical reminders of the hell she'd survived. A flash of rage made his hand clench, but he forced it to soften. As he worked her shirt free, she grew impatient, pulling it over her head herself.

He nuzzled between her breasts, his mouth claiming one nipple while his fingers teased the other. She squirmed, her fingers twisting in his hair as his hand slid down her belly and into her shorts. Scorching heat and wetness greeted his seeking fingers. He slipped one inside, then two, and her nails dug into his back as her hips rose from the bed, begging.

He pulled her shorts off, his mouth tracing a path up her legs until he was at her center. One long lick through her folds made her buck. "Oh, my god," she panted.

He held her hips, sucking her clit between his lips until she whimpered and writhed, her release building. He pushed two fingers inside, feeling her readiness, and she arched hard, her body clenching around him. That was his breaking point.

Standing, Tai shed his pants and retrieved a condom from the nightstand, kissing her as he sheathed himself. He poised above her, waiting. She snaked her hands up to his face and pulled him into a kiss, all the permission he needed.

He pushed slowly into her heat, a shared moan escaping them. He fought for control. The last thing he wanted was to be fast and hard. She deserved better.

"Tai, move," she whimpered in his ear, her nails digging into his back. "Please move."

He plunged into her, and coherent thought shattered into a million pieces of pure sensation. She met his rhythm, her legs wrapping around his waist, pulling him deeper. It wasn't gentle anymore. Her body tensed, and she broke their kiss with a scream as her climax hit. The feeling of her gripping him from the inside shattered his control.

"Laci-baby," he groaned, and let go.

He collapsed onto her, still inside, feeling her arms wrap around him in a quiet sigh of contentment. Later, after he'd cleaned up, he crawled back into bed and pulled her sleeping form against him. Something in his chest warmed. She was safe.

Fingers gently stroked up and down her side, the warmth of his body pressed skin-to-skin with hers. Slowly, Laci climbed from the depths of sleep, her entire body feeling relaxed and languid. Warm, gentle kisses glided from her shoulder and up her neck.

Tai's deep voice whispered directly in her ear, "Good Morning."

Laci rolled over on her stomach, picking up the pillow and covering her head. "No. Sleep."

Tai's laugh made the bed bounce a little, causing Laci to smile. "Come on. We have to get moving and get to work." He got up and out of bed, then she heard the bathroom door shut.

Laci hadn't moved an inch when he returned. "You have to get up."

She lifted the edge just enough so he could hear her. "No, I don't. I know the owner. I can do what I want." She turned her head back into the pillow.

The blankets whipped off to the side, and hands grabbed her ankles and pulled her from the bed up against Tai's body. "I'll make it very worth your while if you get up and come into the shower with me." His deep, sexy voice right in her ear made her shiver. "That's what I thought."

As he warmed the water, she returned to her room for her products. She didn't want to go to work smelling like Tai. Then everyone would be on to them. When she returned, she stopped dead, her brain short-circuiting as she stared at the water cascading over every muscle in his incredible body.

Then he opened the door and pulled her in. He pinned her against the wall with a kiss, and her bottles fell to the floor. The hot water was running over them, turning her on even faster.

He pulled a condom from the shelf by her head, then lifted one of her legs and was in her. Laci couldn't help but moan at the feeling. Not only was he deep inside her, but he also had the strength to move her around as he wanted. But she never felt afraid of it. A thrill, sharp and sweet, shot through her. Here was a man whose strength could be terrifying, yet in his hands, she felt only safety. He controlled every moment, and in his control, she found a tenderness she'd never known.

Once they finished showering, they dressed in their rooms and then met downstairs for breakfast. As they made omelets together, Tai kissed her lips, neck, ear, temple, and the back of her hand.

During the drive to work, Tai told Laci about the cart he would set up on the other side of town, featuring miniature versions of his dishes. It was time to start planning the logistics so he would be ready, and Laci found herself looking forward to springtime in town.

When his phone rang, he answered it with the hands-free system. "This is Tai."

The low, quiet voice came over the line. "It's Vincent. I have some business I need to take care of, so I'll arrive late."

"Understood. I'll see you when you get there." He hung up the call.

Laci turned to Tai. "I think Vincent is a great addition to the team."

Tai lifted an eyebrow at her. "I'm glad you think that, but what will Charlie think?"

She shrugged. "It's one thing for me to be in Charlie's space. It's another for a total stranger to be there. Plus, Vincent is the polar opposite of Charlie, so who knows?"

"Well, that wasn't very reassuring." Tai huffed. "I was hoping his best friend would be able to help tame my worries. It was just bad timing that Vincent couldn't start until the time that Charlie had to leave."

"As tight as Charlie and I are, his energy is unpredictable to even me a lot of the time. I could always rely on him when I needed him, but outside of that, he's a spark all his own." She grinned when Tai laughed.

"That he is."

When they pulled into the parking lot, Laci's senses went off. Fear exploded in her, making her voice rigid. "Tai."

He glanced over to her. "What direction?"

"I don't know. But we have to keep up the appearance that you're nothing more than my boss." Laci's heart rate spiked, and her hands shook. His life was in danger if Tai came across as anything but her boss. The terror of something happening to him had her frozen in her seat.

He picked up his phone and sent a text. "Don't leave the car yet."

Laci sat there, staring straight ahead, trying not to indicate that she had any feelings toward Tai. She knew the threat was real.

His phone pinged with a response.

"Jack is sending officers here," Tai read. "They will stick around until dinner."

He sent another text. He immediately got a response. "Security guys will come in too."

Even though it would take time for their support to arrive, Tai and Laci had to leave the car. They had to look normal to the outside world and couldn't hide away in here. Tai got out on his side first, then approached Laci's as always. Pausing for a moment after her feet landed in the snow, she tried to pinpoint the direction from which she felt the threat was coming. She couldn't. Tai had her walk in front of him to the front door, and once inside, Laci didn't feel it anymore. Someone had been waiting for them to come in, watching the parking lot. Her nightmare from last night came flooding back.

Knowing Tai had too much to do in his office, she assured him she would keep an eye out and let him know if she thought something was wrong. There was some comfort in knowing he would be watching the cameras while he was back there. Benji and Vanessa chatted with Laci about getting together over the weekend. They were trying to decide which movie to watch, and the conversation served as a good distraction.

As Laci worked on getting chairs in place, Tai came out to open the bar for the lunch crowd. She knew something was off when he came into the room. Looking up at him, her heart clenched when he looked right at her and then back down at the bar without his usual smile.

As Laci turned back to her task, she caught Vanessa looking back and forth between the two of them. She could tell something had happened. Laci subtly shook her head at Vanessa to say, "Not now." Vanessa's eyes got huge, but she returned to placing the silverware.

Laci had her back to the door when she heard it open. "Heya, Sugar Daddy, you miss me?" She spun around and ran full sprint into Charlie's arms. "Hey, Baby-girl, I know I missed you something fierce." His arms wrapped around her, and he kissed her temple. All was right again with her best friend back.

Benji called hello to him from the kitchen. Vanessa gave him a quick side hug.

Charlie let Laci go, and when he turned to go to the bar, Tai gave him a quick nod and a curt hello. "Charlie, glad to see you back." Tai barely glanced at Laci as he left Charlie's space behind the bar and returned to his office. Even though she knew he was only following her orders, that one hurt her.

Charlie got all set and then turned to face Laci. "What the hell is going on with the two of you?"

Half shrugging, she looked down at the bar, now focused on wiping down the already clean surface. "What are you talking about?"

Laci caught Charlie's exaggerated eye roll out of the corner of her eye. "That man is looking at you like he had you for breakfast, and it is driving him insane not to be able to touch you."

She whipped her head up to face him, starting to worry. "Is it really that obvious?"

Once he detected her change, he moved quickly to reassure her. "I can see it because I know you both well. I don't think anybody outside of the four of us will notice."

Laci realized she had been wringing the towel in her hands and placed it on the bar. "Last night, I had a nightmare where Tai and I were ambushed in the back lot while leaving. Then my senses went off when Tai and I arrived this morning. Somebody was watching the lot."

Charlie huffed at her. "Well, that nightmare is new. So, you told Tai he can't treat you as more than an employee."

Sadness and regret filled her. "Yeah."

Charlie shook his head. "And that's why he looks like he's lost everything."

Waving her arm out to indicate the windows surrounding them, she said, "It's while we're out here where the public can see us. I can't take any chances."

Charlie rolled his eyes at her again. "That man wants nothing more than to be able to touch you when he wants, be near you, protect you, and care for you. In one sentence, you told him to bottle that all up and put it on a shelf."

"Charlie, we can't..."

"Let me go talk to him." Charlie left Laci behind the bar.

With a sly grin, Vanessa strolled over and asked, "Please tell me your night was hot because that man has the body of a god."

Tai had finished the plans when Charlie stuck his head in. "Can we chat?"

"Yeah, come in."

After closing the door, he sat across from Tai's desk and got straight to the point. "Laci needs to stay with you." Alarm bells went off in his head. It wasn't like Charlie to willingly give up his duty to protect her. "I came home early this morning. Looking around inside, I saw she had gone all out. There were weapons in every room. She was terrified to be there alone."

Tai grumbled. "I tried to get her to come to stay with me."

Charlie put up his hands to calm Tai. "I know. She's also strong-willed. She was terrified to be alone at my house, but she's even more terrified of getting you killed." He shook his head.

Tai pinched the bridge of his nose. "Laci went off the rails the first night at my place. She tried to pack her things and drive off into the night because it would be better if I were alive and hurting than dead. I was barely able to convince her to stay. Then her nightmare that night was about somebody killing me. Laci believes that I'm going to be the one who ends up dead in this scenario."

"Man, can you blame her? It's happened right in front of her. I don't think she's been fully able to grieve for Leo because she feels guilty that he died because of dating her. So not only is she trying to protect you, but she's dealing with her fear and pent-up grief. It's all leaking out via these nightmares. I know you have feelings for her. I know she has feelings for you mixed into that whole vat of emotion inside her. She can't keep it all from being intertwined. Love for you comes across as fear, and she snaps at you or shuts you out completely."

Although her insistence that he treat her as an employee stung, he knew she was doing it to protect him. Tai had to wait it out.

"There's more." Charlie's anger multiplied. "When I looked outside from my back windows, I saw fresh footprints toward the house from the woods. Kathy and her husband confirmed they were new as of last night. Whoever it is, they knew to approach in a direction the cops driving by wouldn't see."

Damnit. "If it's her ex, how bold will he get?"

"He went through a lot to get me away. I would say he's after her and will let her know. Her ex comes from money. He can hire as many guys as he wants. You're way more of a problem for him than Leo was. Leo made her happy. Leo moved in with her, but couldn't directly compete with his money. He hired the goons to kill Leo to take that happiness away from her. You have money."

"So, I've taken the main thing he believes he can control her with."

"Exactly. Except Laci now has a ton of her own money, but he doesn't acknowledge that." Charlie clenched and unclenched his fists in his lap. "He didn't attempt an entry into my house. I guess he figured out she wasn't there anymore. It's likely why she also felt danger in the parking lot, the next best location to find her and confirm she's still in town. You said there was a tracker on her car?"

"Yeah, the police tech found it. Jack figured he used a slim-jim device to get it under your garage door and onto Laci's car. We..."

An alert went off on the security monitors. Someone hit the panic button up front, tripping the silent alarm.

The button was a small, cold circle of plastic under Laci's fingers. Across the bar, his massive, hulking frame loomed no more than five feet in front of her. His hands were on the back of the chair directly before her. Vanessa had been next to her only a moment ago. When Laci saw him, she shoved Vanessa through the kitchen doorway to get out of the way. Now, it was him and Laci face-to-face.

"What do you want, Nathan?" He stared straight into her.

His overwhelming, clawing cologne enveloped her, the memory of it causing her body to revolt, but she stood firm. Her skin crawled at the sight of her ex. The man who stood before her now wasn't the young man she married all those years ago. The changes he made to his body, late nights, and drugs had robbed her of the man she fell in love with. When they met in the college library, he had been this average, quiet guy who constantly showered her with gifts and romantic gestures. Some part of the hole in her heart after losing her parents had been filled. He became a completely different man physically and mentally during their marriage, and everything fell apart. This man nearly murdered her.

He wore a tailored suit and a silk dress shirt over his now massively muscled physique, a diamond chain around his neck, the latest in expensive watches, and multiple gold and diamond rings on his fingers. He'd styled his jet-black hair with so much gel that she knew it wouldn't move. The diamond studs shimmered from his ears, anything to show the world he had money.

Looking at his eyes, though, she could see a significant difference. They used to be an aqua color that matched the most transparent ocean water. Now, they were dull, almost dingy gray. His paranoia was eating away at him and was front and center in his eyes. They bored into her now. He wanted her back under his control.

Laci's hands were still under the counter. She felt around as best she could for anything she could use to defend herself. Her fingers ran over a small knife. They used it to cut up lemon wedges, and it was her only option. Picking up that knife reminded her that she would have to defend herself. Her body knew that being in the presence of this man only meant excruciating pain. Her breathing became too shallow to get enough air into her lungs. No matter how hard she fought to stay calm, there was no stopping it.

Nathan's head tilted almost unnaturally, and a predatory smile crept across his face. "Not feeling so safe out here without your gay boy and new man, are you?" He sneered at the last words. "You thought running away from home would keep me from finding you? Bitch, I can find you no matter where you go, and I can pay as many people as I want to keep track of you for me. He can't have you. You're still mine." He moved between the chairs, right up to the bar to get closer and stare her down.

Laci couldn't see both of his hands now. Nathan looked up through the kitchen window. He must have seen Tai or Charlie coming this way because he grinned and lunged over the bar. Laci had only a moment to react. She swung the knife up, trying to catch anything she could. She felt it go into something soft and heard Nathan scream. A hand clamped a cloth over her face. Too late, Laci realized what it was...but she had already inhaled. Pain exploded in the back of her head, and everything went black.

SEVENTEEN

The world exploded into motion. Tai was on his feet, right on Charlie's heels as they burst from the office. Vanessa ran at them from the kitchen. Through the pass-through window, he heard Laci's ex snarl, "You're still mine." The bastard's eyes met Tai's for a split second before he grabbed Laci's face. A raw, male roar of pain tore through the air. A moment later, Tai's heart stopped as he watched Laci's body crumple to the floor.

Vanessa shrieked, and Benji grabbed her. Charlie was out the door and on his knees next to Laci. When he lifted her upper body into his arms, she was completely limp. Her breathing was slow despite the fear she should have had. Blood coated his skin when he moved his arm from beneath her head.

While Charlie held her, Tai watched in horror as her breathing slowed, faltered, and then stopped entirely.

A ragged hole tore open in Tai's chest, stealing his breath. "Benji, call 911! Tell them we need paramedics!" His own voice sounded distant, thin. He dropped to his knees, helping Charlie guide her back to the floor. His fingers fumbled for the pulse in her neck. It was there, thready, weak, but there. "Come on, Laci-baby," he breathed against her cold lips, tilting her head back and forcing air into her lungs. He tried his best to keep his breaths even so that he wouldn't pass out in the process.

They had to keep this up until help arrived. When Laci hit the panic button, it sent an emergency call to the police station. With each breath, it felt as if her lips were getting colder. It only made the panic in his chest rise. Blood now covered the floor around her head.

The police charged through the front door and quickly assessed the situation. It wasn't long until the paramedics arrived, too. Tai sat back and watched, hearing Vanessa crying in the kitchen. He was on the verge of crying, too, but he had to hold it together.

The team dropped to their knees on the floor around Laci, quickly evaluating every inch of her. They moved together, each doing their tasks. The cops pulled Tai and Charlie aside to ask what had happened. As Tai explained, the medic calling out orders stopped them. "Any idea what drug he dosed her with?"

Charlie whipped around. "That asshole! Is that why she stopped breathing?"

"We gave her a dose of Narcan."

Tai held on to Charlie and pulled him into the kitchen as they waited. Every second they watched felt like it lasted forever. Vanessa cried into Benji's arms.

A knock reverberated on the back door. Tai didn't want to turn away, but he had to. When Jack stepped in the door, his gaze fell on the blood staining their arms and scrubbed a hand over his face.

Tai looked pleadingly at Jack. "Did you get him?"

Jack shook his head.

Damnit! "You have to get him, Jack!"

"Tai, I have everybody I can out there searching for him. We don't know where he ran off to."

The paramedic out front commanded, "Let's get ready for rapid transport. Get the backboard and move her to the cot." She had yet to take a breath. The mask was still breathing for her. Tai watched as they placed her on the stretcher. He called out to her, "Laci-baby, breathe!"

They were out the door.

Everyone stood there, trying to piece together what had happened. Vanessa looked at Tai with tears streaming down her face. "She saved me. She grabbed me and pushed me through the door in here. That put her too close to him. Who was he?"

"That was Nathan, her ex-husband," Charlie replied, his voice shaking.

Benji looked at Charlie and Tai. "Go. Go to the hospital with her. Vanessa and I and the staff can handle everything here."

Jack agreed. "Clean up a little before you go. You don't want to cause a scene in the ER."

They stopped to wash the blood from their hands, then Tai ran to his office and grabbed his keys. Charlie and Tai were out the door and into Tai's SUV in record time.

Charlie was rocking back and forth in the passenger seat, his hands knotted together, chanting a desperate mantra. "She'll be okay. She has to be okay. She'll be okay."

In his mind, Tai chanted with Charlie as they drove to the hospital. He shouldn't have left her alone out there. After what she said in the parking lot, she shouldn't have been alone.

When Charlie and Tai arrived, they remained in the waiting area. The receptionist told them she couldn't get any new information while they were working on Laci in the back. The men sat and stared at the TV, barely paying attention to what was playing. Charlie couldn't sit still. He got up to pace several times.

After they had been there for over an hour, Tai had to keep Charlie in his chair and prevent him from bothering the receptionist again. "Shouldn't you call her kids?"

"Not yet. I don't want them to know until we have answers." Charlie shook his head. "Tai, this is worse. This time is worse than any other time. She was at least breathing in the past. She was lifeless this time. We can't lose her."

Tai looked up as a nurse came out and called them over. "The doctor wants to talk to you before you can see her."

"She's alive?" *Please say yes.*

"I'll let the doctor talk to you."

The nurse moved the two of them into a small conference room. The sterile white and gray walls of the small conference room seemed to press in on him, squeezing the air from his chest. He sat in one of the chairs at a small round table in the center.

Charlie collapsed into the chair beside him, his voice a ragged whisper. "Tai...these rooms. They only bring you in here for one reason."

Tai felt empty, hollow. Did he want the doctor to come here sooner to tell them she was gone? Or did he want to wait longer? The choice wasn't theirs. A doctor walked into the room. Tai could tell he was about the same age as him, but had already seen too much working in the emergency room. The stern look on his face made Tai's stomach plummet.

"Hi, I'm Dr. Kelvin. You're here for Laci, right?"

Charlie introduced them, "I'm Charlie, her best friend, and this is Tai, her partner." Charlie took it upon himself to say that Laci and Tai were a couple. *We are. She has to be okay.*

The doctor continued, "Let me give you some relief. We were able to stabilize her. She's still alive." Tai's heart started beating again. "Can either of you tell us exactly what happened?"

"We were back in my office," Tai said. "Her ex-husband attacked her. We only had a minimal view of the assault."

"I see. So, we had to fight for Laci on several fronts. We conducted a drug test based on the information provided by the paramedics. Her ex dosed Laci with Fentanyl."

"Wait. Isn't that the drug that's all over the news?" Charlie asked.

The doctor gave a slight nod. "It's a powerful opioid that, unfortunately, has made its way into several street drugs. It causes a high, but it can also be fatal. Fortunately, Laci started breathing on her own again in the ambulance."

Tai and Charlie let out a simultaneous breath of relief.

The doctor continued, his tone clinical but his eyes compassionate. "She also suffered significant trauma to the back of her head. Head wounds are notorious for bleeding, as you saw, and we did have to put in several stitches to close the laceration."

"Was it just the wound? Is her brain okay? The way she hit the floor..." Tai's voice trailed off, not waiting to replay that scene again.

"A CT scan showed no traumatic injury to her brain right now."

Charlie sat up a bit. "So she'll recover?"

"She'll likely still have a heck of a headache and possibly some dizziness, but otherwise her brain is not injured. He also dislocated her right shoulder. We were able to set that and are waiting for the orthopedic doctor to assess whether it needs surgery. She won't be going home for a while, and we'll be moving her upstairs soon."

But she's alive. Regardless, she's alive, and they will care for her. "Can we see her?"

"Yes, of course. Please be aware that we had to sedate Laci for the CT scan, and so she'll still be asleep."

The doctor stood, and the two men followed him out the door. There was a dark room located in front of the nurses' station, and the doctor gestured for them to go to it. When they stepped in, a nurse was working to clean up around Laci. She smiled up at them and spoke barely above a whisper. "I'm Kalie, and I'll be her nurse while she's here. You can come around. It's okay to touch her, but be careful of the wires and tubes. Try not to move her right arm. The wrappings are only a temporary hold until ortho assesses her."

The nurse stepped out, leaving Charlie and Tai alone with Laci. Tai took her right hand in his. This morning, it gripped him so tightly. Now, it was cold and lifeless. Charlie took her left hand. His face fell when her fingers didn't curl around his. They sat there, not saying anything in the dark room, listening to the steady beeping of the monitor with her heartbeat moving across the screen. Tai watched it to reassure himself that she was alive. He could see it there. The mask on her face confirmed for him that she was breathing, too. She looked like a mummy, her head and upper body wrapped in bandages.

Charlie leaned his face closer to hers. Tai watched as the other man held back his tears. "Hey, Baby-girl, Tai and I are here. You're not alone. I'll leave Tai here with you while I call the kids." He looked up at Tai. "Call me if anything changes. I'm going to step outside."

Tai pulled the chair to her bedside, ensuring that it didn't disrupt the wires and tubes. He reached his hand through the bed rails to hold hers. He picked it up to his lips, making sure not to move her shoulder, and kissed the back. "Laci, I'm right here. I'll be here as long as possible until you come home with me. You're going to come home with me again, love."

He couldn't believe that the woman who was so alive and thriving in his arms this morning lay nearly lifeless in front of him now. The way he'd treated her, just because she shut him out again, now felt petty and stupid.

Now that he knew her body, knew who she was with her guard down, he wanted to see that fire, that passion, in her eyes every day. When they pulled into the lot, and suddenly there was this substantial fucking wall between them again, he couldn't take it.

He may have tolerated it until they drove back to his house tonight. Except when Charlie walked in, she dropped everything, had that beautiful smile, and ran into his arms. It was too much for Tai at that moment. He had to walk away. He may as well have stamped "asshole" on his forehead. He hadn't handled it well at all.

The image of her lifeless body hitting the floor ran through his mind repeatedly. The feeling of someone tearing his heart out of his chest was something he never wanted to experience again. In that moment, he knew he loved her.

Looking up at her pale face, he finally understood. Her terror that night when he told her about her ex plotting with Charlie's mother, he now felt. What Tai watched as she fell was what she witnessed during Leo's murder. That level of pain she didn't want to live over again. The pain of running away and not taking things further with him was the better option for her.

"Now I understand, Laci-love," he whispered to her. "Now I know what you were running from. It wasn't me. You were running from the pain of witnessing it again. I understand now."

Over the past few months, he had seen her transform into a warm, loving person, and he wanted that to stay. If she retreated into the shell she was when she first arrived, then he would do as Charlie did. Tai would ensure she kept her therapy appointments, hire more security if necessary to make her feel safe, and do everything in his power to show her he loved her. He would do everything possible to protect her and provide a secure living space.

The door to her room opened. Tai expected to see Charlie, but instead, Jack stepped in. "Can I join you?" Tai motioned him in.

Jack took a seat on the other side of her bed. "I figured it would take an army to get you out of here, so I came to you instead. How is she doing?"

Once again, Tai looked at the monitors before turning to Jack. "She's alive. He injured her head and dislocated her right shoulder. Doc said Nathan dosed her with Fentanyl."

The other man nodded gravely. "Can you tell me what you saw?"

Tai had little to give him. "Jack, it all happened so fast, and we could only see through the kitchen window. I heard him tell her that she was his. He looked straight at me, smiled, and then attacked. We heard him scream in pain, but nothing from her. All we saw was when she hit the floor, lifeless."

Jack confirmed. "That is the same thing Charlie told me. I saw him out front. Benji was able to rewind the video footage from your security cameras."

Tai sat up straighter.

"You could tell something was wrong before Nathan walked in the door." Jack continued. "Laci must have seen him outside because she quickly grabbed Vanessa and shoved her into the kitchen. By the time Laci turned back around, he was inside and had made it to the other side of the bar from her. She didn't make any sudden moves, which was a good thing on her part, but had her hands down under the counter. That's how she hit the panic button and grabbed a small knife from the ledge under the bar. When he lunged, she swung. He grabbed her face and slammed her head into the bar. Her arm was yanked backward across the bar in the twist of their movements. He let go of her, she fell to the floor, and the knife was gone."

Realization hit Tai like a physical blow. *She got him. She must have stabbed him.* "That's why we heard him scream in pain," Tai said. "She stabbed him."

Laci's fingers twitched against his palm, a barely perceptible flutter. Tai's head snapped down, his heart leaping into his throat. He tightened his grip. "Laci-love? Can you hear me?" Another twitch, stronger this time.

Jack stood. "I'll get Charlie."

"Laci-love, I'm right here. The drugs are wearing off. Take a breath for me." Kalie pulled back the curtain. Tai couldn't help but smile at her. "She's responding to me."

Kalie stepped in, leaning down close to Laci's ear. "Can you hear me, Laci? My name is Kalie. You're in the hospital." She pulled back, watching Laci's face, but it didn't change. "Laci, if you can hear me, can you squeeze Tai's hand?"

When her fingers didn't move, Tai leaned down to her. "Laci-love, I need you to squeeze my hand." Joy, sharp and overwhelming, surged through him as her fingers finally wrapped around his. "See, she moved."

"What's going on? Jack told me to get back in here." Charlie stepped into the room.

"She moved in response to me." Tai saw hope bloom on Charlie's face just before the other man scrambled to his side.

On the other side of the bed, Kalie was looking over Laci's IV, occasionally glancing up at the screen. Tai looked up and noticed that the numbers were rising. "Is she coming out of it?"

"Slowly, but yes, it looks like she's coming out of it." She shook Laci's uninjured shoulder. "Laci, I need you to wake up for me."

Come on, please wake up. Movement behind her eyelids caused his heart to skip a few beats. "Laci-love, you waking up? Come on, I need to see you."

"Baby-girl, come on, you can do this." Charlie squeezed her knee.

Each blip on the monitor felt like a lifetime until she finally blinked her eyes open. Tai felt as if all of the oxygen had been sucked from the room. Then she looked at him, and her recognition caused him to breathe again.

"Well, hello there." Kalie leaned over Laci, flashing a small pen light in her eyes that caused Laci to jump. "I know that hurt, sweetie, but I had to do it. Can you tell me your name?"

Laci's mouth moved slowly, her tongue darting out a moment to lick her lips. "Laci. Laci Caldwell," she said with a scratchy voice.

Kalie continued with questions, asking Laci to move her fingers, her toes, and her legs. The more she did, the more Laci's eyes cleared up, and Tai could see her coming back to them. "Okay, you did pretty well, Laci."

Out of nowhere, Laci started a coughing fit, her monitors went haywire, and then tears of pain ran down her cheeks. Kalie moved so fast, Tai barely saw her. The head of the bed lifted. "Tai, help me sit her up. Hold her steady right there." Kalie stepped to the cart behind the bed and pulled open the top drawer.

Tai wrapped his arm around Laci's shoulder, and his other hand across her chest. "It's okay, Kalie's gonna help."

"Laci, I need you to take slow, deep breaths. That's good. Open up and I'll swipe this around in your mouth to take care of some of the dryness." Laci opened her mouth, and Kalie swabbed the inside. Tai wiped the tears off her cheeks. "Tell me where you are hurting, and I'll talk to the doctor about pain management."

"Everywhere from here up." Laci motioned with her hand from mid chest to her head.

"Got it. The doctor will come in when he has a chance, and I'll be coming in every fifteen minutes or so to do assessments. I'll be back as soon as I can with something to help the pain." Kalie whisked out of the room.

Charlie returned to the other side of the bed, retaking his seat. Tai sat back down in his chair.

Laci slowly looked between the two of them. "Vanessa?" She barely whispered.

Tai reached up to push a lock of hair back from her face. "She's okay, love. You got her out of the way in time. He didn't hurt anybody else."

"Nathan?"

Tai shook his head. "The police are still looking for him."

Kalie stepped back in, this time with a syringe. "Got something for you."

"Tequila?" Laci asked.

Kalie gave a small chuckle as she wiped the IV on Laci's hand and then pushed the syringe into it. "Of course. Top shelf. Only the best for my best patients." Then she zipped out the door again.

Jack stepped back in, peeking around the curtain. "Knock knock. Are we good?" When he saw Laci sitting up, he smiled. "Hi Laci, I see your bodyguards have returned to their posts. At least now they are smiling."

Laci squeezed their hands. "Well, what can I say? I found the two best-looking ones, and they stuck with me."

Jack chuckled. "I hate to be the downer, but I need your statement. Can you tell me what you remember of what happened?"

Tai watched Laci's eyebrows pull together as she tried to explain everything. He had to resist the urge to jump in with his own details.

Jack pulled a photo from his jacket pocket. "Any of you recognize this man?"

Tai took the photo and examined it closely. It was a security camera still, a tall, slender man with blond hair, at the bakery on the far side of the square. He handed the photo to Charlie so he and Laci could look at it. "I don't recognize him."

"I don't either, but he fits the description of the man who came to my parents' door," Charlie answered.

"He also fits the description of the man that Kathy saw snooping around your house when Laci was at the store," Jack added. Then he turned to Laci. "We asked several people around town, and they said this guy had been here asking about you a while back. They didn't give him anything, and they denied knowing you at all. I'm sure Mark told him exactly where to find you in town, and that's how Mark got that additional info about you."

Laci held out her good hand for Charlie to give her the photo. She moved the photo closer to her eyes, and Tai caught the wince of pain before she lowered it again. "I know this guy." The men all froze. "I don't know his name, but he's a higher-up manager in logistics at my last company."

Charlie's head whipped to her, his eyes wide. Then Laci's eyes went wide.

"What is it?" Tai asked them.

"He was part of Leo's reporting structure," Laci whispered.

Jack took the photo back and noted everything Laci could tell him about her company and what she knew of the guy.

"Jack, Tai said Nathan got away. Have you found him yet?"

He shook his head. "No, we know he took off around the back and across the parking lot, but we lost him after that. He seems to have disappeared. Given he's now sporting a stab wound, he has to be hurting and maybe looking for medical care."

A chilling certainty settled in Laci's gaze, a look that made Tai's blood run cold. "He won't go to a real hospital. He knows we'll be looking. He'll find a back-alley doctor, somebody his money can buy. He'll dull the pain with whatever drugs he can get his hands on... and then he will come for me again. This isn't over."

EIGHTEEN

Packed up and driving home in Tai's SUV, Laci enjoyed the bright sunshine reflecting off the snow and the fresh air instead of hospital antiseptics and cleaning supplies. She was so happy to be released that she didn't care they were on their way to Tai's house and not Charlie's. The first day or so had been tough. The head injury caused dizzy spells so bad that the nurses had to catch her.

The orthopedic team delivered good news. There was no surgery required, just several weeks in a sling to let the shoulder heal. Through it all, Tai was a constant, solid presence at her side. Watching him try to sleep on the recliner in her room made her uncomfortable.

"Tai, please," she'd grumbled on the second night, her voice rough with sleep. "Go home. Watching you pretzel yourself into that tiny recliner is more painful than my shoulder. I'm in the middle of a hospital. Nathan isn't going to attack me here."

Tai refused.

Charlie came in each morning, relieving Tai to go home to refresh for work. He snuck in pancakes one morning, then had her laughing uncontrollably as he regaled her with the story of how he met Vincent.

"I thought you were my best friend. You didn't tell me he's Adonis." Charlie wildly gestured as he spoke. "I damn near dropped a new bottle of top-shelf whisky when he walked in the door."

Jack arrived around dinnertime to sit with her. He brought food for them both from Blackwood, and they ate together. She giggled when the nurses on the floor asked where Laci found the pool of good-looking men.

"It's a long story," she told them, looking over at Jack, who was trying and failing to hide his smirk behind his reports.

Her friends happily greeted her as they walked into the house. Tai kept a close presence to ensure no one jostled her shoulder or head too much when they hugged her.

Benji held her gently. "We brought brunch so you can enjoy being with the team again."

After they left to get to work, Laci could barely keep her eyes open. While Tai went over care instructions with Jack, who was staying behind with her, she lay on the couch.

The couch dipped when Tai sat on the edge and gently kissed her temple. "Laci-love, I'm getting ready to go to work now. Jack is upstairs getting settled." She barely nodded. "I'll see you tonight. Tomorrow, I'll help you shower so you can get the hospital smell off of you."

Giving him a sleepy smile, she murmured, "Sounds like fun."

He chuckled, kissed her lips, and she fell back to sleep before he walked out the door.

Evening sun streamed through the windows when Laci opened her eyes. Attempting to get her bearings, she looked around the room. Jack sat on the other side of the sectional, quietly watching TV.

When he caught her waking, he moved to kneel in front of her. "You slept for quite a while there. You want to sit up and see what you need?"

She tried to push herself up with her good arm. Jack waited until she struggled, then slid a supportive arm around her waist to help her the rest of the way up.

"Thanks," she said. "I still get dizzy when I change positions. If you could help me stand, I should be able to walk to the bathroom alone."

As she asked, he put an arm around her to assist. The room spun a little, but he held on until she could walk to the bathroom. When she came out again, he set two places at the table, and the room smelled amazing.

"Do I smell pasta?" she asked.

He chuckled from the stove. "Yes, chicken alfredo. Have a seat, and I'll get it plated up for you. I made it with penne instead of linguini, so you don't have to twirl your fork. I left an appetizer on the table for you."

She sat, finding a med waiting for her to take. After serving them both, he sat across from her. Laci knew very little about him, so she asked about his life growing up.

Jack smiled at her. "My parents still live in the house I grew up in. They were a good combination of being strict and allowing me to learn my lessons. I was in at least one sport all year, mostly football and baseball, to expend my energy healthily."

Laci grinned, remembering the days of chasing after two energetic little ones. "What made you decide to become a cop?"

He finished his bite. "I knew I wanted to do something to help people for a career, but I wasn't sure exactly what. I joined the army right after graduating from high school. My mother was proud but extremely anxious about her only child going off into the worst parts of the world. When I came home, I enrolled in the police academy as soon as possible. I didn't want downtime in between. I love my job on most days."

Of course, he turned the tables on her. "Laci, I already know a lot about the bad side of your life. Tell me more about the good parts."

Laci relaxed since he'd avoided asking for more details about Nathan. "I grew up in a small middle-class suburb. There is a twelve-year age gap between the younger of my two brothers and me, so they were off doing their own thing at college, and I was practically an only child."

Jack's eyes widened. "That is quite a gap in ages."

Laci softly grinned. "You would think my parents babied me, being the youngest and the gap, but no, my brothers taught my parents lessons they used to raise me." She pushed a piece of chicken across her plate. "Shortly after I graduated from high school, my parents were killed by a drunk driver." Laci took in a deep breath to keep the memory at bay. "My brothers lived far from home, so I would have been alone, except I had Charlie with me. I inherited the house, but it was too much for me to care for. I sold it, and Charlie and I found an apartment near our college."

"So, you and Charlie have been attached for most of your lives."

"He lived with me after my divorce and helped raise my kids. He's a major part of their lives, too."

The conversation continued as they cleaned up the dishes, but on more practical matters. "Are you here just tonight, or did Tai ask you to stay with me whenever he's gone?"

Jack turned from the sink while washing dishes. "I volunteered to be here. It'll help give Tai peace of mind knowing you're not here alone, and it helps me know you're safe while Nathan is out there. We both want you to concentrate on healing. You'll be alone from when Tai leaves for work until I finish my shift, but at night, you'll never be alone."

This house was so open that she felt exposed when moving around, and having another person here to keep an eye on things helped. The familiar drowsiness of her meds snuck in, and she opted to go upstairs to lie down. She said goodnight to Jack and made her way to her room.

Laci's clothes still smelled like the hospital, and she desperately wanted to get them off her body. She got out of her yoga pants and into her sleep boxers, but the top would be an issue. While she sat on the side of her bed contemplating how to manage it, her eyes drifted shut.

"Laci-love, it's me, I've got you." Arms lifted her off the bed. Tai walked her to his room. He sat her on the edge of his bed, then stepped away to the dresser. When he came back, he cupped her face. "Let's finish getting you ready for bed. I'm going to take your sling off, don't move your arm."

She managed a faint nod, sleep pulling at her. Tai carefully removed her sling and then her shirt and bra, all without jostling her shoulder. He slipped one of his T-shirts over her and carefully repositioned the sling. The softness of the well-worn fabric and the scent of clean laundry mixed with a hint of his cologne brought a deep comfort to her. He laid her down and pulled the blanket over her, and she was already drifting away.

⚠

"I am capable of picking up the bowls," Laci grumbled.

Tai gave her a sweet smile, then kissed her cheek. "I've got it."

The man was driving her nuts. Whenever he was home, he did practically everything for her. Of course, she needed help with her shoelaces, but she was capable of pulling her own clothes out of the closet.

Over time, Laci had gained limited use of her right arm, but the doctor had not yet cleared her for full use. Working regularly with a physical therapist increased her mobility, but it was sometimes painful. Under an abundance of caution, she didn't leave the house unless it was for a doctor's appointment. Tai invited the friend group to his home for a game night last week. She and Tai shared a smirk, seeing that Charlie had brought Vincent with him.

"The doctor's office moved your appointment back. I won't have time to bring you back here before I go to work. Jack suggested I bring you to the police station, and you can sit with him until his shift is over, then he'll bring you back here." Tai was cleaning up after their own popcorn and movie session that evening.

"Got it. I've been moving my arm around, so I'm sure the doctor will clear me to start working out again." Laci had to turn away before he saw her smile.

Tai caught her in the gym working out by herself a couple of days ago. He was not pleased. Arms snaked around her waist, then pulled her up against his body, his voice low in her ear, "If the doctor clears you, then you can go in the gym on your own."

She giggled. "Aw, but I quite enjoyed the punishment I got last time." He kissed her neck and smacked her butt as he let go of her.

"Why don't you go to our room and get ready for bed?"

Laci walked around and up the stairs. When she opened the door, she stopped dead in her tracks. Every surface in the room had lit candles. The sky was clear, the moon shining past the mountains through the balcony doors.

Tai silently walked behind her. "I have to work tomorrow and serve all the happy couples on Valentine's Day. So, I thought you and I could celebrate a little early."

He took her hand and led her into the room, grabbed a blanket at the foot of the bed, and guided her onto the balcony. Placing the blanket over her shoulders, he then wrapped his arms around her from behind, and they looked out at the moon and the shadow of the mountains below. Tai's hands shifted around her, and when she looked down, there he held a small red box.

"Go ahead and open it," he said.

Inside lay a stunning platinum chain necklace with two diamond-encrusted hearts intertwined. Four smaller platinum hearts formed a drop loop between the larger ones.

"For the two of us and the people who are most special to you."

Laci turned to him in confusion. "Four hearts?"

He pulled the necklace from its box and fastened it around her neck. "I'm sure you can guess three."

"Yes, my kids and Charlie."

"Right. But you had another love, and your time with him was cut short. I can have a place now in your life, but I want you to know that I'll always help you keep a piece of your heart for remembering him." Tears streamed down her face. Some for the love she lost, and others for what she now had.

When he wrapped his arms back around her, she leaned into his strength, letting his solid presence hold all her shattered pieces in place.

After his shift, Jack drove Laci to his house so he could change out of his uniform and gather fresh clothes to stay with her that night. They pulled up to the huge two-story craftsman home, and Laci admired the details. She especially loved the expansive front porch, where she could imagine having rockers and enjoying cool drinks on summer evenings.

Jack shut off the truck and turned to her. "Come on in. Getting changed and grabbing my things won't take me too long. Then we can head back to Tai's house." They walked in through the back screened porch and into the large kitchen, which had an eat-in nook. "Make yourself at home. I'm going to run upstairs." He walked through the archway to the stairs up front.

Laci followed him into the living room and took a look around. Given that Jack was a single guy, she expected a man's den, but it wasn't like that. The muted green walls and cream-colored furniture surprised her. A massive stone fireplace sat at one end, framed out by built-in shelving, with photos lined up along the mantle.

The first photo showed Jack on his high school graduation day, grinning between his parents. Next to it, he stood in his army uniform, arm slung around one of seven buddies in a tight group. Then, a much older photo, three skinny young boys standing together, smiling and eating popsicles. It was clearly Jack, Tai, and then a younger version of Tai.

"That's Felix. We're hanging out in their backyard." His voice came from behind her. "Felix and I were best friends until late in middle school, then I hung out more with Tai."

She looked over her shoulder at him. "Tai said his brother got into trouble a lot. Given your parents wanted you on the straight path, that wouldn't have been somebody good for you to continue hanging out with."

"Yeah, that and Tai and I connected because we had ideas about what we wanted to do, where we wanted to go. Since he was ahead of us, I learned more about life after high school from him, and we became friends as a result. When I left the military, he was among the first people to call and welcome me home. Been close ever since."

Laci moved to the last photo, where he and a beautiful, petite blond girl were featured. The way they looked at each other in the picture made it clear they were deeply in love.

"That...is Nikki. We were together for a few years, but she was gone when I returned from my last deployment. She'd packed up and left town." The sadness in his voice tore at her own internal scars. Then she remembered the story that Charlie told her in the movie theater.

Laci turned to him. "I'm sorry, Jack, that must have been devastating."

Jack looked right at her. "It's nothing close to what you've been through. I know she's still alive and out there. I understand a small part of your pain, and that's why I'm here to support you through all this. If you need somebody to talk to, who at least understands a little, know I'm here for you."

She walked up and hugged him. His arms came around her and squeezed tightly. They stood like that for a few minutes, supporting each other in their losses. When he stepped back, he grabbed his bag from the couch and motioned for her to head back through the kitchen to his truck. "Come on, we need to get you back in time for your appointment."

◢◣

"Laci, how is your recovery going?"

Dr. T's face on her computer helped to bring some normalcy to her life. "I got clearance to remove the sling, but I still have some minor restrictions."

He smiled. "That is good to hear. And how has Tai been doing now that you have received the release?"

She tried not to roll her eyes but didn't quite succeed. "Tai is still trying to keep me from moving it around too much, according to him. Moving it makes it feel better. It's stiff from being locked against my body. Moving it is like scratching a major itch."

"Do you think it's your arm he is trying to protect, or is he trying to protect you as a whole?"

"He and Jack talked about bringing me back to Blackwood. Since then, he's been agitated and in my space." It was getting to the point of aggravating.

Oh no, Dr. T stopped writing to look at her. "Let's set aside your frustration for a moment. What do you think Tai was feeling at the restaurant, right after your attack?"

The question caught her off guard, but she considered it. "Terror. Absolute Terror."

"Exactly. He experienced a trauma, too. He watched the woman he loves nearly die. Now, put yourself in his shoes. If Leo had survived that night, how would you have treated him in the days and weeks that followed?"

It felt as if time stopped around her. That scene flashed in her mind again, Leo's lifeless body hitting the pavement. What if they had been found and rescued in time? What if he survived? "I guess I would be scared to let him out of my sight. I would have done everything possible to make sure he was comfortable..." Her voice trailed off as the realization hit her. Dr. T simply nodded, letting the silence do the work.

Glancing at the screen again, Dr. T looked right at her. "Laci, you are working with me due to the repeated trauma you suffered over your adult life. Tai suffered trauma watching the woman he loves being attacked and lying lifeless. But you survived. Tai got another chance with you. Remember, he saw you when you arrived in town and could barely function. Tai is doing everything in his power to help keep you from going back to that. He doesn't want to lose you physically, emotionally, or mentally. Words are not going to go far enough here. Show him you appreciate his efforts and that you are stronger now than you were back then."

The underlying fear she had been holding back came to the surface. "They haven't found Nathan. It could still happen. Nathan could still kill Tai. What if we make a wrong decision, thinking we can go about our lives like I did with Leo, and my worst nightmare comes true again?"

"All of those homework assignments I gave you, what did they do?"

She took a moment to consider. Each had her stop and focus on what she was doing, feeling, or internally saying to herself, all things she could control.

He smiled at her. "All of those homework assignments helped bring a level of empowerment back to you, didn't they?"

She nodded.

"You're afraid your worst nightmare will come true again," he said, his voice gentle but firm. "Let me ask you this. What did you do when Nathan walked into Blackwood?"

"I pushed Vanessa out of the way. I hit the panic button. I grabbed a knife."

"And the Laci who first called me, would she have done all that?"

She stopped. The woman who arrived in town, a ghost drifting through the world, would have frozen. She would have given up. But she hadn't. "No," she said, the word filled with a new strength. "No, she wouldn't have."

He smiled at her. "You've built your own power, piece by piece. Don't let this one incident convince you it's gone. This time, you have a support system in place. It's not only you and Charlie anymore. You have a team behind you, and they won't let you fall."

Well damn.

Laci wasn't so sure about this plan. But she also knew she couldn't hide forever. They all agreed she wouldn't work out front, but people in town needed to see her. Tai kissed the back of her hand as they pulled into the lot. "Love, you won't be left alone at any time. I'll be in the office with you while you work, and then you move to the kitchen area while I walk the floor."

"I got it. Nathan needs confirmation that I'm still in town. He'll only make a move if guaranteed to get what he wants. Failure enrages him."

Laci waited for Tai to come around to open her door. As he did, he looked down at her.

She paused to feel the environment and said, "Nothing, I don't feel him nearby."

They made their way inside and back to the office, where Laci was surprised to find a new desk added to the space for her. They heard the staff come in and call out their hellos, and then Charlie came charging around the corner to hug Laci. "I'm so glad you're back!"

As Charlie lifted her into a hug, Tai's voice cut in, "Her shoulder."

Charlie gently placed her back on her feet. Laci had been officially freed of her sling, but Tai heard the doctor tell her to be careful with it, so he protected her.

When it was time to move to the kitchen, Tai and Laci stood and walked out together. Tai cleared his throat to get everyone's attention. "I'm sure nerves are a little high having Laci back here, but it's necessary. We're making a few changes, and she'll be in the office with me or in the kitchen. She doesn't work the front at all, got it?" Everyone agreed. "We have security teams open to close daily, and officers are patrolling outside. We're trying to make this as safe as possible while still working to remove the threat." There was a momentary silent exchange between Tai and Vincent that Laci caught when everyone moved to their stations.

Tai kissed her quickly, then headed out front to greet customers. There she stood, watching through the window as Tai talked to customers, while Charlie and Vincent moved behind the bar, feeling miles apart from them. Benji grabbed her attention. "Hey Laci, if you don't mind helping back here, I can show you where we could use support."

She smiled as she turned to him. "Good job distracting me, Benji. How can I help?"

He handed her an apron and a knife. Benji had her on chopping duty for salads. "Look, my wife had a similar issue when the twins left. She was a part of every aspect of their lives, and when the Navy sent them off to parts unknown, she had the same lost look in her eyes for weeks. The only way I managed to get her out of it was by distracting her and finding a more positive outlet for her energy. You've had a lot happen and change lately. I can give you a routine back here."

"So, you're saying you're some type of woman whisperer."

"Darling, I wouldn't be back here cooking if I were. I would be on the road making millions!" They both laughed.

Laci found that Benji was right. Having some positive tasks to focus on really helped. She was still helping keep the restaurant moving, just not out front. Intensely focused on her tasks, she didn't notice when Tai came in. His warm hand on her shoulder and a kiss on her temple brought her out of her zone. When she looked at him, she realized he wasn't only checking on how she was doing but reassuring himself that she was safe and happy.

In front of the grill, Benji grinned while waving his tongs at Tai. "Hey, stop distracting my kitchen helper! You get back out front where you belong."

Tai laughed at the ridiculous order. "Got it! But your helper is good-looking, and I couldn't help myself."

Laci kept chopping, but she leaned into Tai to let him know she appreciated him stopping in to check on her. He must have watched her and Charlie work together so much that he learned how she needed these small moments to bring her back to her center. It was second nature to Charlie since he'd been doing it for years.

However, that didn't stop her from adding fuel to the fire. "Benji, I need to file a harassment charge against him. He's all up in my personal space, and he kissed me without my permission."

That got a round of laughs from everyone in the kitchen. Tai threw up his hands and walked out the doorway to the dining area. As he passed the window, he looked back at her and winked. She smiled and winked back.

Nineteen

The room was dark when Laci woke to Tai's hands traveling over her body. His lips gently feathered across her shoulder blades, then down her spine. She felt his hands kneading her ass, his mouth a hot trail moving ever lower. "Open for me, love."

Laci spread her legs to give him better access. Fingers slipped into her, eliciting the electric current that ran through her belly. He drew out her pleasure with long, slow strokes of his fingers while his mouth began a worshipful pursuit of every inch of her back. She felt the path of licks, nibbles, and kisses climb her spine to her neck, and when he found that perfect spot and sucked, a moan escaped her lips.

He settled beside her again, his gaze locking with hers as his fingers continued their slow, intimate rhythm inside her. "Good morning, my love," he murmured, his voice a low, rough velvet against the quiet.

She smiled. "Well, it's a good morning for me so far."

Laci kissed his lips, then made her way down his chest, kissing and licking as she slowly moved, gently running her fingernails down the sides of his body. It wasn't fair that she was the only one now ramped up and on the edge. When her hands ran down to his thighs and then inward, ever so gently over the inside crease, a hand gathered her hair and gently tugged. Moving her mouth lower, she kissed and licked down one thigh and back up the other.

Tai let out a low growl of frustration. Ending the teasing, she took one slow, long lick up his full length, then flicked the tip of her tongue on the head. She felt the fist in her hair tighten, his sharp breath a ragged curse against the quiet morning.

Tracking up and down his legs with her fingers, Laci stopped to wrap her hand around the base. His breathing ramped up, each breath becoming ragged. Tightening her grip, she slowly took him deep into her mouth, her hand moving in tandem. She felt the muscles in his thighs bunch and tighten, the fist in her hair no longer gentle as he tried to guide her pace. When she let go with her hand, taking all of him, a guttural sound was torn from his chest, and he nearly bucked off the bed.

"Fuck! Love... Shit!"

She pulled back, a smile playing on her lips as she looked up at him. The look in his eyes stole her breath. Gone was the teasing man from moments ago. This was pure, undiluted possession. Before she could blink, he flipped her onto her back in one fluid motion, his powerful body caging hers.

He was already between her legs when his mouth came down on hers, a kiss full of the frantic need she'd seen in his eyes. He broke away only long enough to grab a condom from the nightstand before pushing into her.

Laci's scream of pleasure was swallowed by his kiss. All semblance of control was gone. He moved with a raw, frantic rhythm that stole her breath and sent spirals of light dancing behind her eyelids. Her world narrowed to the feel of his body in hers, his mouth on hers, until everything tightened into one unbearable knot of pleasure that finally, blessedly, snapped. A moment later, she felt his release deep inside her, his own groan lost against her lips.

Tai collapsed on top of her, his face buried in the pillow next to her head, his breathing harsh in the quiet room. Laci ran her fingers gently up and down his slick back, her own body humming with contentment. He turned his head, his lips finding the curve of her neck, and placed soft kisses along her skin.

Lifting to be nose-to-nose with her, Tai kissed her lips and then smiled. "I have a surprise for you. Get up and quickly get dressed so we don't miss it."

Oh, is that why he woke at this ungodly hour?

Laci took a quick shower, got dressed, and headed downstairs. It was dark in the house, but she knew exactly where he was. It comforted her to know she could fully sense his presence. As she came down the stairs, he moved from the kitchen, grabbed her hand, and led her to the garage.

On the drive, Laci watched Tai expertly navigate the tight turns as they climbed higher. "So, will it be warm today? Or will it snow today?"

Tai shot her an amused glance. "Still not adjusted to spring here, are you?"

"The town is beautiful with all of the trees, just like Charlie told me it was. But it's a little daunting to carry four seasons of clothing with me every time I leave the house." She smiled when he chuckled. "By now back home, I'd be dealing with humidity and wetlands instead of lawn. I like how much drier it is here, that's for sure. And the river along the far end is so loud now."

"I don't know how long you had planned to stay," Tai quickly glanced at her, "but summers here are probably very different, too. It's cool in the mornings, then dry and hot during the day. We usually get an afternoon storm, and then it cools right back down after sunset. We don't use a lot of air conditioning."

Laci looked toward the window so Tai couldn't see her face. "I didn't have a timeline set. My plans have completely changed, and now…I'm not sure about anything."

Tai laid a hand on her knee and squeezed. "Would you consider staying long-term?"

It took a moment before Laci shrugged. "Possibly. I miss my kids. They are the only reason I would want to move back home."

Tai guided his SUV off the paved road and over a gravel pathway, heading into a small space between a grove of trees. They soon reached a clearing and parked. Opening the back hatch, he pulled out a blanket and a basket. He motioned for Laci to join him further out on the clearing, where he laid the blanket down. While she sat and unpacked the basket, he closed up the car.

As the sky lightened, Laci found Tai had prepared and packed a full breakfast. Omelets, bacon, muffins, juice, and coffee lay out in an intimate buffet. While they ate, the sun rose. The sky lightened, bleeding through shades of red, orange, and yellow. It looked like someone had delicately painted the colors and blended them with such precision that you could barely tell where one ended and the next began.

"Damn, I wish I'd brought my camera. This view is amazing." Laci stood, walking closer to the edge of the clearing.

The view was similar to what they could see from Tai's bedroom balcony, but it was much higher and turned more to the south, offering a more expansive view from east to west. The sun peeked over the hills to Laci's left, and she watched in awe as the mountain tops in the distance to the right, still covered in deep snow, were now glowing the same colors as the sky.

Laci turned to look out over the town where she had come to find refuge several months ago. When she arrived here on Charlie's doorstep, she was a shell, barely going through the motions of day-to-day life. With his help and Tai's, Laci felt like herself again, or even better than she had been. Having their support while she worked with Dr. T, she realized that she was hardly living even before Leo's death. Now, she was open to new friendships, meeting new people, and embracing a new life.

Yes, Nathan was still out there somewhere, but Laci knew now that she had the support she needed. But she also had to be able to stand up for herself. She had much more to live for now. She wouldn't let Nathan continue to ruin things for her and could no longer live in fear.

Tai's arms snaked around her waist, and he kissed her neck. "This spot is where I come to get away from life. It always gives me a fresh perspective to see everything in such a grand view, yet also shrunk down so tiny."

Laci laughed a bit, looking over the lush, green valley. "The town is tiny down there."

He chuckled. "Yep, little ant village now. Until several months ago, I was doing well in my life. I had my home, my business, and my friends. I kept myself busy and was happy. Or so I thought. Then, this beautiful woman stepped foot in my restaurant, and time froze for me."

"Who was she?" Laci asked. "She sounds intriguing."

"When you turned and smiled at Charlie, the warmth and love in that smile blew me away. I realized I was missing that in my life. Somebody to smile at me like that every day."

He took a deep breath and continued, "Somehow, I would fight the world if I could get you to smile like that. Having you in my home, where I felt I could protect you, brought me comfort. The day Nathan attacked you, and I watched your lifeless body fall to the floor, I felt my entire world shatter. Charlie and I grieved, but I also realized then that I couldn't continue without you."

When his arms tightened a bit around her, Laci stroked her hands along them to calm him.

"Since then, I've cherished every time I've seen your smile directed at me with the warmth and the love you have for me."

Tears welled up in Laci's eyes. Hearing him say all this, she knew she'd found where she belonged.

"Laci, I want you to stay here with me. I want to be by your side through everything. I want to return to this spot in forty years when we're old and gray, barely able to walk, and admire this sunrise together as we are now." His voice dropped, thick with an emotion that made her own heart ache. "Laci-love, will you marry me?"

Laci looked down where his arms were around her and saw him holding a small box with a stunning diamond ring.

Around the center stone were a rainbow of birthstones for each person in their lives. Unable to speak yet, she nodded her head.

Tears were now falling as she turned in his arms and put hers around his neck, whispering in his ear, "Yes, I will."

And Tai kissed her. As his lips met hers, Laci felt a profound sense of peace settle over her. For the first time in what felt like a lifetime, the future felt brighter than the shadow of her past.

On their drive into Blackwood that morning, Laci now saw the town with a fresh perspective. She could make this her home. Her kids were grown now and didn't need her back in Ohio. There was nothing else back there for her except memories.

Tai's fingers, entwined with hers as he drove, gave her hand a slight squeeze. "You ready to face the family?"

They had called the kids after they got back to the house. Initially, Laci was worried about their reactions. Sure, they got along with Tai over Christmas and had a few video calls with him since then, but they still didn't know him. Laci's world felt right again the moment she heard Alie's squeal of joy.

"We are going to get bombarded, aren't we?" She asked.

"Yep. The challenge will be to keep this under wraps for a while. We can trust our inner circle, and with you staying in the kitchen area, it should be fine." He glanced over to her. "I was thinking maybe you'd like a bigger part in the business."

Laci turned to look at him. "How so?"

"With your background, I was hoping maybe you'd like to take over the financials. Manage the office for me?"

When he gave her a sly smile, Laci couldn't help but laugh. "Oh, now I see how this is. You loop me in with your sweet proposal, all so you can have somebody else do your paperwork that you hate."

They pulled into the lot, and Tai leaned over to kiss Laci. "Let's do this."

Falling back into their familiar roles, they operated as if it were any other morning. It wasn't until she brought out a package of napkins to stock the bar that Charlie made a fuss.

"Whoa whoa whoa. What is that?" He questioned loudly. Everyone in the place froze and turned to look at him. "Do I get to start calling you Sugar-Mommy now?"

Vanessa gasped and ran full speed around the bar, reaching for Laci's hand. "Oh my god! Yay!" She jumped up to hug Laci.

Tai's arm pulled Laci to his side, and he looked around at everyone now gathered out front. "This morning I asked Laci to marry me, and she said yes." The screams of joy were deafening. "But!" Tai called out over the noise. "I'm asking you all to keep this between us here. You know how news travels in this town, and I'd rather not be the main topic of conversation."

"Well, that means I won't be telling my wife," Benji said under his breath.

As the celebratory chaos settled back into the familiar rhythm of the lunch rush, Laci slipped into the office to begin learning the financials. Her new role felt real, solidified even more when Tai brought in a stack of her photos, newly framed in stark black and white. He hung them around the restaurant, and seeing her art become a part of Black-wood's atmosphere made her feel, finally, like she was truly home.

Summer was practically here now, and tourists increased around the town. Each day, a line would form at the door at Blackwood. Charlie explained to Laci that tourists enjoyed stopping in the hills because it was a "quaint life and relaxing." The faux snobby accent he adopted as he spoke made Laci giggle. Vincent took over serving the high-top tables closest to the bar to relieve Vanessa.

"Yeah, we'll be closed for those two days. We could make it work if I flew in and out within twenty-four hours. If you can set up the viewing shortly after I arrive, we can discuss logistics that evening."

As Tai paced the office on the phone, Laci admired his body and enjoyed the deep timbre of his voice. Nothing calmed her nerves faster than his deep voice. "Got it. I'll be there on Sunday morning and fly back on Monday. Don't start with that whiny 'Oh, I miss you. Can't you stay longer?"

There was a pause, and Tai's eyebrows rose. His voice dropped to a threatening tone. "Do I have to remind you about the time you abandoned me at the airport? You still owe me." He looked at Laci and winked. "Yeah, I'll see you Sunday."

A laugh burst from Laci as he dropped his cell onto the desk. "Abandon you at the airport again? You mean he's done it before?"

Tai smiled. "I came home to visit my family during my junior year, and Dan promised to pick me up when I returned after the break. I confirmed with him at least ten times my scheduled landing time. I arrive, and he's nowhere to be found. I called him, but there was no answer. I had to call another buddy to come to get me, and he told me Dan got hammered at a party the night before and passed out in his underwear in the backyard. I have photos."

She laughed when she pictured this image.

He stood. "Stay here for a moment." He only stepped far enough out into the kitchen where Charlie could hear him, but he wasn't far from Laci. "Charlie, can you come back here for a second?"

In unison, Laci could hear Vanessa, Benji, and Vincent say, "Oooooooo, somebody's in trouble!"

Charlie was right behind Tai as he stepped back in. To get back at the others, Charlie said rather loudly, "Okay, Sugar Daddy, but please don't spank me as hard this time." There was a massive round of laughs outside as he closed the door.

Pinching the bridge of his nose, Tai turned back to Charlie. "You know, I fully accept that you're a package deal with Laci, and I'll have to put up with you for the rest of my life, but seriously, do you have to make it so damn difficult?" Charlie beamed at Tai and winked at Laci as he sat on the couch. Tai moved back behind his desk.

"I'm going out of town this weekend." Tai's tone had turned serious. "I'm flying out on Sunday and coming back on Monday. I don't have much choice. A friend wants me to look at a property he's interested in to open a nightclub, and we have a small window to decide."

Recognition crossed Charlie's face. "You're not taking Laci with you."

Tai shook his head. "No, Dan won't talk business with me if she's there. He's cagey about his finances around strangers."

Tai continued, "Is there any way that you and Vincent can come stay at our house?"

Charlie smiled at Laci, "Oooooo oooouuuuur house." Tai smiled.

Laci cooed back at Charlie, "Oooooo, you and Vincent."

Chuckling, Charlie didn't even hesitate. "I will, for sure. I'll ask Vincent. That is a delicate situation for an outsider to walk into."

"I fully agree. Let me know as soon as you can, and then I can at least relax knowing she's not alone."

Charlie agreed and headed for the door, pausing to look back at Laci. "How much background can I give Vincent?"

"Top level. Try not to get into the details." He gave Laci a thumbs-up and walked out.

The dinner rush started early, so Tai and Laci moved to their respective areas. As Laci moved around the kitchen helping Benji, she couldn't help but catch glimpses of Tai through the window. Seeing him chat and laugh with patrons warmed her heart.

Tai glanced over at one point to catch her staring at him. They exchanged a smile, a silent promise that passed between them before they returned to their tasks. He was in his element, a man who had built this business from the ground up. Laci watched him, a fierce hope warring with her fear. This new, beautiful life they were building together felt both incredibly real and terrifyingly fragile.

TWENTY

Laci was helping Benji with morning prep work when Vanessa came running in. "Vanessa, what's wrong?"

Vanessa pushed a hand back through her hair, her eyes wide like a spooked deer's. "Uh, during our morning jog, somebody stopped me and asked about Tai being engaged."

Benji put his knife down. "Who told them?"

"Mrs. Murphy." Vanessa twisted her hands in front of her. "I know I have to tell Tai, but I don't know how."

Laci looked between the two of them. "So a couple of people know. They don't know who he is engaged to."

Wiping his hands, Benji looked back at Laci. "You don't know how small-town gossip works." He led the way to Tai's office. "Tai, we have a problem."

Tai looked up from his paperwork, and his eyebrows dropped the moment he spotted all three of them in the doorway. "Who is the problem?"

Vanessa pulled in a deep breath. "Mrs. Murphy."

Charlie stepped into the office. "What's going on?"

"It was Mrs. Murphy," Vanessa rushed on, twisting her hands. "She knew about the engagement. She and Hester must have noticed something when they were here for dinner. I swear, I didn't say a word. I didn't confirm anything, and neither did Brent."

"Oh." Laci dropped onto the couch.

"Crap. If Nathan is still around, then he will hear enough to put the pieces together and know that it's Laci." Charlie's hand clenched into a fist, his jaw set. "Tai, I promise you, Vincent and I have her covered this weekend. We won't let him get to her. We'll stay at your place. We won't go out."

It was clear that Tai was uncomfortable with leaving Laci as he sat down with her on the couch. "I should cancel this trip. Dan is a big boy. He can do this."

"No, Tai, you have to go," Laci insisted, her voice firmer than she felt. "This is a huge opportunity for you. We can't let him dictate our lives from the shadows. I'll be fine. Charlie and Vincent will be here. We can't stop living. We don't even know where he is. We still have three days to monitor for any changes. Go ahead and do what you need to. I'm stronger now than I've been in the past."

The arm he had around her stiffened. Laci could feel the tension in his body, but eventually he agreed.

As Tai and Charlie discussed the security system at the house, Laci realized she had no choice but to act now. This was her time to stand up for herself. Laci wouldn't stray from what Charlie wanted her to do this weekend and wouldn't let her nightmares take over again. She worked too hard to let them win.

"Laci-love." A kiss to her temple. Reaching out a hand, Tai wasn't next to her.

Laci groggily sat up. "Tai?"

He came around to her side of the bed. "Hey, Laci-love, I'm leaving for the airport."

She opened her eyes to see Tai in a full business suit. Even at Blackwood, he never wore more than his dress shirt, pants, and a tie. The sharp lines of the jacket and vest were a stark contrast to his usual style, and the fabric was cut to fit his athletic form perfectly.

"You look fucking hot," she breathed.

He shook his head and chuckled. "You'll have to hold that thought until I get back," he murmured against her lips. "Charlie and Vincent are here, so you're not alone. I'll be back tomorrow, my love."

He cupped her face and kissed her lips. "I love you."

"I love you too." And then he was gone.

The smell of Charlie's irresistible pancakes woke Laci from her deep sleep. Rolling out of bed, she threw on sweats and a T-shirt. Sure enough, he was at the stovetop, flipping pancakes like at a 1960s roadside diner. Vincent was sitting at the bar, drinking orange juice. She took a moment to glance outside, scanning the yard up to the tree line.

"How is it that I can't resist those damn pancakes?" Laci smiled as she walked in. "Good morning, Vincent."

He gave her a single nod in response.

Charlie grinned. "Because I know you're an absolute carb monster."

She grinned widely. "Agree."

Laci sat next to Vincent, his quiet presence balancing out Charlie's overly chipper energy.

"So, what are we going to do today?" Charlie asked.

As she prepared her plate, she pondered, then ticked the options off on her fingers. "Well, we could work out, rob a bank, or watch movies, or," she paused, her expression perfectly deadpan, "we could hire strippers, or play video games."

Vincent's head slowly swiveled in her direction. "Please tell me that you only mean every other one of those options."

Her lips twitched. "Yeah, you're right. Options two and four sound like the best ideas." She popped a slice of pancake in her mouth and avoided looking at Vincent.

Charlie started laughing hysterically. "Seriously, I wish I'd had my phone to snap this image. Laci, I not only love hearing your jokes again, but I also love seeing you deliver them with a straight face. And Vincent, your eyes are ready to pop out of your head."

While washing dishes, her eyes scanned the backyard, looking over every possible inch. Charlie stepped up beside her, placing the pan in the sink. "Don't. I can tell you want to pull out all of your equipment again and set it all up."

"I can't help it. You know he's out there." She looked over to him, seeing a hint of the same fear she had.

Charlie wrapped his arm around her, squeezing her shoulder. "You heard Tai go over the security system. I promise you it's armed, and I don't plan on disarming it until he comes back. Plus, you see those walls. Somebody would have to seriously risk their life to scoot around the end by the drop-off. No way Nathan is doing that."

In the gym, Laci was back to fully working out, no longer protecting her shoulder. She was happy to see her muscle definition return.

Vincent was watching her from the weight bench. "Laci, can I make some suggestions?"

She put her water bottle down and looked over. There was an unease to him, especially when he looked back at Charlie. "Vincent, it's all good. I'm open to any suggestions you might have." Laci motioned to his body. "I'm pretty sure you know what you're doing."

It took him a moment, but he agreed. "I had a situation in the past where I was dating somebody close to their best friend. If I said or did one thing wrong to her friend, my partner would go off. So, I tend to tread lightly."

"Not gonna happen here," Charlie spoke up. "Neither one of us is that fragile."

Laci gave him a moment to digest what Charlie said. "I don't know if you noticed," she loudly whispered, "but we're all adults here and act like it...most of the time."

Vincent stood and had her pick up the weights she was using. He looked her in the eye before touching her, but she gave him an encouraging smile. He then helped her refine her form and maximize the value of her reps.

The three were curled together on the couch by the night's end. Laci yawned. "That was a good movie, but I'm freaking tired." The guys agreed.

They shut everything down and headed upstairs into their respective bedrooms. Tonight would be the first time Laci slept in here without Tai. There was a pang of remembering when there was another first time sleeping without her partner.

Tai is alive. Tai will be back. Tai is alive. Tai will be back.

Not feeling secure sleeping with the balcony doors uncovered, she pulled the curtains shut. They faced out the back where no one could see in, but it creeped her out to feel exposed when she was alone. When she got into bed, Laci reminded herself again that she wasn't alone. Charlie and Vincent were close by. She picked up her phone and saw Tai's message.

> TAI: Laci-love, you're not alone. I'll return to you. Charlie and Vincent are right there with you. I'll be back soon. I love you.

She typed back a quick I love you too, the words feeling both simple and monumental. Plugging in her phone, Laci settled into the massive bed that now felt like hers and let the exhaustion claim her.

A whisper in her ear woke her, "Laci, be very quiet. I need you to wake up."

Charlie. Charlie was scared. Laci opened her eyes. It was dark, but she could make out Charlie's face mere inches from hers. "Quickly and quietly get up and get dressed."

Laci moved with quiet urgency, pulling on yesterday's clothes and her gym shoes. In one swift motion, she twisted her hair into a secure bun. Finally, she unplugged her phone, popped it in her pocket, and was ready.

Charlie came to her and showed her his phone. It displayed a simplified layout of what seemed to be Tai's property. A small red box blinked in the top right corner of it. Someone was in the far-right corner of the backyard.

Laci leaned close and whispered in Charlie's ear. "Where's Vincent?"

Charlie leaned close, his breath warm against her ear. "You're not going to believe this," he whispered. He put a finger to his lips, gesturing for silence before cracking the door open. On the bridge, Vincent was a dark, prone shape on the floor, utterly still.

He was using some type of scope on a tripod, looking out the back windows. He motioned for them to lie on the floor without looking at them. From the back corner of the yard, anyone would have a clear line of sight to the bridge.

Vincent belly-crawled over to Charlie and Laci. "There is a guy way out there." He spoke so low his voice didn't carry past them. "I can see him. I don't think he'll come any closer. He's on the other side of the wall, moving back and forth to set off the sensors and create a distraction."

Laci knew something else was coming.

Charlie looked at them both. "Laci, we can get out in your car before anybody tries to get in the house. We'll head to my house and stay there." Vincent agreed, but Laci shook her head. They looked at her as if she had lost her mind.

"Think about it. What is the best way for them to reach me? You know I'm the target. Leaving the house is what they want because ambushing a car is much easier than targeting a huge house with its gated driveway, perimeter privacy wall, and security system. That guy is out there to create the illusion that attackers are coming. He's purposely moving around to trip the motion sensor, but we should still prepare for the possibility that somebody might break in. Did you call the police?"

"Yeah," Charlie answered. "I called before I got to you. When Vincent confirmed movement."

"Good, then staying inside will also buy us time for the police to get up here." She blew out a breath to try to expend a little of the nervous energy that was building inside of her. "Alright, we have to move quickly, but I know exactly where to go."

Vincent returned to his position to scan the right corner of the yard again. They watched as he moved left and right, then turned completely around to check through the front windows. He gave them a thumbs-up.

To avoid being seen, Laci stayed on her belly, turned her legs first, and slid down the stairs. The last thing she wanted to do was let the dancer out back know that they were on to him. She crawled behind the kitchen counter to the hallway to the left. Charlie and now Vincent were right behind her.

There was a door on the right to the gym. Laci opened the door to the left and crawled into Tai's office. Once she confirmed the blinds were closed, she stood and went to the bookcases along the left wall. In the middle one, on the third shelf down, was an ornate box. Laci lifted the lid, reached in, and removed the false bottom to push the button underneath. The quiet click gave her relief.

She replaced the box's innards and then pushed the entire shelf back to reveal a hidden room. It had no windows and no lighting, so it was completely dark. Once they were all inside, Laci turned and locked the secret door. When the lock flipped, tiny glowing green LEDs lit up along the ceiling. It wasn't nearly enough to light the room, but enough that they could make out the furniture and sit.

Charlie looked at her with wide eyes, "What in the rich people fuck is this?"

Half smiling, Laci turned to him, "This was a walk-in closet. It was unused since it's in Tai's office instead of a bedroom. He had the bookshelves and the secret door installed when he had the security system upgraded."

Charlie rechecked his phone and showed it to her. They could see the remnants of their movements as they entered this room, but nothing more than the dancing man outside.

Laci noticed the notification. "Charlie, you have to text Tai."

She watched as he typed the message.

CHARLIE: She's safe. We called the police and made it to the hidden room.

TAI: Thank you. Stay put, but also be silent. The room isn't soundproof.

Vincent made his way around the tiny space, inspecting its build. Tai had shown it to Laci once, in case she needed it. The door was metal, and the wall had a metal frame and panels between the studs. A human couldn't kick in the door, but the space wasn't entirely impenetrable.

Two small loveseats were in an L-shape against the back walls. A cell phone sat on a small table in the back right corner between the loveseats, plugged in but shut off. In the back left corner was a cabinet with bottles of water and some food items. The ceiling and walls featured sound-damp-ening panels, and carpet with extra padding covered the floor. Everything reduced the chances of anyone on the outside hearing breathing or movement.

Laci had Charlie turn the brightness level of his screen as low as possible, and she did the same to her phone. Vincent then picked up a bag that Laci didn't see him bring in. He pulled out two handguns, loaded them, and stowed them on his person. He then pulled one of the loveseats out, facing the other, so its back was to the door.

Charlie and Laci gaped at him. Their attention snapped back to Charlie's phone as the front property line blinked red. Someone else was here. While Vincent moved to double-check the locks, Laci was on the phone with the police, confirming the officers hadn't arrived. The dispatcher said they were only halfway up.

They watched as two red boxes moved up the dri-veway. When Charlie switched to the outside cameras, they saw black-clad figures had climbed over the walls and were heading for the house. It was clear that Vincent wanted to be out there where he could have a tactical advantage, but he had also put himself between Charlie, Laci, and the door.

Vincent motioned for them to get down on the floor. They did, between the furniture. He motioned to Laci, pointing at the LEDs. Before moving to the switch on the wall, she approached Vincent.

"My ex has hired professional killers in the past," she whispered. "That may be what we're up against now."

He nodded in confirmation. She crawled over to a switch and hit it. Darkness once again surrounded them.

Laci felt her way back next to Charlie. He looked at the cameras again. The first two figures attempted to enter through the back doors, and now two more had reached the front door.

Laci got up in his ear. "You need to shut off the screen now. We can't risk the light."

He put it away. They heard the front door open. Involuntarily, Laci's breathing ramped up, so Charlie rolled on his side and tucked her up into his chest. It was hard work for her to stay in this moment, ready to fight if necessary. She couldn't go back to that time. Things were different now. Nathan couldn't get her here, and she wasn't alone. *Oh god, Tai must be absolutely out of his mind.* They knew this would happen while he was gone. It was Laci who convinced him to go. The image of him holding on to her formed in her mind, and her muscles relaxed.

They heard the footsteps move up the stairs. In her pocket, Laci's phone vibrated, a distinct pattern she assigned to Jack. Placing it on the floor between her and Charlie, she pulled up the message.

JACK: How many? Armed?

LACI: Inside, four, yes.

Shutting it off again, she put it away. They lay there listening. They could hear the men cross the bridge. Shortly after, they traveled back and were now in the rooms above. Then they heard movement outside the door of the hidden room. More men must have come in. Steps moved around the office and came to a stop. Charlie and Laci held their breath. Laci could feel Vincent move, but he didn't make a sound. He was now on the same side of the furniture as she and Charlie, but crouched and was aiming at the door. Finally, the footsteps left the office, and Laci heard the door to the gym open and close.

She concentrated on breathing as slowly and silently as possible. There was no way Nathan was here. Nathan hired people to kill someone or operated alone to get to her. He'd hired men to kill Leo, but he'd come into the restaurant alone. If this were to kill Tai for asking her to marry him, Nathan would have done it soon after the engagement news spread through town. He wouldn't wait three days and attack when Tai was out of town. When he got angry, Nathan wanted instant results. Something was wrong with this.

Outside, they could barely make out a shout. "Police! Freeze! Put the weapon down now! Get down on the ground!"

The three in the room didn't move a muscle. It felt like forever. Heavier boots moved through the entire house. At different distances, "Clear" was called out. Soon, "Get them up and out of here."

Laci's pocket vibrated with Jack's signal.

JACK: Nobody can see you come out of that
room now. I suggest you tell Vincent to stand
down.

What the hell? Laci rolled over. "Hey, Vincent, Jack said to stand down."

Vincent stood and flipped on the LEDs again. He gave them a big grin, his teeth showing up in the green light. "Navy SEAL," he whispered. He laughed at her and Charlie's reactions, then put the handguns away in the duffel and slid it under the couch.

Charlie helped Laci up from the floor, and she heard Charlie say under his breath, "Damn, he's hot when he does that."

Laci opened the door for them, and as soon as they were out, she turned and shut it again.

They came down the hall and found Jack standing in the middle of the living room.

"Jack?" Laci exclaimed. "When do you sleep?"

He turned to Laci's voice and huffed. "Pretty much never. Dispatch called me when they heard that it was Tai's house. I was right behind the cruisers. We'll take these guys back and question them. At least this could lead us to where Nathan is hiding."

Laci remembered what she was thinking in the hidden room. "Something isn't right. It's off track from what Nathan would usually do. If he wanted to kill Tai, he would have hired professional thugs and had them strike immediately after discovering the engagement. He would have done it himself if he wanted to get to me."

Charlie concurred. "Yeah, that's out of character for Nathan. Something isn't right."

"I'll defer to your expertise." Jack looked at the bridge overhead. "I have a tech upstairs right now. He's checking over the house for anything they may have left behind. We don't need any more surprises. Laci, you'd better call Tai before he climbs through my cell phone."

Walking across the house, she stepped into the laundry room, the only room where cops weren't working, phone in hand. But the moment the door closed, her body shook. She dropped her phone on the washing machine and gripped the sides, concentrating on breathing as slowly as possible. Finally, her muscles relaxed, and she took a step back.

Picking up her phone, she dialed Tai, and he picked up on the first ring. "Laci-love, are you okay?"

She took a breath before responding. "Yes, I'm okay. All three of us are. Jack is here, and they got the guys."

A relieved sigh came over the line. "Thank goodness. But Laci," his voice dropped, full of concern, "how are *you*?"

She realized that in all of that, she hadn't panicked. There was no dissociation, no frantic spiral, just a clear-headed focus on survival. She'd stayed alert and in the moment. "I stayed completely calm. I got us downstairs to the room, and then I followed Vincent's directions from there. Oh, and don't tell me you had no idea about Vincent's background."

That made him break his concern a bit, as he laughed. "I knew. Jack knows. That's it. Vincent specifically asked that we not reveal it, so we kept it quiet."

Laci smiled. "Well, Vincent has much explaining to do in the morning, but I'll make sure Charlie knows to keep it quiet."

There was a pause. "Are you alright sleeping there tonight without me?"

Laci whispered back to him, "I have a Navy SEAL sleeping next to our room. I think I'll be fine. Tai, I love you. I'm okay. I'll see you when you get home."

"Goodnight, Laci. I love you too."

TWENTY-ONE

THE ADRENALINE FROM THE overnight attack had worn off, leaving Charlie and Laci drained that morning. Vincent, on the other hand, looked as if he'd enjoyed a refreshing walk in the park. He was at the stove, the smell of bacon and eggs in the air. "Morning. Coffee is in the pot for you."

"You are a god," Charlie mumbled as he and Laci dragged to the counter.

The first few sips were enough to perk them up, and they began setting the table. Vincent dished up the food, and they all sat together. While swiping butter over his toast, Charlie turned to Vincent with a raised eyebrow. "So, how does a Navy SEAL end up working behind the bar in a small-town restaurant?"

Vincent swallowed the bite he had taken, pausing only a moment before answering. "I finished my time with the Navy and had no idea what to do, especially moving back here. Don't get me wrong, I love living here, but I kept thinking, 'What could go wrong that would require my skills?'"

Charlie and Laci shared a look and exchanged sardonic chuckles.

"Yeah," Laci said. "Then I moved to town."

Vincent smiled. "I'm starting to get that. Jack called me and mentioned that Tai needed unique help at Blackwood. I figured, what the hell. I could talk to Tai and see what this was about."

"The night you came in with Jack," Laci remembered.

"Yes. Tai filled me in, but I wasn't convinced at first. I was fine with the security part, but being a bar runner? Still, I started working with you all, and when the attack on you happened, Laci, I knew why Tai needed me. Then I met Charlie, and let's just say, I knew I'd found my place." Charlie grinned, and Vincent's expression softened.

Laci had to ask, "How much did Tai tell you about me for security purposes?"

Vincent's gaze softened with understanding. "Honestly, not much. Just that there had been attempts on your life, and he and Charlie couldn't be everywhere at once. He said he needed me as backup. It wasn't until we were coming to stay the night that Charlie filled me in a little more. But all he said was that you have a psycho ex-husband who won't leave you alone."

Charlie shrugged. "You said high-level. I figured it was just enough to get the point across."

Vincent's expression softened. "You don't need to tell me anything else, Laci. Details or not, I'll protect you to the best of my ability."

But he had to know. Laci gave him the condensed version, and Charlie went pale when she got to the attack at Blackwood, the memory still too fresh. "Last night's attack doesn't match what Nathan would do," she finished. "He believes he's smarter than me, but I've spent years learning his patterns. Plus, I can usually sense when he's near. It feels like this icy cold wave of danger."

"We had a name for that in training," Vincent said. "Situational awareness. It's when you're so pinned down you can't move a muscle. All you can do is feel the world around you, waiting for the moment it's safe to breathe again."

Charlie looked at them both. "I don't have that, but I never doubted her feelings."

Vincent grew thoughtful. "Now that I have a better picture, I have an idea. Some former military buddies of mine live around town. They'd be willing to help. With your permission, maybe I can have them keep an eye on things. In the meantime, Laci, you and I are going to do some defensive training."

He'd barely finished the thought when a sharp rattle from the garage door cut through the kitchen's quiet hum. Laci's breath caught in her throat. She looked to Vincent and Charlie, and they were smiling. "Go on, go look. It's safe."

Tai slipped through the door, his exhaustion from the red-eye flight weighing heavily on him. He'd needed to get home to Laci. He set his bags down and looked up to find her standing in the dining area, staring right at him.

After everything she'd endured last night, sleep-deprived and dressed in sweats with her hair piled in a messy bun, she was still the most beautiful woman he'd ever seen.

Then she gave him that smile, the one that made warmth bloom in his chest, and ran down the hall toward him. Tai caught her easily as she jumped, her legs wrapping around his waist, and kissed her deeply. The feel of her body in his arms and her lips on his chased away his deepest fears.

She pulled back, resting her head on his shoulder. "I missed you. I'm so glad you're home."

With her here, it is home.

Tai walked them toward the dining area, Laci still clinging to him.

"Uh, Tai," Charlie said. "It looks like you have a bit of a monkey problem."

He looked at Charlie. "I take it you didn't tell her I got an earlier flight."

Charlie smiled cheekily. "Nope! We wanted to see her face when you walked in."

"Well, I need to change, and I have a feeling she's not letting go." Laci shook her head against his shoulder. "We'll be right back."

Tai carried her upstairs, his self-control fraying with every step. He barely resisted slamming the bedroom door. He pinned her against the wall, his mouth crashing down on hers in a frantic kiss. *She's here. She's alive. She's safe.* The thought repeated in an attempt to calm the terror that had almost consumed him. He hooked his thumbs in the waistband of her pants and tugged, his urgency palpable.

Within moments, their clothes were a tangled heap on the floor. He lifted her, her legs wrapping around his waist as he slid into her heat. The warmth of her body silenced the chaos in his mind. He stilled, burying his face in the crook of her neck, and just breathed her in. The scent of her skin, the weight of her in his arms, the reality of her safety washed over him.

Leaning back just enough to see her eyes, Tai whispered against her lips, "No screaming, Laci-love. You don't want them to hear us."

Laci's fingers dug into his shoulders, her head thrown back against the wall. "Tai...I can't...you feel too good."

A low growl rumbled in his chest, a sound of both pleasure and warning. He fought to keep the pace slow, to savor the glide of her body around him. But her ragged breaths and the tiny tremors already starting deep inside her were shredding his restraint.

"I need this," he breathed, the words rough with emotion. "I need to feel you, right here, safe with me."

Laci held on, her body melting into his rhythm. He felt the exact moment her climax built, the subtle tightening of her muscles telling him she was close. Pressing his lips directly in her ear, he commanded in a low, rough tone, "Now, Laci-love. Let go for me."

As she shattered, he pressed his mouth hard to hers, swallowing her cry as his own release tore through him. He shuddered against her, both of them panting, her body lax and boneless against his. His voice was thick and unsteady. "I love you."

Her face was pressed into his shoulder, and her muffled reply was almost a sob. "I love you too."

Tai stayed like that for a long moment, memorizing the feeling of her in his arms. He slowly withdrew, letting her feet slide to the floor but keeping her caged against the wall with his body. He pushed the damp hair from her face, cupping her cheeks and pressing his forehead to hers. He gave her one last, tender kiss.

"Okay," he said softly, his breath ghosting over her lips. "Get yourself pulled together. I'll change, and we'd better get back down there before Charlie starts making obnoxious jokes."

Tai reluctantly let her go and turned for his closet.

Just as they reached the bottom of the stairs, Tai's phone rang. He answered, his voice tight. "Jack."

"Hey Tai, are you back?" Jack asked, sounding exhausted. "I need to come over and talk with all of you."

"Yeah, I'm home. We'll wait here."

When Jack knocked, Tai had just finished making a fresh pot of coffee. As they gathered around the kitchen table, coffee mugs in hand, Jack looked at each of them grimly. "Each of you has a different perspective on what happened. I need to hear it all, from all your points of view. Maybe then I can tie some of these pieces together."

Charlie started, replaying the events of the night, with Vincent and then Tai adding their parts. The different perspectives painted a clearer, more terrifying picture in Tai's mind.

When they were done, Jack looked through his notes. "This is what we gathered from the thugs. The worst thing on any of their records was a drug trafficking charge."

"Why would drug dealers want to ambush her?" Tai asked.

"They said they were hired by a messenger who paid them in cash. The messenger was supposed to tag along, but they figured he'd get in the way, so they sent him to trigger your alarms, hoping it would flush Laci out of the house."

"The guy in the back," Vincent concluded. "That was the messenger." He shook his head. "Seriously, that guy wasn't even worth our effort."

Jack agreed. "They were counting on Laci's terror to make her run. When nobody came out, they changed the plan and went in, assuming she was asleep inside."

Tai's jaw tightened. "I was watching the cameras. I saw the first four, then two more. That's when I called dispatch. I turned off the house alarm so it wouldn't chase them off before your guys got there."

"Right. Two others remained in the ambush spot to act as lookouts. They bailed when they saw us coming," Jack continued. "The six who entered the house couldn't find Laci. When they saw the unmade second bed and the luggage, they realized she wasn't alone as they had been told. They decided to cut and run, but we arrived before they could." He turned to Laci. "You said last night that this isn't how Nathan usually operates. Does any of this help?"

"The money has to be from Nathan," Laci murmured, her gaze distant. "And banking on me being terrified enough to run...that's definitely him."

Tai added, "What he wasn't ready for is how much work you've done. He hasn't seen how strong you've become. At Blackwood, he was sending a message to me."

"And since Vincent and I drove home with you two Saturday night," Charlie added, "they had no idea we were here."

"So, they weren't watching Blackwood anymore," Vincent weighed in. "They were watching the house. They would have seen four of us get into the car, but with the tinted windows, they only saw you and Laci."

Laci's eyes narrowed. "Whoever this is must have put a plan together in a hurry when they realized Tai was out of town."

Charlie shook his head. "Hiring goons, yeah, that's Nathan. But using street-level drug dealers to do it? Not his style."

"He's right," Laci said. "The last time, he hired professional killers. Even his drugs come from high-level suppliers. Nathan would never deal with street-level people. His money buys him a higher class of criminal."

"Their orders were to contain you and wait for instructions," Jack said, watching her closely. "Does that sound like Nathan?"

Charlie and Laci looked at each other, and both shook their heads. "No," Laci said. "The men who killed Leo just held me back. When they were finished, they left me with his body. They didn't take me with them." She saw Vincent flinch. That wasn't a detail they'd told him. "Nathan doesn't like other men handling me. He wants that for himself. Somebody else set this up using his money. They tried to get him what he wanted, but they lacked his precision and his access to better criminals." She looked up at Jack. "What about the guy who was asking about me around town?"

Jack pulled out a headshot, placing it on the table. "David Jansen. Police in Ohio tracked him down, but they can't get him to talk. He's terrified of Nathan's connections. He thinks talking is a death sentence."

"Not surprising," Laci said quietly. "I've seen his temper."

"His wife, on the other hand, was somewhat cooperative. She confirmed that he did work in logistics at your former company, Laci, and also did contract work on the side. Last year, he left the company to become a full-time contractor, as it offered a more lucrative opportunity. I confirmed that he switched about a month after Leo was killed."

Laci's brow knitted. "How is that connected? I'm not really following."

"His wife provided bank statements. He was receiving regular deposits for several years, then there were three major bumps." Jack turned to Charlie. "About when were your parents bribed?"

A muscle ticked in Charlie's cheek. "I don't know exact dates, it took almost an hour of me screaming at them for them to reveal the bribes in the first place. Best I can put together is a short time after Laci arrived here, and then right before my mother went into the hospital."

"Three deposits," Tai repeated. "Two bribes, and the money to travel here with the cover of taking his wife on vacation."

"Exactly." Jack continued. "There were charges from around here back when he was spotted in town asking questions, and then again recently, up until about the time of when Nathan attacked you. He got pulled over for speeding last night in Ohio."

"That's not the guy in the back yard," Vincent said quietly. "The guy I saw had dark hair and was neither tall nor thin."

A heavy silence fell over the table.

Tai broke it, his voice low. "So, it's Nathan's money and his obsession."

"But it's not his plan," Laci finished, a new chill running down her spine. "His money just pulled the strings."

Charlie looked from face to face. "Nathan has a puppet. And we have no idea who it is."

TWENTY-TWO

Tai met with Vincent's contacts to create a plan. To convince any locals that they had let their guard down, the security guys gradually returned to their usual schedule.

"I'm still not good with this. You are out in the open." Tai grumbled as they strolled through town.

Mrs. Peterson waved, her shuffle quickening as she approached them. Laci had to hold in a laugh when Tai spoke under his breath, "I'm pretty sure that woman has been in her nineties since I was a kid."

It had become a familiar routine on their strolls, someone asking to see the ring they'd heard about. Despite Tai hating that his personal life had been put out there, Laci reminded him that it worked as part of their plan to flush Nathan out.

The self-defense program that Vincent developed helped Laci gain strength, mobility, and defensive moves. Tai enjoyed watching her body tone from the morning workouts, but grumbled about how rough Vincent got with her and the new bruises.

One night in the shower, he held on to her as the hot water ran over her right shoulder. "Can you please move me back a little more?"

"This is getting to be too much. Your entire arm is black and blue, and you can't even lift it." Tai grabbed her hand, gently rotating it to help her loosen up her wrist. "Vincent needs to lighten up on you."

Laci tilted her head back. "No. He can't. And I don't want him to. There is a chance that Nathan will get his hands on me." She shushed him when he argued. "There will always be a chance, even if you hire a hundred men to protect me. I have to train for the worst-case scenario. He won't handle me with care, and you know it."

The late morning sun warmed the air on the day Tai picked to go out with Laci. The food carts surrounded the town square, where a band played and tourists and locals strolled. Tai's cart was running well, and his staff was keeping it stocked. Perusing a few of the other carts, Laci learned about the different offerings available in town. Tai seemed to relax, surprising her with random kisses as they browsed.

A cold, electric hum vibrated just under Laci's skin, the air suddenly thick and charged. Every nerve ending screamed a single, silent warning. *Danger*. He was here. He was watching. She forced her lips into a smile. "You know," she said, her voice a pitch higher than usual, "I'm suddenly craving a cupcake."

He saw the change in her expression and agreed. She put her hand in the back pocket of her jeans, and they moved toward the cake shop on the other side of the square, holding hands and smiling.

They entered the bakery, placed their order, and sat at a small table by the front window. Though Laci saw Tai's eyes flicker to the window, he feigned a relaxed smile, looking happy just to enjoy her company. Scratching the back of her neck, she couldn't get her body to stop vibrating. He was watching them from somewhere with a clear view of the square. They were still conversing and eating, but Laci was having difficulty keeping up. Tai did his best to cover, then leaned over and kissed her, gently holding his lips to hers. The contact brought a level of peace to her nerves.

The two cleaned up their wrappers, and Laci's skin crawled again as they stepped into the street. Something was wrong, very wrong. She couldn't get back to Blackwood fast enough. With her fingers entwined with Tai's, she tensed her hand to let him know. They couldn't walk any quicker, however. They had to look casual. A man stepped out of one of the shops and turned in front of them. He seemed to be walking in the same direction, so they slowed to stay behind him.

Tai asked Laci what she thought the lunch crowd level would be today. Looking around, she responded, "Given the number of people, I would say high. They will want to come in and cool off. But I think the storms predicted for tonight will probably keep our late diners low."

As she looked around, she spotted a couple behind them, also walking in the same direction. They were almost at Blackwood, with just three blocks to go. Laci's skin was on fire now. She was in imminent danger. It took everything in her not to sprint off.

When they turned the corner, she smiled and offered the suggestion, "It's much cooler here in the shade. It would be nice to have benches out here for customers to wait."

Tai looked at her. "I might have to think about that one."

The man in front of them kept walking as they reached the front door, and the couple behind followed them inside to sit at a table. Charlie was on edge. Vincent must have been keeping him informed.

"Laci, did you enjoy the stroll?" Charlie asked.

She grinned. "I did. Tai bought me a cupcake!"

"Well, because you're a carb monster, he knows how to keep you under control."

As Tai and Laci stepped through the kitchen doorway, she heard Tai add, "Well, it's one way." Charlie burst out laughing.

Tai and Laci made their way back to the office, closed the door, and Tai grabbed her in a hug. Laci's body shook uncontrollably. Holding in her reaction that long was too much.

He whispered in her ear, "Laci-love, you're safe. Take a breath." She took one breath. "Another, my love." She took another.

The shaking subsided. Tai held on to her.

Laci looked up at him. "He's beyond angry. We kicked the hornets' nest."

A knock sounded at the door. Tai opened it and let Vincent in. "They have all reported in and confirmed that there were no visuals on the ground. Wherever he was, he must have been inside and looking out. Good job on the signals, Laci. The team moved the moment you let them know."

Laci stopped and tried to play it all back in her head. "Vincent, he was up higher. He was looking down on us. I felt as if, at one point, a sniper would hit me. When Philip stepped out in front of us and slowed our pace, it built rapidly. Even with the two guards behind us, by the time we got to the movie theater, I wanted to run."

Vincent looked guilty. "At least now we have confirmation that he's in town. Rooftops were clear, so he must be watching from an upstairs window."

Tai's arms tightened around her. "Vincent, we can't-"

"We have to, Tai," Vincent interrupted. "I promise I don't want to do this, but we must appear as if we're not on to him. Laci has to be out front. I'll update the team to look at the windows. And I'll let Jack know Nathan is still in town."

Vincent left the office and closed the door behind him.

It took Tai and Laci a little longer to cool down and prepare for the crowds. Tai's act was more challenging, but Charlie helped them as they made their way out front.

"Hey, Sugar Daddy, when are you going to buy me a cupcake?"

Vincent turned to Charlie and responded in a deadpan tone, "If you want one, I'll give you a cupcake."

Tai and Laci both started laughing from either side of the kitchen window.

The lunch crowd came and went. Concentrating on serving customers helped everyone. The team reset, and then it was time for dinner. By dusk, they had a line out to the street waiting for tables. Laci stepped out of the kitchen on one of her rotations and spotted Mark in the queue.

Sliding behind Vincent, she spoke low, "Charlie, discreetly describe Mark to Vincent. He's halfway back in the line. We need to let him in without a scene. Tai can't react."

As Charlie described Mark, she pretended to do tasks that took her closer and closer to the kitchen and farther from the front door. The last thing they needed tonight was Mark's shenanigans. They had enough on their plates. On her next rotation, Laci crouched down, working the lower part of the bar next to Charlie. Vincent was at the tables, but heading back.

Under his breath, she heard him say, "High-top right."

While washing dishes, she moved her head as naturally as possible and caught Mark out of the corner of her eye. He was staring straight at her. When it was time to rotate to the bar, Laci came out from the kitchen but only scanned the tables on the left side of the room. Tai stepped behind her, grabbed a glass, and filled it with water for himself. He leaned over for a kiss, and she gave him one. He looped his arm around her, kissed her again, and whispered, "I'll avoid that side for now. You keep avoiding eye contact."

Pretending that he had said something funny, she laughed and kissed him again, going on her toes to whisper in his ear, "Got it," before returning to the kitchen.

Among all of them, Vincent was the one who could freely move around the place and gather information to determine if Mark was going to cause an additional problem for them tonight. To Mark, Vincent was just another staff member. Charlie, Tai, and Laci were known enemies. They kept up the act. Vincent and Laci maintained their rotation, and Charlie remained busy with the people directly at the bar. Each time she scanned the room close enough to see Mark in her peripheral vision, she could see his anger and frustration grow.

When Vincent came behind the bar again after serving Mark his food, he whispered to Laci, "He hasn't taken his eyes off of you for more than a moment. The lust he has for you is overwhelming, and I can't believe you have the strength to stay out here in his range. Your skin must be crawling."

She squatted down with supplies behind the bar, restocking the shelf next to Vincent's legs. "It is crawling. I want to go back and hide in the office, but I have to stay out here to keep him as under control as possible. I have all of you to watch my back out here."

A ragged sigh of relief escaped Laci's lips the moment the door swung shut behind Mark. She planned to stay where Tai could see her, just in case, but now she could move around more freely. Vincent came into the kitchen, dialing his phone.

Vincent looked at her as the other person picked up the line. "Jack, yeah. Mark is the puppet."

Her heart nearly stopped. She stood there listening as Vincent ran down the details about seeing the text messages on Mark's phone and even overhearing a call he'd taken. Plus, Vincent was the only one to see the dancer in the backyard on the night of the break-in and confirmed it was Mark.

Not only were there two known predators hunting her, but they were now working together. She and the others couldn't do anything about it. They had to keep moving with the dinner rush. Laci quickly stopped in the office and then reappeared on the floor. Tai was looking for her because she had missed her rotation. As she stepped back out behind the bar, she gave him a calm smile, and he visibly relaxed.

As expected, the crowds dwindled early, given the rumbles of thunder outside. Tai let the bulk of the staff go early and was able to convince Vanessa and Benji to leave as well. As the four of them wrapped up the closing tasks, they repeatedly tried to get in touch with Jack, but he wasn't answering their calls or returning their texts.

"I'll go out and take a look around," Vincent said quietly. "Lock the door behind me."

They all watched in awe as Vincent disappeared into the night, a flash of lightning not giving them any sight of him. One moment he was there, and then he was gone. Laci paced the central walkway, unease making her skin crawl. A light rap on the glass door made her jump.

Charlie opened the door, and Vincent stepped in. "Looped around and didn't see anything. I checked over your car and didn't see anything wrong with it. We can get in the car and leave here. Charlie and I will stay at your place tonight."

Agreeing, they all stepped out, and Tai locked the door. A low rumble of thunder rolled over them as they approached the back lot. The air hung still and humid, awaiting the storm to clear it out. Now out from the safety of the building, Laci's senses started going off like a firehouse alarm.

"No," she breathed, her fingers digging into Tai's arm, her voice a raw, desperate whisper. "Tai, we have to go back. *Now*."

"We're almost to the car, it's closer," Charlie whispered in her ear. He wrapped an arm around her shoulders.

Laci looked back over her shoulder and saw the figures in the back alley. "Oh god no."

"Where do you think you're going?" Nathan called out from the darkness.

Instantly, Vincent and Tai formed a wall between the men and Laci. Behind her, Charlie wrapped an arm around her waist, ready to pull her clear.

Tai took a step forward. "This isn't going to end the way you want it to."

"It's either going to end with me taking her, or a whole lot of blood." Nathan sneered. He motioned with his head, and Mark pulled out a gun, aiming it directly at Tai.

Nathan charged towards Tai, a meaty fist flying right at him. Tai was able to dodge to the right in a smooth motion despite his size. Laci flinched at the sickening thud of Nathan's fist hitting Tai's shoulder, but Tai's stance barely shifted.

Meanwhile, with Mark distracted, whipping between the fight and Laci and Charlie, Vincent was able to silently get up close enough to grab Mark's wrist and twist it, causing Mark to drop the gun. As Vincent moved to gain control of the weapon, Mark pulled a taser from his pocket and jammed it into Vincent's neck. A blue spark lit the darkness as Vincent's body locked up and he dropped to the pavement.

"Vincent!" Charlie cried out. He took an instinctive step toward his partner before forcing himself back to Laci's side. He wouldn't leave her.

With Vincent convulsing on the pavement, Mark scrambled for the fallen gun.

Tai threw one hard punch into Nathan's side. Nathan roared and fell backward into the brick wall. When Tai turned to get back to Laci and Charlie, Mark's arm swung up.

Three sharp cracks echoed off the brick, brutally loud in the sudden silence. Laci's world fractured. She saw the impact, the way Tai's body jerked, a marionette with its strings cut. His eyes, fixed on hers for a split second, went vacant before he crumpled to the pavement. A soundless scream tore from her throat, the world dissolving into a black-and-white nightmare.

"No!" She took a step towards Tai, but Charlie pulled her back. "Don't stop me! Don't make me watch again! Let me go!" She fought against Charlie's arms, pushing and clawing, but he held her against him like a vice.

Vincent pushed up from the ground, getting to his knees. Mark turned and fired three more shots directly into Vincent's chest. His body convulsed and went back down hard.

"You need to go now," Charlie whispered to her. "You need to live." He pushed her towards the car, moving forward to put himself between her and the men.

Everything in her refused to run. She couldn't leave them here to die.

"Laci, if you run, I'll kill him." Mark's sinister words echoed through the space.

Looking up, she saw the gun pointed right at Charlie's head.

"Laci, go." Charlie calmly commanded. "Get in the car and go."

Mark moved his finger to the trigger.

"I'll go with you!" Laci called out in tears. "Leave him alone, and I'll go with you."

"Laci, don't do this," Charlie called out to her. "Just go."

"I can't," she could barely talk now. "I can't lose you, too."

Nathan's huge hand wrapped around her wrist, pulling her to him. His other hand clamped over her mouth and nose. A foul, bitter liquid spilled onto her tongue, the taste overwhelming her as it coated her throat. There was a sudden, sharp pinch in the side of her hip, and as blackness swallowed her, her last conscious thought was of Tai and Vincent, their faces already burning and fading into static behind her eyes. As blackness took her, his whisper coiled in her ear, "I told you that you're mine."

TWENTY-THREE

THE SOUNDS OF DISTANT sirens filtered into the void. Tai let out a groan at the pain radiating through his upper body. Attempting to push off his stomach and roll to his back caused fire to cascade through his ribs.

"Oh my god, Tai!" Charlie's voice was a choked sob. "We thought... We saw you go down. We thought you were dead." Hands gently lifted his shoulder and hip, giving him momentum to roll over. "How are you alive?"

Tai opened his eyes, staring up into the darkness as a flash of lightning traveled across the clouds. Breathing felt impossible, the weight around his body seeming to hold him together at this point. Red and blue lights ricocheted off the buildings around him, the sound of engines filling the silent lot.

Charlie's face appeared above him, his eyes puffy and bloodshot, raw with a devastation that stole Tai's breath. "I thought you were dead. Mark shot you and Vincent."

As if saying his name resurrected him from the grave, Tai heard Vincent swearing a blue streak. Charlie scrambled to his feet and disappeared, calling to his partner.

Booted feet rapidly approached, a stranger's face above him, flashlights moving around his body. "Hey there, we are going to take care of you. Can you tell me what happened?"

Hands now moved over his head and limbs.

"Shot." Tai coughed out.

"You were shot? Where were you hit?" The medic asked.

"Back."

Hands rolled Tai to his side. Unable to hold it back, he let out a roar of pain.

"I see three holes but-"

"He's got a vest on. We both had one on." Vincent's voice carried.

Rolled back, the hands now quickly pulled off his shirt, and the straps of the vest were undone. The moment the pressure was released, Tai tried to take in a deep breath, but the pain still radiated through him.

Tai turned his head to see Vincent standing by him, using one hand on Charlie's shoulder to hold him steady. "Laci?"

Charlie shattered. "They have her."

Rage, pure and cold, flooded the pain from his mind. "Up." He demanded. "Get me up."

"Whoa there." The medic tried to put a hand on his chest to keep him down. "You're not going anywhere. Your vest saved your life, but your insides are rattled. You need to be evaluated."

"They will kill her if we don't find them. My injuries can wait. Get. Me. Up." Finally taking the hint that he wasn't going to cooperate, the medics helped Tai sit up and then got him to his feet.

"At least let us check you over in the ambulance. If you have any broken ribs, that could puncture a lung."

"Fine. But I want to talk to the cops while you do that." Tai saw an officer approaching. "Where is Sergeant Mathison?"

The cop followed the group to the ambulances. Vincent sat down in one, Tai went to the other, the sharp smell of antiseptic and cleaning agents wiping away the humid air outside. "Sergeant Mathison's tied up on another scene. He told us to get the full report from you."

"What happened is we were attacked by my fiancé's ex-husband and his lackey. They took her from us, and they will torture and kill her if we don't find her." Tai kept his voice civil by the thinnest of threads. He wanted to tear apart everything within a fifty-mile radius, starting with Mark's apartment.

A female voice chirped codes over the radio as the officer stepped away for a moment. When he came back, there was a new determination to his face. "We have reinforcements coming in, and while we wait for them, I need you to tell me every detail you can of the attack."

As he spoke, the medic finished listening to his chest. "Breath sounds are clear and equal. Vitals are stable for now. I don't feel any obvious displaced fractures, but you're going to have some spectacular bruising."

"Thanks." Tai pulled his undershirt back over his head. "Are you done?"

"If you aren't going to the hospital with us," the medic continued, "then we need you to read this and sign at the bottom. It says you understand that refusing transport could lead to permanent injury or death."

Tai grabbed the pen, scribbled his signature at the bottom, and carefully climbed out of the back to where Charlie and Vincent now stood. He opened his mouth to give an order, to get them moving, but the haunted look in Charlie's eyes stopped him. The earlier words echoed in his mind. *"We saw you go down. We thought you were dead."*

Ice flooded his veins. Laci. Laci believed he was dead. She had been forced to watch it happen all over again. The thought of her breaking under the weight of that repeated horror was more painful than any bullet.

Don't give up, Laci-love. Wherever you are, keep fighting.

He shoved the thought aside, forcing himself back into the moment. "Let's get everybody inside," he said, his voice rough. "It's about to pour. We need to find her. Fast."

⛰

The world was a heavy darkness. It felt like being stuck underwater in a vast ocean at night without knowing which way was up. A primal part of Laci's mind screamed that she wasn't safe, though she couldn't remember why. They had finished up for the night, cleaned up, and then there was a haze of memory of stepping out the door, but then it was blank. Little by little, the heaviness lifted. She knew she was breathing fine, not drowning, so this was letting her mind clear, like when taking the sleeping meds.

Soon, she returned to her body, and she was able to start taking stock. As far as Laci could tell, all of her clothing was still on her body, undisturbed. Her arms, though, were at an odd angle in front of her, and it took time to realize that someone had tied her wrists. She was a bit dizzy, still making her way from the blackness, but she could tell she wasn't injured anywhere. A distant clap of thunder told her she was inside, but not far from the exterior.

Concentrate. Keep your breathing slow and steady. The cold of the surface Laci was lying on registered through her body. It wasn't soft, like a mattress, but solid and somewhat rough, like a concrete floor. The air smelled faintly of cleaning products. She sensed Nathan wasn't near, but was she alone? She held her breath, listening. The room was silent, with no other breathing or small movements. Opening her eyes a crack to assess her situation, she could now see she was facing a cinderblock wall, but not on the floor. It was a raised platform protruding from the wall.

The silence was broken, shattered by the sound of two men arguing in the distance, their footsteps echoing closer. Laci closed her eyes and concentrated on keeping her breathing even and slow. Until she could figure out a plan, they had to believe that she was still unconscious.

"Man, she's been out this whole time. You could have fucked her three times by now," the first male voice complained.

"How many times do I have to explain this to you? Fucking moron. It's not just her body. I need her mind too. When I take her, I want to break her." *Nathan.* Laci worked hard to keep from reacting to his voice. She kept her attention on her breathing.

"I have no problem fucking a drugged bitch. Maybe I can warm her up for you." That was Mark.

A dull thud echoed in the distance. Laci cringed, the familiar sound pushing her back to the memories of Nathan's heavy fists. "Nobody else can have her."

Laci's senses were on high alert. He must be in the room. She couldn't move or give away that she was awake. A hand groped between her legs, but she continued to breathe steadily, and her muscles remained relaxed.

Nathan's anger increased. "She's still fucking out. How much did you give her?"

"Exactly what you told me."

"Fucking lightweights, can't handle anything." She heard two distinct sets of footsteps as they left the room.

The echo of their footsteps faded. Silence pressed in, thick and heavy. Laci counted to sixty, forcing her breathing to remain slow, even. Every instinct screamed at her to move, but she waited. Finally, she risked opening her eyes. Empty. Now. The time was now.

Laci looked at the bindings on her wrists. They were made of rope and looped through an eye hook in the wall. Scooting herself up so that her arms were down straight, she could get her fingers into her jeans and underwear. Grabbing the pocket knife she'd hidden against her belly, Laci flicked open the blade and got to work, cutting quickly enough to get detached from the wall so she could flip around and sit up. Tiptoeing slowly to the door, she peeked out, looking right and left.

There were long hallways with multiple doors, reminiscent of a school, and another hallway lay straight ahead. When they left, Laci heard their footsteps go to the right. If she ran left, she might be visible when they came back, so she ran straight ahead. Keeping her footfalls as soft as possible to avoid her shoes squeaking on the linoleum floor, Laci stuck to the walls where the shadows were darkest. She kept working the knife against her bindings as she moved and finally got through the first strand.

This hallway connected to another long one that led either to the right or left. This time, turning left, Laci hoped it would have a door to the outside at the end. Needing to get her hands free to fight, she turned her concentration to the bindings on her wrists again. After working the knife back and forth, they snapped free so Laci could bundle them up and shove them in a garbage can. She closed her knife and stuck it back against her belly.

In the darkness, she could make out an exterior door and picked up her speed. A flash of lightning illuminated the hallway, revealing the chain and padlock binding the door handles. *No!* It shattered her hope for an escape. The next option was a window, so she ducked into a nearby classroom. However, the windows were narrow, tilt-in type, and there wasn't enough space for her body to fit through. Rain ran down the glass like a waterfall, and a clap of thunder shook the panes.

The voices returned, echoing from the area where she escaped. "You fucking idiot, I told you to tie her to the wall!"

"I did!"

"Find her now!"

"Where am I going to put you?" *Put him?*

"Leave me here. There is no way she could have gotten out. The only exit was past us." *Well, shit.* "Look inside closets and bathrooms. She's probably balled up somewhere, barely breathing." *That's what you think, asshole.*

Tall cabinets lined two walls in this classroom. There was barely enough space for Laci to lie between the top of them and the ceiling. She closed the door to match the others down the hallway. Hearing Mark's stomping footsteps, there wasn't much time. She stepped up on a filing cabinet and hopped up, slinking her body into the tight space. As she pulled herself up, she heard him approaching this hallway. She lay face down, flattening her body on top of the cabinet as much as possible, moving against the wall so she wasn't visible from the front side of it. Legs up and tucked, hair tucked in, and arms tucked in now, she had to wait, hoping the storm wouldn't reveal her position.

He was across the hall. Laci could hear him opening every door and cabinet, and her heart raced. *Keep it cool. You can do this.*

Laci-love, breathe. Her mind conjured the reminder in Tai's voice.

Oh god, Tai. A flash of him falling. *Don't think about it.* Vincent crumbling to the pavement. Charlie's scream. *Breathe.* Mark stepped into the room. *Hold it in.* His heavy, stomping steps crossed the room.

Laci-love, breathe. She took slow, silent breaths. *That's it, keep breathing.*

Mark checked the cabinets at the back of the room, then turned to the ones she was on.

The first door opened at Laci's feet. *Silent breath in.*

The next one was by her knees. *Silent breath out.*

The next one was by her hips. *Silent breath in.*

Then, the one by her middle. *Silent breath out.*

Her shoulders. *Silent breath in.*

Her head. *Silent breath out.*

He stopped moving. *Why isn't he moving?* Stars formed behind her closed eyes.

"Laci-love, take a breath."

Laci took one long, silent breath and held it. The seconds felt endless. Finally, he walked out of the room, but she didn't dare move a muscle. The steps were outside the classroom. She let her breath out silently and then pulled another one in. That's when the storm lit up the room. *Thank you for waiting.*

The steps were now moving away. "Man, she's not hiding down this fucking hallway."

"Then check another. Do I have to do all the thinking for you? If you hadn't fucked up so many times, we wouldn't be here." Nathan snapped. *He's unraveling.* This only made him more dangerous.

Laci's body wanted to run, and she also wanted to climb down and stab the ever-loving hell out of them, but she stayed put and stayed still. Mark's footsteps moved further away. As long as she could hear him moving, she knew she was clear. Slowly, she lowered herself off the cabinet. At the door, she stopped to listen. The two of them were arguing on the far side of the building again.

Moving silently, she searched for an interior room. The storm outside was too much of a risk to illuminate the exterior spaces, and she knew she was lucky Mark hadn't seen her in the last room. Laci tested one closed door, blowing out a breath when it opened. In the dimness of the exit sign over the door, she could see it was a file room with rows of shelves filled with boxes.

Quietly moving halfway down the rows, she picked a wide set of double shelves. Using the frames as a step, Laci quickly pulled herself onto the top. These weren't as high as the cabinet in the classroom, but they were still much taller than Mark. Once again, she tucked herself into a long, narrow form, arms in, legs in, and lay face down to concentrate on her breathing. She knew this cat-and-mouse game only bought her time before the cops found her, if they even knew how to track her. She was trapped with only one way out of the building, requiring her to pass Nathan and Mark.

Since the two psychopaths knew she was trapped, Nathan wouldn't let Mark stop searching for her. If Nathan wanted her, he would get her. She knew this all too well. He used it to win her over in college, and then turned it into a weapon against her when he started using drugs. But maybe somehow she could wait for them to move to a different area of the building and then make a dash for the door.

Footsteps again sounded in the hallway. Laci's heart rate picked up, but she focused on her breathing, staying steady, silent, and slow. He was in the classroom where she was last. She imagined Tai wrapped around her, keeping her safe. The door to the file room opened. Laci turned inward, unmoving, keeping her breath as slow and silent as possible, in and out, in and out. She listened to him step past the shelf she was on, his heavy footsteps letting her know how close he was. He went down to the end, around the far side, and back up the other side. The door to the room closed hard, but Laci didn't hear Mark's footsteps in the hallway. Her body tensed, but she kept silent.

A hand grabbed her and pulled her off the shelf. "Got you!"

The fall from that height was brief since she was quickly wrapped in arms and pulled against a body. One hand was squeezing her throat, and an arm pinned Laci up against a sizable male frame. She tried to thrash, but the hand on her throat squeezed tighter. Oh god, the more of a fight she put up, the more turned on he became. She could feel him hardening against her back. She stopped thrashing and saw stars. He was cutting off too much of her air.

His breath was panting fast in her ear. "Maybe I should fuck you right here before I take you back to him. I know I could slide into you hard and fast before he even knows what I'm doing."

She didn't even have the strength now to shake her head, and her body was running out of oxygen. When he let go of her throat, there was a moment of terror, believing Mark was going to do what he suggested, but instead, he opened the door. She was able to get in two breaths before his tight grip returned as he dragged her down the hallway. With each of his steps, her vision got darker.

"If you kill her, I'll cut off your balls and shove them down your throat," Nathan growled down the hall. Mark barely released his hand, enough that Laci could breathe again.

"Bring her here." Mark dragged Laci closer to Nathan as ordered.

Just the thought of Nathan putting his hands on her made Laci's skin crawl. Forced inches from him, the victorious grin across his face sent ice down her spine. Nathan grabbed her left hand, and she felt a ring placed on her finger.

He raised her hand in front of her face. "Now I have what is rightfully mine again. I'll have the body and mind in a moment, too."

Laci fought the urge to puke. It was a replica of her wedding set, including the huge, gaudy diamond on a wide, diamond-encrusted band that scratched her fingers just like the original had.

Nathan grabbed Mark's shoulder, limping as he clutched an arm against his side. The stab wound she had given him months ago. It must have been agonizing, especially if he hadn't treated it properly. He must have been seeking out doctors for help, which was why they couldn't find him. And that is precisely where Tai had punched Nathan, on that side.

Mark carried Laci to what appeared to be the gym. *No, no, no, no!* On a desk sat a cell phone, the camera lens facing the center of the room. Bile rose in her throat when she realized how bad this was going to be. Mark dragged her to the center and turned to face the phone while Nathan picked it up, typed into it, then set it back down. She scanned for an exit, her hope sinking as she saw the thick chain and padlock binding the external door.

She could barely see Nathan sitting to the side, in the shadows. *Was he shooting up?* Yes. She saw the moment the drugs took effect. His face relaxed, and then a familiar mask fell into place. Pure hatred and rage. He stood, and Laci flashed back in her past of him coming after her. *Stay in the moment. You have to focus.*

"What the fuck do you think you're doing?" Nathan roared.

Mark's grip on her lessened slightly. "You told me not to let her escape."

Nathan charged at them and grabbed Mark by the throat. His fist went right into Mark's face over and over again. "Nobody touches her but me!" He released Mark, and the body dropped to the floor, blood pouring from his nose and mouth.

Before she could run, Nathan turned around, grabbed Laci's face, and licked her cheek. The look in his eyes told her that all semblance of sanity was gone. He wanted control again, and he was going to take it.

A low hum of voices filled Blackwood, the noise raking against Tai's frayed nerves. Charlie kept himself busy serving coffee to the techs that Jack's captain woke and sent over to the restaurant. The entire team came in carrying laptops, screens, and radios. A huge, laminated map of the valley was taped to the front window. Sheets of rain rolled down the glass behind it, washing out the town and trapping them all in the bubble of the restaurant.

Tai paced his office, Jack's latest update not doing much to help calm him. "I've been on the phone with the cops back in their hometown," Jack said, "the prison, and even the prosecutor. I'm trying to get anything possible on how Nathan thinks and where he might go."

"But he's not from around here." Tai reminded him.

"Yes, but guys like him have a set pattern," Jack replied. "Everybody said the same thing, that he has to have control. That means he would be using Mark's knowledge of the area, but Mark is just the tool. Nathan's telling him exactly what to look for."

"So where would Mark go?" Tai asked.

"We're on our way now to his parents' house. I'm hoping they can give us some ideas on possible favorite hang-out spots that Mark had growing up, or something to give us a clue."

Now, Tai laid out a spread of food on the bar for the team to eat and keep themselves fueled. It wasn't the full menu, just items he could offer as snacks from the remnants of the week's leftovers, but it seemed to be enough. He'd carefully watched as techs would approach the map, placing small X's on some locations as law enforcement eliminated hiding spots.

"Sir, I may have something," a female tech called out from the back corner. Two men and Vincent approached her. "I've been working on tracing her phone, figuring that even if they took it from her, it might give a direction at least to where they would have dropped it."

"A breadcrumb," the lieutenant said.

"Exactly. Except I have one solid ping from this tower when she was first taken, but nothing after." Tai could see her screen change as he approached. "I just got a faint hit, actually, more like echoes."

"Well, we at least have a possible direction. They went away from the city, which is what we expected." The lieutenant sounded defeated. "It doesn't give us enough to go on."

"Not necessarily." Vincent's voice stopped them all. He got up and walked to the map. "Your ghost signal hit this tower and this one." He made two red circles. "I know this area, several high ridges and deep valleys. We had a similar issue in Afghanistan. Signals reflect off of these ridges, causing an error in calculating the phone's location. We need to focus on this area here."

The lieutenant shook his head. "Vincent, that's a hundred square miles of forest and four towns. I can't have my guys kicking in doors based on a ghost signal."

As Vincent was about to argue his point, Tai's phone buzzed in his pocket. The notification of the text showed a blocked number. The message read, "Watch me take her from you."

Hands shaking, he clicked on the notification, watching as the text message came up with a link. A rock of pure dread formed in his stomach. The chatter in the room seemed to fade to a distant hum.

"Tai, what is it?" Charlie quietly asked from beside him. "No." He read the message.

"I have to know," he said quietly.

His thumb inched up to the screen, hovering momentarily before he clicked it. A website displayed a black rectangle with a spinning blue circle. With each rotation, Tai's vision blacked out to that one pinpoint spot on the screen. He felt his heart beat in time to it.

When the feed cleared, the air left his lungs. Laci. She stood in the center of the frame, pinned tight against Mark, whose hand was wrapped around her throat. Somehow, by the way she was standing there, Tai could feel her determination. Her eyes were focused on a spot behind the camera, but he could see her determination to stay calm and focused.

"Tai, look," Charlie's voice broke him out of his tunnel vision. "You can just barely make out a clock on the wall. It's right now. This is live."

Vincent rushed to Tai's side, looking over his shoulder. Now that Charlie pulled Tai's focus from Laci's face, he saw other details in the dim light around them. The lights reflected off what had to be windows high up on the wall. The room was vast, with a slatted, glossy wood floor, and about ten feet behind Laci and Mark were painted blue lines.

"It's a gym," Tai concluded.

Vincent moved fast. "Her signal is weak because it's in a building made of cinderblock. Get all locations in this area that could have a gym. Rec centers, schools, anything you can think of.

When Laci's eyes changed, Tai caught it. "Something is happening." He quickly moved around the bar to the group, Charlie right by his side, not taking his eyes off the phone. Then they all watched in horror as Nathan stepped into the frame, his fists clenched. His roar of anger overwhelmed the phone's mic as he charged at Laci and Mark, one fist landing squarely in Mark's face, again and again. They watched as Mark crumpled into a bloody heap. Then, Nathan turned, his predatory eyes focused on Laci.

Tai's thumb stabbed the screen, killing the feed. He couldn't watch another second. "I can't just sit here." He stormed back to his office to grab his keys.

"Tai, you can't go in there yourself!" The lieutenant called after him.

Keys in hand, he looked to Charlie and Vincent on his way to the door. "We're going. We'll be in the area, ready to move the second they get a location." He looked back at the lieutenant. "Find her."

Keeping as rag doll as possible with her eyes straight ahead, Laci knew Nathan would ramp up faster if she gave any visible fear reaction on her face. That's what Nathan wanted. It repulsed her to have him touch her, but for now, she had to tolerate it.

Laci slowly walked her fingers up to the waist of her jeans. Nathan pulled his head back a bit, and her hand froze. He leaned in and licked the other side of her face. She swept her thumb in her underwear and under the knife. When her fingers solidly wrapped around the warm handle, Laci pulled the knife free. There was one chance to do this quickly before he heard it and reacted.

One deep, centering breath, *for Tai, for Vincent, for Charlie*, and she moved. The knife snapped open with a sharp click. She didn't aim for a killing blow. She aimed to maim. To create an opening. She drove the blade deep into the soft flesh of his side, twisting as Vincent had taught her. Nathan made a wet, gurgling sound, his grip spasming on her face, pain turning his eyes feral. His fingers were digging in harder, making it unbearably painful. Yanking the handle toward her, she ripped the blade through his flesh.

Laci pulled the knife out and turned it in her hand for another attack. Nathan was still standing, still holding on to her face with his body pressed to the front of hers. The drugs were holding him up. She could feel the warm wetness of his blood seeping into the front of her clothes.

The last flicker of sanity in his eyes died, replaced by pure rage. "You bitch," he snarled. "You'll pay for that." His hand on her face twisted viciously, and white-hot pain shot down her neck.

"I don't think so!" She swung her free hand up and nailed him in the Adam's apple with her lower palm.

A choked, gurgling sound tore from Nathan's throat. His hand flew to his neck, his grip on her finally breaking.

She turned to run, but her head yanked backward, sending a searing pain across her scalp. Nathan had grabbed

Laci's hair to try to pull her back into him, so she spun and slashed. She ended up getting his neck. With a grip still on her hair, as he fell, he took her down. No matter how hard she pulled, his grip held fast in her hair. The drugs were energizing him. The smell of blood was overpowering, nearly making her gag. It pooled on the floor, growing with every second, and she was now sliding in it with her struggles. He couldn't have that much left in him.

"Let go of me!" She made one final move and sliced his wrist. His hand released.

She flipped over on her hands and knees and crawled away toward the door. *I need to get out. I need to get to the door.* As she progressed, a hand grabbed her ankle and yanked her backward, causing her to fall flat and almost smack her face on the floor. Then, an arm grabbed her around her waist. Her mind was confused as to how Nathan could still be moving until she realized, *Mark.*

He yanked her under him, pushing her flat to the floor. Laci looked over her shoulder, expecting to see rage, but instead saw uncontrolled animalistic lust in his eyes. *Oh god, the violence was a turn-on for him too.* Rising to one knee, Mark pulled her up, and his fingers grabbed at the top of Laci's jeans and tugged. She couldn't swing her arm back to stab him with enough force. She took a breath to clear her head and think.

Come on, you know how to do this. Vincent trained you. When he shifted his arms to try to undo her jeans, she took her opportunity. She dropped, using his momentum against him, twisting her body down and out of his grasp. As her shoulder hit the slick floor, she hooked her legs around his torso, just as she'd done with Vincent a hundred times on the mats. With a surge of adrenaline, she squeezed and rolled, throwing his larger body off balance. He hit the floor with a sickening, wet smack. She scissored her legs, her thighs like a vice, pinning him.

"I'm done with you, too!" Before he could move, Laci sat up and swung the knife down hard with both hands into his chest.

She pulled it out and put her hands behind her on the floor to push herself back and get her legs out from around him. But Mark was still moving. He rolled to his belly and smiled, blood trickling from his mouth as one arm reached for her. Laci tried to get up and run, but the blood made her shoes slick on the floor. Crawling across the cold wood until she hit the hall where a rug runner lay, she kept her eyes forward.

Get to the door. Just a little further. Laci grabbed the wall and stood up. As she held on to the wall, her feet faltered, and she tripped but caught herself and stayed up. *Come on, you can do this. Make it to the door.* Not knowing if Mark and Nathan were dead scared the hell out of her. *You have to get away before they come after you.* Looking back, she couldn't see anybody, but the fear still kept her adrenaline high. Another step, but when she tried to move her legs again, she couldn't go any further. The knife dropped from her hand. She fell to her knees.

Tears fell now, fearing she would never see her family again. She had fought. She thought she had won. And she was going to die here on this filthy floor. The thought was a final, quiet surrender as darkness flooded her vision. Her arm came up instinctively, a final, futile gesture to shield her face as she fell.

TWENTY-FOUR

YELLOW POLICE TAPE BLOCKED off the parking lot. When Tai pulled up, a cop approached his window. "This is an active scene. I'm gonna have to ask you to leave."

There was no way Tai was backing down. "It's my fiancé they have in there."

"Mr. Jackson?" The cop asked. "Can I see some ID?" Tai quickly pulled his wallet from his pocket, handing the cop his driver's license. "Sergeant Mathison has given you clearance to come in. Let me get some help to lift the tape, and you can pull in and park off to that side."

As Tai pulled past the tape, he noted the police cars and SWAT vehicles filling the lot, not a single one of them with their lights on.

"They run dark, so nobody inside can be alerted to their presence," Vincent said quietly.

"Can we get out? I can't sit back here anymore." Charlie asked from the back seat.

Vincent opened his door and climbed out, Tai and Charlie following on their side of the SUV. The noises outside the vehicle were quite different from the silence they had been in. Radios chirped, boots stomped, and there was a constant clank and rattle of men gearing up.

In moments, the cacophony of noise from the team gearing up dropped to silence. The group stood there, listening to one man give entry instructions before they moved in. Tai wanted to open the video feed to check on what was happening to Laci, but he couldn't bring himself to do so. Again, he scanned the dark windows for any sign that the three of them could be in there, but nothing moved. The fear that this wasn't the right place and that they were expending valuable time tightened his chest.

With one hand signal, the air changed. The team moved toward the door as a unit, and the heightened concentration and adrenaline were palpable. Swiftly pulling open the doors, the men disappeared into the building before the blink of an eye. Tai and Charlie stood there watching. Vincent moved up with the remaining officers outside to gather information.

The world around them stopped. Tai's every breath felt like an eternity. He was waiting for anything to tell him that Laci was inside and that she was alive. Despite the vehicles, radios, and remaining officers outside, Tai stood in a bubble of silence. His entire life depended on what they found in that building. He focused on the door where the teams disappeared.

That was until Vincent turned to look back at Tai and Charlie, nodding his head. They had the correct building. Laci was inside. But was she alive? Was she hurt?

Charlie's relieved cry broke through the night. Seeing his partner in distress, Vincent took a step toward them. Suddenly, his feet stopped, and his head whipped back to the officer beside him. After listening, he jogged to Tai.

"Tai, they found her," he said, his voice grave. "They want you to go in." He pointed to the door where an officer in full gear stood waiting. "You will follow him in and have to stick right with him. Don't move or look anywhere else."

Nodding, Tai didn't hesitate. He started jogging toward the officer. No matter what happened in there, Tai would not let Laci go. He would help her through this.

The officer blocked Tai from entering. "I need you to follow me and stay in the center of the hall, got it?" He agreed. He would do whatever it took to get to her, so he could see that she was alive. The officer turned and reentered the building. As Tai entered the hall, cops were moving everywhere. There was a heavy smell of iron in the otherwise stale air. The officer he followed stopped, turned, and motioned for Tai to move more toward the left side of the hall. Another officer was kneeling on the floor near the wall past him. As Tai approached, he saw her lying there, drenched in blood. *Oh, god, no.*

Tai dropped to his knees next to her. They killed her. Nathan had finally succeeded and killed her. The cop put a hand on Tai's shoulder. "None of this is hers. I already checked her. She has no wounds. We think she passed out from exhaustion. We wanted to move her before she woke up near this mess, and we didn't want her to fight us."

Tai looked up and realized several cops were standing at the gym door.

It didn't matter. The officer said he could have her. He said he could take her. It wasn't her blood. Tai moved his arms under her body. He didn't want to scare her, so he spoke in her ear, "Laci-love, it's me. I've got you. You're safe."

As Tai stood with her, she tucked her head up against his chest. He stepped outside, and Charlie came running. It was clear he thought the same thing Tai had.

"She's okay," Tai repeated, his voice thick with relief. "The blood isn't hers. They just wanted me to get her clear of the scene." The three of them sank onto a low retaining wall, the adrenaline finally giving way to a bone-deep exhaustion.

Charlie looked at him with bewilderment. "What happened?"

Tai shook his head. "I honestly don't know, Charlie, and I'm not sure I want to find out."

Vincent lifted her left hand. He pulled a ring off her finger, but it wasn't Tai's engagement ring. "By the looks of her, I don't think I want to be picking any fights with her ever." Tai looked up at Vincent. Vincent looked down at her, a slow, grim smile touching his lips. "Our girl didn't just survive. She won."

Running water. A shower. Laci felt strong arms surrounding her body, lifting her from a soft surface. There was a deep grunt of pain on the lift that sounded like Tai. *But Tai is dead.* Slowly, she was lowered to a cold, hard surface, the sound of the shower now echoing around her. The arm behind her back didn't let go, but the one under her legs let them drop over an edge. A large, warm hand stroked her cheek.

"Laci-love. You coming back to me?" Tai's voice sank into her mind.

Her eyes fluttered open, immediately recognizing their bathroom. She picked up her head and looked right into Tai's eyes. "How? I...I saw you die."

Tai pushed back her hair, but instead of softness, it was stiff. Laci turned to look in the mirror and gasped. Blood covered every inch of her. The horrific scene of fighting for her life, scrambling in pools of blood, played in her mind. Her body began shaking.

"Hey, you're safe now. Let's get you undressed and into the shower." He tugged up the bottom of her shirt, and she lifted her arms for him to pull it off. As her pants came off, her cell phone dropped to the floor. Tai picked it up and held it. "Is this how you kept it on you?"

"Yeah. I turned off the ringer, then slid it against my thigh, and used my jeans to hold it in place." She shrugged. "They would have tossed it if it had been in my pocket, and it was the only thing I could think of to help somebody trace my location."

Tai gave her a gentle smile. "It worked."

When he tried to pull his shirt off, he grunted again, unable to remove it. He could only lift his arm so far before it stopped.

"Let me." Gently working her hands under the fabric, she pulled it out so it would loosen enough for him to work one arm out, then the other, and she lifted it over his head. As she tossed it on the floor, she saw the black and purple bruise spanning his side. "What is this? Turn around."

"It's fine. I'm okay," He assured her as he unbuttoned his pants and dropped them to the floor.

"You can't lift your arms, you aren't okay. Let me see." Laci gently ran her hands along his skin as he turned, showing her his back where three gigantic black and blue bruises spread across his sides, nearly meeting in the middle along his spine. "This is where he shot you?"

"Yeah. After we walked around town yesterday, Vincent was concerned that Nathan might escalate, so he put a bullet-resistant vest on me. We figured he would do something to me to manipulate you." Tai pulled in a breath, wincing when his chest expanded. "I had my eye on Nathan, not realizing it would be Mark that was the bigger threat."

He held out his hand to her. "Come on, let's get you washed up."

Sliding off the counter, she stepped into the shower and got under the spray, feeling the stickiness wash off of her, and when she looked down, she watched the blood swirl around and into the drain. The last of the night was now washing away. She smiled up at Tai. "Okay, now you." She switched places with him, watching his sigh of relief as the hot water ran over his body while she shampooed her hair and washed her face.

Large soapy hands moved over her shoulders and down her body. "I'd like to wash lower, but I'm afraid I'll get stuck in here, unable to get back up." Instead, he turned Laci back under the spray, massaging his fingers through her hair as she wiped away the soap on her face. "There you are." Tai's lips touched hers in a gentle caress. "I will never take for granted being able to do this."

While they were drying off, Tai took her left hand in his. "Did he take your engagement ring?"

Laci gave him a small smile. "No. After Vincent called Jack to tell him that Mark was the puppet, I ran back to your office and hid my ring and necklace in your desk."

"Why?"

"I guess Vincent and I were thinking along the same lines. I knew Nathan was about to strike, and his motivation has always been to retake his position in my life as my husband. He would have destroyed the ring you gave me, and I couldn't take that chance." Laci looked at her bare hand, a shudder passing through her. "He'd already taken so much. I couldn't let him take that, too."

After they dressed for bed, she paused. "Charlie and Vincent?"

Tai gave her a half smile, rapping his knuckles three times on the wall. The door to the other bedroom opened, and then their door opened, Charlie's face popping in. "Hey Sugar-daddy, is she awake?"

Laci spun and wrapped her arms around Charlie's neck, holding tight and appreciating the feel of his arms enfolding her. "Is Vincent okay?"

"I am." His soft voice carried from the doorway. He stepped into her hug with Charlie when she lifted her arm to him. "I put a vest on right before I put one on Tai. I knew the moment I made a move, I would become a target too."

"When we saw you drop from the taser..." Laci couldn't finish the thought. She didn't want to drag that whole scene up again. "Are you as badly bruised as Tai?"

Vincent gave a slight shake of his head. "Don't worry about me. I've had worse."

Charlie let her go, a smirk on his face. "Don't worry, Baby-girl, I'll kiss all his boo-boos better." His face fell a bit. "I called the kids. I let them know there was a big incident, but that you were okay and would tell them the details when you were able."

"I should call them." Laci turned for her phone.

Charlie grabbed her arm. "No. Right now, you need to rest. They know you're safe and that you'll call them after you get some decent sleep."

Tai spoke up behind Laci. "How about we all try to get at least some sleep?"

Sunlight filtered in around the curtains when Tai's phone began vibrating on his nightstand. When he moved to roll over, he hissed loudly. "Son of a..."

Laci lifted her head. "Don't move. I'll grab it." She got up on her knees and gently reached over him, seeing Jack's name on the screen as she handed it to him.

"Jack," Tai answered. "Yeah, come on by. We'll see you when you get here." He hit the button, but before he could say anything, it rang again. "Vanessa." He clicked the button to send her to voicemail. "We can deal with everybody else later."

Getting up, Laci returned from the bathroom with pills and a glass of water. She climbed back in with Tai, handing them to him. "You'll need these for a while. And we should probably get you checked out by a doctor to make sure you don't have more damage than you think."

Tai took the pills, pulling Laci back down against him. He gently ran his fingers through her hair. "Let's steal a few more minutes. The moment we step out that door, the world rushes back in. Police, doctors, our friends... everybody will want a piece of us. But right here," he whispered, his breath warm against her temple, "it's just you and me."

Unfortunately, there was a time limit on their quiet since Jack was due to arrive. Tai went downstairs, and Laci called her kids. Of course, it took a lot of effort to reassure them that she was okay. As she walked out of the bedroom, Charlie and Vincent emerged from their room as well. The sun lit up the house, streaming in through the front windows. Somehow, everything seemed brighter to Laci. This house, this town, was no longer a refuge. Now, it was her home.

Charlie answered the door when Jack arrived. "Dude, really? Donuts? Could you be any more cliché?"

Laci nudged Charlie out of the way. "Gimme carbs."

Jack let out a visible sigh of relief when he saw her. He stepped in the door, handed the donuts to Charlie, and pulled Laci into a tight hug. "I'm so glad to see you."

"I'm okay, Jack. Thanks to everybody's efforts, I'm here." She patted his back.

He let go, and they headed for the kitchen where Tai had started the coffee. Tai held up a hand when Jack went to hug him, too. "I love you like a brother, but if you do any sort of manly back-slapping hug right now, I'll have to kill you."

Jack chuckled. "Got it." Then he joined everyone at the table after grabbing his own mug of coffee. "I feel like this is partly all my fault. You all were trying to reach me, and I had the ringer off while we interrogated the doctors Mark took Nathan to. I should have been watching the time, knowing you needed protection at closing."

"No," Laci broke in. "You can't carry that burden on your shoulders. There were so many things any one of us could have done differently, and yet we didn't. Let's just appreciate the fact that we all came out on the other side of it, with our lives."

"You, Laci, are one hell of a bad-ass." Jack grinned at her. "That phone they used to live broadcast, it was also recording. I saw what you did."

Laci looked around the table at the men with her. "Well, thanks to Vincent's training, and Tai having a pocket knife in his desk drawer that I could grab, it all worked out."

"That's why you were covered in blood? You stabbed them?" Charlie asked.

"Oh, she didn't just stab them," Jack answered. "She annihilated them."

"I had no choice." Laci pulled in a shuddering breath. "The moment Mark grabbed me, I knew I had to do it. I...I wasn't even sure if they were dead when I crawled out of there."

Jack's lips half lifted. "You killed them both. Nathan was dead when the cops arrived. Paramedics couldn't save Mark, and he was gone before they could move him. You are free now, Laci. You are free to live your life however you want."

Tai reached for Laci's hand and squeezed it. She squeezed back, feeling the warmth, looking up to the man who risked everything for her. Now, she really was free. Free from the fear that had held on to her for so long. The decision was hers to make. Her past was back in Ohio, but her future was here with Tai. And this was where she would stay. This was her home now.

Laci saw Charlie and Jack exchange a look. It wasn't just her that was free now, with Mark gone, Nicole was too, and both men knew it.

EPILOGUE

Seven Months Later

Tai and Laci were married in September in their back-yard. Alie, Mason, Charlie, and Jack stood beside them as they said their vows. As Laci walked down the aisle, the stoic control Tai was known for completely shattered. Tears tracked freely down his face, a raw, beautiful display of emotion that had every guest reaching for a tissue. After the ceremony, Carla, their wedding photographer, joined them for the drive up to the private clearing where Tai proposed. Before sunset, when the sun was still peeking over the mountains, they recreated the same pose as when Laci said yes to Tai's proposal.

By the time they returned to the house for the evening festivities, everyone was seated at their tables, ready to eat the catered meal. Laci had expressly forbidden Benji from cooking, ordering him to sit back and enjoy the party as a guest. After dinner, everyone danced the night away on the patio.

Given that the threat to Laci was gone, she could now move freely around Blackwood and town. Tai loved having her out and about, where he could see her every day. Vincent had recently moved in with Charlie, and Laci took every opportunity to call them her sugar babies.

Alie and Mason were now visiting for the holidays, staying with Tai and Laci, and helping them decorate every inch of their home. Charlie and Vincent joined them in the morning to continue the holiday traditions. This time, though, Tai was included in calling the kids down from upstairs, and he loved it. They spent the morning opening gifts and having Charlie cook breakfast for them. Tai and Charlie told everyone about the day she arrived in town, and Vincent laughed at Tai's reaction to seeing Charlie plant a kiss on Laci.

After cleaning up breakfast, they moved to the living room. Laci smiled and looked around at her family. Here they were, gathered together and enjoying each other's company. Laci realized, while watching Mason show off his company's latest game to Charlie and Vincent, seeing Alie lean into Tai as they worked together on her new puzzle book, that this was the feeling of being whole. Tai got up and brought out a large flat package for Laci. He smiled as he sat beside her and gave it to her.

"Something for you, Laci-love."

Laci sat forward and unwrapped it. She gasped as she realized what it was. The image was a side-by-side of the day Tai proposed at sunrise in the clearing on the left and their wedding day recreation at sunset on the right.

She looked at Tai. "But how?"

"When I had you unpacking the basket, I was setting up your camera. Carla gave me a remote button and taught me how to take pictures. I must have clicked that remote a hundred times. I cleaned up the equipment and put it all back in the car when you weren't looking. I took the images to Carla soon after so she would know exactly how to take the same shot on our wedding day."

Laci was amazed at the two photos, each with stunning qualities. The others also commented on their beauty. She expected to see a harsh line dividing the two moments, but Carla had masterfully blended the sunrise and sunset, the colors melting into each other to create one seamless, breathtaking scene. Then, she noticed the words engraved into the black metal frame surrounding the images. On the proposal side were Tai's words when he asked her to marry him, and on the wedding side were their vows. She was speechless and kissed him.

That night, as Tai and Laci lay in bed admiring the moon over the mountains, she couldn't help but reflect. It felt like a lifetime ago that she had arrived on Charlie's doorstep, a broken, hollowed-out version of herself. So much happened, but she was where she belonged, surrounded by friends, family, and a man who would love and protect her.

She rolled into Tai's side. He leaned down and kissed her. "I love you."

Laci grinned back up at him. "I love you too."

Laci had never felt this loved or safe in her adult years. It wasn't a fragile, temporary peace. It was a deep, foundational strength. A home. And she planned on living there for the rest of her life.

Jack sat in the darkness of his living room, holding the photo he cherished most in one hand and his fifth or sixth beer in the other. Christmas had been her favorite holiday. He remembered her squeals of joy when it was time to bring out the decorations and put up the tree, which never failed to bring a smile to his face.

She would hide a box in his gear if he deployed over Christmas. Then, on December 1st, he was allowed to open the box. It contained twenty-five dated envelopes, and the instructions she included stated that he had to wait to open them until the corresponding dates. Every envelope held a handwritten note from her. A memory, a hope for their future, a reminder of why their love was strong enough to survive the distance. Each one was now a testament to a life he no longer had. The two boxes sat on his dresser. Every morning when he woke up, he would read one note. They each brought a mix of comfort and pain, but he couldn't put them away.

Besides having dinner with his parents, he couldn't celebrate the holiday with anybody else. Nothing had been the same since he'd returned from his last deployment five years ago to find her simply...gone. The photo in his hand showed the two of them lying on the lawn in the park, the camera above their faces. They were soaking up the last moments together before he shipped out. He'd taken the photo with him on that deployment so her smiling face could keep him going.

While he was gone, though, she disappeared. He'd arrived at her apartment to find it empty. He knew Charlie held a piece of the puzzle, but Charlie would never break his promise to Nikki. Nikki's parents were a brick wall of silence. His life was empty without her. As days passed, he realized her best friend, Vanessa, was just as devastated and confused. If Vanessa didn't know where she was, he knew it had been catastrophic because they were inseparable.

Over the years in the police force, he'd gained the resources to help track her down. He knew where she was, and he watched her from afar. Seeing her alive had brought a sliver of peace, but also the agony of not being able to touch or hold her. Then, he found the police report of what happened. The factual text of the report swam before his eyes. Each word was a punch to the gut, stealing the air from his lungs. The rage came first, a boiling hot inferno. Then came the cold, crushing wave of guilt and devastation. He was a soldier. A cop. A protector. And he had failed to protect the one person who meant everything.

He saw her at the wedding. While standing with Laci and Tai, he saw her face among the guests. He wanted to run to her right then, pick her up, hug her, and kiss her. But he couldn't. She made eye contact with him once. The sadness in her eyes nearly killed him. The second he was free of his duties as a groomsman, he'd scanned the crowd, his heart hammering frantically against his ribs. But once again, she had vanished.

He knew at that moment that he would never give up, and he would get her back.

ALSO BY TK SUNDERLAND

<u>South Hillsbend Series</u>
Shattered Pieces
Frozen Silence (Coming Soon)

About the Author

TK Sunderland has always had a vivid imagination, creating stories in their mind from the simple sparks of daily life. Any conversation or occurrence could become the seed for a full story, complete with characters and plot twists.

TK lives in the Great Lakes region with two teenagers, a cat, and three energetic dogs who keep life interesting. When they aren't writing tales of romantic suspense, TK enjoys exploring new hiking trails, getting lost in a good book, or spending quality time gaming with their kids. *Shattered Pieces* is TK's debut novel, inviting readers into the captivating world of South Hillsbend for the very first time.

Visit **TKSunderland.com** for new releases and updates.

www.ingramcontent.com/pod-product-compliance
Lightning Source LLC
Chambersburg PA
CBHW020339010826
48970CB00012B/1576